Coon Run Paradigm

James Hendershot

Order this book online at www.trafford.com
or email orders@trafford.com

Most Trafford titles are also available at major online book retailers.

Print information available on the last page.

ISBN: 978-1-6987-1834-7 (sc)
ISBN: 978-1-6987-1833-0 (e)

Trafford rev. 11/21/2024

www.trafford.com

North America & international
toll-free: 844-688-6899 (USA & Canada)
fax: 812 355 4082

Dedicated to page

Thanks to all those who helped bring the special project to a printed manuscript.

Dedicated to paige

Contents

CHAPTER 01

The Memories

During the previous four months, I have not slept well. When I do get to sleep, I simply wake up early. I can think of no logical reason for this, even though I have been prescribed some powerful sleep medication, all that does is make me sleepy the entire next day. Therefore; I have been avoiding these medications and take my chance and maybe get a good night sleep. Even my Sleep On ring continues to give me extremely low scores, like in the 30s. I used to freak out with a 95. I just cannot figure out why I cannot sleep. I know there's something wrong; nevertheless, I cannot figure it out. The last thing I can do is to worry about it. I do not have anything to worry about; our finances are solid, and I have everything I would ever need for the rest in my life, and then even many boxes extra.

So much so, I went on a campaign this last summer to start throwing things away. The worst thing, or among the worst things, I think is to have something and not be able to find it. That is one thing that drives me up to the wall, although I'm sure there are a lot worse things that we must face in our life. Overall, the last almost 15 years that I have lived in Washington were great. I like the mild winters, as compared to those miserable ones in Ohio, plus the summers aren't that bad, with only a few weeks getting hot enough to turn on our central air. That was one fear that I had. I faced my fear and decided to test it out, because it sounded too good to be true. In Ohio, our smaller house had nine air-conditioners spaced evenly throughout our rooms. Because of the excessive electric bills in Ohio, we would only have the ACs on in the rooms that we were in. Therefore, if I went to the vacant room, I had to turn on another AC to cool it down, and let me tell you the summers in our part of Ohio could be miserably hot. However, now with my central air, and thermostat that works with Alexa, one simple command from anywhere in the house turns on our central air; which, immediately cools down the entire house. What is great that once the hot air is cooled down, I can turn off the AC.

In addition; it has had no impact on our electric bill. It almost makes me wish that the sleeping problem was because of the heat, which unfortunately it is not. Moreover; I then must ask myself, why can I not sleep well? I have a feeling that something is missing in me, but cannot think what it is. All my kids are grown up now and actually have very well-paying jobs and secure futures if such a future is available to anyone. I'm often thankful that I am not

starting off in today's world, even though everything is going well, to my thinking it is like a domino set, waiting for one domino to fall, then they all come tumbling down. I've always been a history fanatic and yet I really could not find any time in history that things were going on this good for so long. Even our preceding century endured two horrifying world wars, some atrocious pandemics, and hundreds of other wars that reshaped just about every continent on the Earth. Notwithstanding, we are already almost ¼ of the way through this century, and even though the world is plagued with wars, that have not reached the degree of misery caused by her previous world wars. In fact, at this time in our previous century, WW1, and Spanish Flue struck devastation on humanity.

The one pandemic that we faced we were able to, so far, been able to contain it, with its major victim, the one who saved countless millions of lives, being punished for it. Let's just say that let him was without sin be crucified. No matter how much good someone does there will always be those who say that it is bad. Nevertheless; that has nothing to do with me not being able to sleep. One comfort that I have experienced is that during the sleepless nights, at least some good memories of my childhood surface. Rather oddly; these memories seem to focus on the time I spent with my grandpa Hendershot and on his farm. I always attribute this, to all those animals and wide-open hills to climb and the play endless hours as compared to going home and sitting in a school classroom throughout the day. How could they even compete? Even though we had a 19-inch black-and-white TV with an antenna that we could adjust from the front of the TV compared to grandma who had a 12-inch TV with an antenna that took two people to adjust, one by the TV, and one up on the hill to manually adjusted it. At home, we lived on our TV as those were the days of only NBC, ABC, and CBS. They all three have such wonderful shows many of which are still shown as reruns to this day. We never watched TV that much of grandma's house because there was so much else to do. The last thing I wanted to do was be glued to TV whatever so many hills to climb and animals to chase we were playing with. I remember one time while watching TV with grandma, grandpa who slept in the next room was snoring so loud we can I hear the TV.

Subsequently; I complain to grandma about grandpa snoring, which he replied that he was not snoring. Grandma and I just looked at each other and laughed. Needless to say, we found something else to do during the remainder of that evening. I would often visit grandma and grandpa during my Air Force leaves, and of course visit Uncle John, who lived just up to the road a few hundred feet. One evening I saw a box of photographs that I had never seen before. Being curious I brought the box to my grandparents and started looking at the pictures. Accordingly; I did not recognize most of the people. Fortunately; between the both of them, they quickly recognize these people and told me many stories about them. I think that's when I got my first real taste of the impact of World War II, which ended 12 years before my birth. We see pictures of young man, which grandma would say that he died at so-and-so battle and pictures of older couples who they would tell me had lost children in World War II. I asked grandpa if we had any relatives who fight in any other wars, and he told me that his father fought in the Civil War, a few battles not far from their house. Their home was only I say less than 20 miles from the Ohio River. Before Ohio drove the South out of the Western part of West Virginia, it was Virginia. That left them with the constant fear of rebels stealing their food.

Somehow, they made it, and the war eventually ended. Washington County had fought an ongoing invisible war, until the South was driven back to the present-day border of Virginia and West Virginia. I remember my grandfather showing me his father's sword, which is broken at the end. He broke it during one of the battles, therefore, he gave it to his son. I was so shocked to hold his sword that was used in combat that had ended only 92 years before my birth. Another event I remember with my grandfather was when he thought he was going to die soon; consequently, he took me around the area showing me where he went to school and where he used the black Smith to get work done on some of his broken farm equipment, and many other places unfortunately which really did not interest me at that time. He did recover and lived for at least another 30 years after that time. It was so strange to think of him being a school's student, especially in a one-room school. Naturally, he told me he had to walk five miles to school each day, which based upon the distance between that building and his farm, I could see it was a long way to walk. Speaking of death, my father moved to Florida because of his health conditions. While in Florida, both of his parents died. When he finally got to return; I got to go riding with him one day to each of the many different places in the area that he had played in or done things as a child. I was shocked that he showed me places that he had played considering he always told me he never a chance to play as a kid but only had to work.

That was a memory I kept in back my mind and my mouth shut when he was sharing some issues with me. Soon after, we ended up at Paw Paw Cemetery, which was just around the bend from to Coon Run Road. Both my grandma and grandfather were buried here and my father had me take pictures of their grave stone with him. I actually signed his name, per his request, on the visitation logs at the funeral home during the funerals. As he was their oldest son, he felt a need that his name appears on the log. Ironically, his health began to improve in Florida, and personal relationships turned disastrous; it was my brother who went down there and brought him back to Ohio where he has lived for the last many with no more health issues. Their son with dreadful luck for him to be away and have your parents die. I also got a taste of that so-called bad luck during my stay here in Washington when my mother died. Always hate going to funerals, because I have such difficulty crying considering that they are in a much better place than what we are. That was why I did not cry at grandpa Jackson's funeral, because I considered her a Saint. I remember the Friday before she died, she called my sister's house, whom I was staying with at the time, and asked if I come over and have pizza and soda was her.

Being a very poor student, I readily agreed. We had some unbelievable conversation that night, as I was so shocked that she was so well in tune with the world. Somehow that night we got from the conversation to that she wanted to be cremated when she died. She said people walked over her whole life, she did not want them walking over her when she was dead. I got a phone call while in class that next Monday that she was in the hospital and was not expected to make it. Her insides were completely eaten out with cancer. I immediately rushed across town to the hospital which was less than two miles away only to find she had just died.

My sister told me that even if I had been there, she was so drugged up, she would not have known me. I thought of her last request that she gave me concerning cremation. I told that to my mother and all my aunts, which they refused to have her cremated. I kept telling them that was what she told me that she wanted. When they had the funeral, I attended but did not cry one tear. I figure she was much better off where she was there with these disrespectful children she had raised. I still think about that to this day, yet I know I am sure she knows and all her daughters who are now with her know there was nothing that I could do about it. Any ways, switching back to my grandpa Hendershot, I remember when staying with her during the summer and other events, on Sunday mornings she walked from her farm that is on Coon Run Road to Paw Paw church.

It was probably only less than two miles, but she enjoyed the walk immensely. One year, my father had to return to construction work and thus moved the family up north before my school year ended. Grandma and grandpa agreed to have me live with them until the remainder of the school year. They notified the bus driver and the school and all arrangements were made, and each morning for the remainder my fourth grade, I would catch the bus there. One morning I was running down the hill to catch the bus, of course wearing white pants; I slid into the mud. Grandma was watching me and helped me because my grandpa had to stop the bus when it came back from where it was turning around. I quickly put on my clean pants and ran down to the bus, actually, just as it was arriving. The bus driver was a friend of my grandparents, and must've thought they were really doing a diligent job of taking care of me, which they were. My grandpa's house, set on halfway up a hill, with a valley separating it from another hill with a small creek flowing between them. This valley was called Coon Hollow. As a kid during my exploration adventures, I traveled up and down both Hills extensively, up to grandpa's fence that kept his ponies, and a few heads of cattle fenced in. My exploration was made easier by the paths that his farm animals had created from their normal searching for grass to eat.

I marveled at how efficient these paths were, most often running horizontal and not vertical up to these steep hills. Plus, they helped me feel that I would not get lost as easy as I would have without these paths. One of my discoveries while in the big hill across Coon Hollow was an old graveyard. There probably were only about a dozen gravestones, and each old-style gravestone was maybe two feet tall and a foot wide with the name chiseled on it. The stones were so old that the chisel names had faded. I was surprised how it was so blended in with the trees around it, and practically stumbled on this by accident. Be that as it may; I actually discovered a long-lost graveyard. When I went back to my grandpa's house and told my grandpa, father, and Uncle John, that I discovered a graveyard of which none of them knew anything about, they argued about the possibility of such a graveyard existing. Grandpa finally revealed that he heard his father talk about a graveyard which contained people who died prior to their arrival, and estimated this to be in the early 1700s. They traveled through dangerous Indian lands unprotected without the permission of the British government. And through time were forgotten. I returned home that day with my parents, only to discover accidentally through my grandma, that both Uncle John and grandpa searched for and found that graveyard. I think the graveyard added depth to this farm in that people had lived there before them. I think also that respect that at least currently they were not forgotten, although in no way remembered.

Considering this is a story that grandpa's dad told him casually as a child. I apologize for the way that these memories are not coming back in sequence, but are coming back randomly. I need to get them off my chest while I recollect them, as there has to be a reason. Why am recalling them? One of the proudest moments of my childhood while I was visiting grandpa during summer school, in which he was one of two bus drivers. The other bus driver with my other grandfather grandpa Jackson. Each day they would remain at the school, since by the time they drove back to their home, it would be time for them to drive back to school, since it was only summer school. During this break they would meet at the gas station at the bottom of the hill in front of the school. Each day they got me a bottle of pop. They called it pop, whereas today some call this soda. My proudest point was we were taking the student's home, I could brag that one grandfather with driving this bus while another grandfather with driving the other bus. Naturally, there were few kids who did not believe this, and I would ask my grandpa who would verify it. I got a lot of wows. As I think back about it that was kind special and one of those at the right time to the right place sort of situation.

Subsequently; each summer always spend one week with our grandma and grandpa Hendershot, plus another week with our aunt Mary, our father would give us a couple of dollars for spending money. Considering that there were four of us in this rotation I can see where we ended up costing our father a few dollars. The only place we could spend our money was at Guy Hendershot's store in Germantown. Germantown was probably three or four miles away, much closer than going to Marietta, which was 19 miles. I would buy a soda and the rest on cough drops. Especially the cherry flavored ones were my favorite. Grandma and grandpa were not into cough drops, but my cousins at Mary's house were. These would give me some exceptional favors for trading. I don't remember the special favors that I exchanged for these cough drops. One of my cousins, named Donna Kay, would always pester me; therefore, I knew that a couple of the cough drops got me sometime without being bugged. I also know I gave her two younger brothers the cough drops for them to pester her. Oh, the joys of being a kid. However, back to Guy Hendershot store, he was my grandpa's cousin. Furthermore, I discovered years later he was one of the main directors of the Salem Liberty School. It was now an elementary school; however, previously it was a high school.

My father graduated from this high school. That was one of the pride and joys of us being a Hendershot was that our family had to store, and it was right on the end of Germantown, with Guy's house right across the street. At one time, there were a lot of Hendershot's in this area; however, most of us moved on. I lived in a town called

Warner; which is probably about 10 miles from Coon Run Road, for almost 11 years? By the time I returned in 1999, my grandpa and grandma were living in a small apartment in a town about also 10 miles from my house. Having a wife, three kids, was a sucky job that took a lot of hours I didn't really have a chance to visit with them that much. I did have them meet my wife and youngest son and daughter. I was glad to give them a chance to see that part of my life. I would occasionally visit Uncle John or invite him into our house. Somehow, all the years I had been gone had we drift somewhat apart, but our blood kept us from drifting completely apart. Now when I moved to Washington, there were two people that I kept in contact with over the phone. The first was my mother with the second one being Uncle John. Within a few short years of moving here both died. I have as of yet to replace them as people to call. Uncle John was only about 10 years older than me; therefore, as a kid a lot of my memories of Coon Run were with Uncle John. I was following them over to Bill Bigley's house, which was across the stream on the south of Coon Run Road.

Consequently; I was amazed back there as it had actually some very big rocks, which have been left by the glaciers of the last Ice Age. I just couldn't comprehend that something could move such big rocks. Notwithstanding; however, they were before my eyes. Uncle John also built a cabin halfway up the opposite hill. He did a very good job on this, as I used to enjoy playing there a lot. It was a good base for my exploration adventures. Another thing that amazed me when grandpa told me that their house had been taken apart and moved from a place just above Germantown. I believe this was done well before the Civil War. Board by board, removed and hand carried over this hill, across Coon Hollow, and halfway up to their hill and then reassembled. The state bought the farm from grandpa Hendershot. That house fell apart and was eventually taken away and was disassembled completely from the farm. A place that I enjoyed so many Christmases, Thanksgivings, and usually the great Sunday meal, was gone forever. There was also so many great conversations and just the completeness of being a part of that extended family I will cherish for the remainder of my days, although sadly they are starting to fade away.

The farm and all the junk that grandpa Hendershot has scattered over it, was gone. Both grandma and grandpa were gone. Uncle John built a nice house across the road from grandpa. That house, upon his death, was sold, and therefore, gone. Every link that I had to Coon Hollow was gone. Now with the state owning grandpa Hendershot's old farm, there probably would not be too much fuss over me strolling around it. Actually in 2010, I did go there and take some digital pictures; however, a few years later only to discover that I lost them. I cannot figure out how I lost them and keep expecting someday that they may show back up. I took pictures inside grandma and grandpa's house, which had been ransacked by robbers, who even busted the windows. That just goes to show you what scum actually exists among us. I think that was one reason why I didn't really end up going out to Coon Run Road that much was my disappointment in the people who lived in this area. In reality I did most of my work in West Virginia. I still like my house that I have there, and actually just waiting for a good opportunity to sell it. Although actually it does give me a foothold near what I consider the foundation of our family, and that is on Coon Hollow. The joy of getting the drinking water from a well, that was in the front yard; and with a hand pump filling a bucket up with water. Afterwards; taking it inside and placing it on a corner table where grandma kept it.

The water did taste good; however, the water at Mary's house, which was from a spring, taste better. The point being, neither one had running water, plus both had outhouses. That was as close to wilderness style, but I have never been. The bath consisted of heating up a bucket of water and having some cold water just in case the hot water was too hot and washing yourself. I definitely like my showers better. Another great adventure I had was with the help of Uncle John. I would have even my father, one of my brothers, mother, I think one-time grandma Hendershot. I would have my back turned to them with three quarters on a table, and they were only touch as many as they wanted or none if they wanted, and I would tell them which one they did or did not touch. When I touched them, John was a smoker if I touched a point that someone had touched, he would take a drag from the cigarette. I can see him smoking without looking at him. Because when he exhaled the smoke, I can see it. We did this for four hours and never made a mistake.

That was the thing about smokers back then, non-smokers simply ignored them. No one ever suspected, and we kept it a secret, in case they wanted a rematch in the future, which they never brought up, attributing it to one of those things that cannot be explained. Another great experience we had on this farm was riding grandpa's horses. That was when life took on the whole new arena of excitement. And grandpa patiently would stand beside his pony making sure he didn't get spooked and walked his ponies for a long time. I remember one time my father was yelling at me and acting crazy, when my grandpa asked my dad to relax on me. My father began screaming that my grandpa whom he never took it easy on him, and he rounded us all up to his home. I said that was so sad, but those are the kind things that can happen on Coon Run Road.

I must confess that reliving these Coon Hollow events helped me a little, but not completely. Something inside me is trying to get out. I just don't think I can get that out from here in Washington. Like a cry the distant past I can feel that something is trying to tell me its message. For some strange reason, they cannot get the message to me here in Washington.

Consequently; I do remember three or four caves that were on the hillside south of uncle John's house across the creek that formed the border between grandpa Hendershot's farm, and whoever owned the property that ran up the tall hill across from the creek. Remembering; there were at least three or four caves that ran into this hillside. My uncle John warned me, as a kid, not to go in there because it was dangerous and could fall in on me. I asked him what was the point that these caves? He explained they were digging for coal, which they would sell and make very little money because what they sold, they had to hand carry, and for heating. Accordingly; I always did want and still do want to explore these caves. Therefore, it looks like I will have to go back physically to see what is going on. I will fly on one of the big planes to Ohio; then take a little plane to a city not far from where I need to go, thereafter, I will rent a car from there because I want the flexibility to search as hard as I need to, I think the best if I sneak back and try to get this solved, that is if it can be solved, then to my visitations.

CHAPTER 02

The Arrival

I gave into my temptation, my credit card out and booked a flight to Columbus, Ohio. From Columbus, I would catch a small plane that would take me to Parkersburg West Virginia. Parkersburg was only a 30-minute drive to Warner. I made this drive almost every day for 10 years while working in West Virginia. From the airport, I was going to rent a vehicle. I told my wife to keep this a secret, which I guess in women's language meant to tell everyone possible as soon as possible. My sister was there to meet me. I told her that I really wanted to rent a vehicle, which she said she would take me to Marietta the next day to rent my vehicle. Thus, off we headed to her house.

My sister lived about a mile and a half from my house in Warner. Notwithstanding; I wasn't too far from the place I wanted to be. Originally, I made a hotel reservation for that evening. My sister insisted that I cancel that reservation and stay with her. Therefore; I canceled that reservation. I didn't really feel like spending a ton of money for a hotel room any ways. When we arrived at my sister's house, both my brothers and their families were there to meet me. I guess we were going to have some sort of celebration party. That tends to happen when you have been away for 15 years. They also brought my father out there as well. He was staying in assisted living in Marietta, yet could get permission to visit with us this evening. Everyone asked me why I came and did not bring my wife. I explained that she was busy right now and couldn't really get aside because of so many church activities. With my family being actively involved in church, I figured I could get off with that excuse.

Moreover; I also told them that I wanted to go out to Coon Run Road and check out grandma and grandpa's old farm. I saw some strange looks come over their faces, especially my father's face. My father, who was getting way up there in age, grew tired within a few hours. Especially, since we were all talking at the same time about everything possible, except for Coon Run Road. Therefore, my one brother and his family, since he lived in West Virginia, agreed to drop my father off in Marietta, which was on the way. My other brother, who is a minister in a church about 70 miles north, also had to excuse himself and his family so that he could get home at somewhat a reasonable hour. We bid them all farewells, as we prepared to finish cleaning up after a rather large festival style welcome home meal. As things started to settle down, my sister and I had a little cup of wine, told me that this could help me to sleep tonight. This told me that my wife had told her I was having trouble sleeping. Which is no big thing, except for when you're not sleeping? She then asked me what the real reason I was back there for. I decided to be honest, considering that the more people that were involved could help me find the answers that I needed quicker. I told her I just have been having a really strange feeling about Coon Hollow. She asked me if I had any dreams or anything of that nature?

Consequently; I think it was just to nothing more than a peculiar feeling, as if I needed to find some answers to some questions that I did not in spite of know. She also confessed to having these strange feelings, and even a couple of dreams. Asked her what she had dreamed about? She said the details were extremely vague; however, it had something to do with Indians and a lot of people living in Coon Hollow. I cannot think why they are, could be a lot of people living there, etc. I remembered vaguely once that grandma Hendershot had told me that at one time there were 13 families who lived up Coon Hollow. Even though, I think they were all gone only after World War II. I did not have many details, and just a passing casual conversation without going into any form of detail. Sort of oh, by the way, there were 13 families that lived up this hollow. I remember discovering somewhat a shallow pond just up to the hill behind her house. The pond now had cattails growing in it. I believe I asked my grandma why no one used this pond. She said something about, they had a well, therefore, did not need the pond, which had been used by the families who previously lived up to the hollow. I know that afterward,

I searched every inch of the creek up to the fence line and both sides of the hill that ran along the creek. I never even found so much as a small rock, which if there had been that many families living there, I would have suspected that there should be a bunch of junk or something somewhere, unless they buried it.

However; I assured my sister, that unless we took a backhoe up there, we would find nothing, and if we ever did find something, it will be totally worthless and most likely provide no detail. If we are going to have any detail, then we have to talk to someone who knew about this. Unfortunately; all such people were now dead. I probably should've had started this investigation much younger, instead of waiting until I was 67 years old. Furthermore, I consider that back then they most likely did not cars, and all the transportation would have been by horse. With so many people living in such a small hilly area, they most likely did not have a horse or horses, which would've required a lot of hay, and cleaning up their horse poop. We jumped in her car, what to Marietta to get my rental, then went to Coon Hollow. When we arrived there, I noticed that many things were so different. My Uncle John planted some pines to divide his property from my grandpa's fields. These trees were now humongous, to say the least. Additionally, my grandparents' house had been dismantled and hauled away with all the other junk my grandfather had stored, to include a lot of old cars. His barn and a few other buildings such as a building to store his corn in, plus a chicken coop and a few of the other odd buildings I vaguely remember seeing but never went into.

These buildings were gone. I'm not saying that this is a bad thing, because actually is a very good thing. The difficulty is that they allowed the brush and small trees to take over what little open space they had, plus the hillsides. These hillsides were currently forests. Notwithstanding; across Coon Run Road in front of what used to be grandpa's barn was at the present time what appeared to be a bunch of tree-cutting equipment, plus remains of trees they formerly attempted to process into boards. My difficulty was locating where they were getting these trees from. Because the area around here was still swarming with trees. Upon examining this equipment, we determined that it had been not used for quite a long time. Thereafter; after seeing some phone numbers painted on the sides of the vehicles, we called one of these numbers and asked them why they left this equipment here. The man, who answered the phone, started to become rather hostile, demanding to know who we were. We explained that our grandfather had once owned this land, and we were just back here to explore some childhood memories. This seemed to appease this man, who immediately apologized for his hostility. He further cited that some corrupt government people had sabotaged their operations. Additionally; he claimed that the government officials took all the money that had been earned from cutting the trees, leaving them nothing to pay for the expenses of cutting those trees.

Moreover; he argued they sued them for their equipment, only to leave it there and go bad. Additionally, the workers complained about freak accidents, dangerous things that were happening that should not be happening. One such thing; was one of the blades come flying off their saws? They could live with this until one day one of the flight blades cut off a coworker's hand. This was when the employees up and quit. I asked him if he had any idea that was sabotaging their equipment? He claimed that he had set up security cameras that monitor the equipment 24/7 revealing no one touching the equipment; nevertheless, the equipment malfunctions continued. Further, he added that this had reached such a level of concern for his company that they refused to even attempt to retrieve their equipment. Subsequently; I asked him where they kept all the cut trees or where they cut the trees from. He claimed that they got them from the two hilltops on the old Hendershot farm, and dragged them down to some paths that they had cut out with some portable bush hogs, and finished dragging the logs down with horses.

My sister added that she was still thankful that no one had gotten killed. She also appreciated their warning concerning the corrupt government officials. When she hung up the phone, we walked over to where the barn used to be, and sat down on some old buckets that were there. We had to scratch their heads for a minute, as we both agreed to have an intuition or feeling that was inside us that was growing faster now, we were in reality here. Compounding this, with what the company man had just revealed to us, we decided that this actually did warrant additional consideration, at the very least. My concern, was since we now had evidence that whatever this was it could strike dangerously back at us; we should proceed with extreme caution at the bare minimum. Moreover; my additional concern was trying to define what we were dealing with, if we were at all dealing with something or just playing with figments of our imagination. I recommended that we walk around this farm area and of course Coon Hollow and try to get a feeling for this area. This would not be an easy task, as the brush now grew where a house and barn, plus tons of junk, once dominated. I figured a good place to start would be to see if we could locate the pump well that was in the front yard. I remember grandma telling me that this well were only 15 feet deep, which ironically since it sat on a hill, would place it somewhat level to the creek who flowed about 30 feet in front of the old house. Believing that we both felt a bit not at ease, I recommended that we both start taking pictures from our cell phones. Additionally, I felt that by looking and taking these pictures, we were more apt to discover any potential irregularities. Considering that everything had been removed or leveled out, to include a strange partial concrete foundation that once existed through the gate and up to the hill about 20 feet.

It often times asked my grandfather what this was and what had been in there, he continuously ignored giving me an answer, and being a kid with a vivid imagination, I would just forget about it and move on to another unsolvable mystery. I knew that if we came back, we would need to bring a weed eater, or sickle, and many other tools to help us clear out enough space, so we could see the ground that we were walking on. One pleasant thing that we noticed was that there was a wide variety of wild flowers now growing. This kind of flowers added a special touch to the fields. Strangely; with this many flowers, there should have been small birds and bees making some noise in their dire attempt to make whatever they make, or eat something for the continued survival. Notwithstanding; it was eerily quiet. I did not even detect any small creatures trashing through the brush. I realized that I had to be careful not to be reading something into approximately a situation which did not have anything to cause me to worry. Be that as it may; every time we stepped on a trig, we both jumped. I commented how lucky we were that we were not carrying weapons, or both of us may have already shot ourselves.

It was nice to at least discover that the tiny creek that ran down Coon Hollow was still flowing with water. We all enjoyed playing in this water and watching the crawdads the minute minnows swim back and forth as they were carried towards a little larger creek across the road down at the end of the grandpa's property line. We now discovered that there were no more crawdads nor other fish of any sort swimming in these waters. I thought that maybe since there were no longer any outhouses being used on this creek than a major food supply for these creatures may have been eliminated. Yet again, with only two elderly people living here for so many years, this should not have been a primary food supply for these creatures. We now elected to sit alongside the Coon Run Road, and rest a few minutes. Quite soon, a vehicle pulled up, stopped, and the man exited the vehicle asking us what we were doing? I told him that our grandfather had once lived here, and we were just looking forward to seeing if there had been any major developments since our childhoods. He then asked me if we knew a John Hendershot. I next asked him if he meant my deceased

Uncle John, or my cousin John, for my son John? He said the only one he knew with my cousin who sold him the house that he now lived in. I asked him how he enjoyed living on Coon Run Road.

He said it had a few ups and downs, but for the most part, it was a life. My sister asked what he meant by a few ups and downs? He acted rather reluctant to answer this question. I explained that we had spoken on the phone with the logging company ceased doing work here because they felt it, there, were strange mitigating circumstances that could be dangerous. He confessed that there were times that he and his ex-wife had concerns here. Therefore, I asked him what he meant by his ex-wife? He cited that she finally one day refused to live here any longer and took their two kids and moved into Marietta. I then told him that the reason we were actually here, was to investigate some uneasy feelings that we now had concerning this area. He invited us to my deceased Uncle John's house, that he at present owned, and discuss these issues over some fresh coffee. We accepted this invitation, if not for anything but to see what the inside of John's house looked like now. When we entered, we were surprised to see how sanitary it was, considering that except for constantly washing his hands, Uncle John never occupied himself too much with keeping his house clean. He always kept it right at the borderline of clean and dirty. We commented on how washed the house was now, in which he answered that they needed a long time to get it to a condition that they could occupy.

Consequently; I told him that, for the most part, my Uncle John had to live here alone; he was never concerned about keeping it clean. The new owner verified they took many months to remove the dirt and the films of cigarette smoke that had embedded itself into this house. I asked him if he still had to use propane for heating. He said that a mission initially; however, after he petitioned the state to allow him to tap into one of the old wells on my grandpa's previous farm for gas. He agreed to pump the well in order to ensure a supply of natural gas for his house. By pumping this well, it also provided the state with some oil that they could sell. He seriously doubted that the money received from this oil actually made it into the state treasuries. I recommended that he keeps these concerns a secret to ensure his continued access to the natural gas, in which he readily agreed. Out of curiosity, I asked him if he ever attempted to explore the caves on the hillside behind his house across the creek? He said that some of his friends actually went in there and braced up the entrances, going in about 200 feet for each one before becoming too bored and scared to continue. I asked him it would be okay if I went in there and checked them out, being something that I always wanted to do ever since I was a kid. He agreed to go with me and grabbed two flashlights. He recommended that my sister guard the entrances in case something happened, and we would need rescued.

Accordingly; I asked him if his friends had discovered anything in the caves? Consequently; he verified that they found a group of skeletons at the point where they quit bracing up the caves. Furthermore, I asked him if this was found in all three caves, which he replied that they found it in simply one cave. To me, I felt that they may have only been using this as a graveyard. Our guide, agreed that they had reached a similar agreement. This was further based upon no signs of physical trauma and that the bodies were stacked neatly with a few personal items nearby. Naturally; I asked him if they found anything else in these caves? He claimed they came up empty-handed, and it was a waste of time considering that even all the coal had been removed. With this, we proceeded back to the entrance and when we were within 30 feet of the entrance to the cave, it started to shake. We could run as fast as we could to the entrance, arriving there before it collapsed. Consequently; neither of the other two caves were affected. This left us both at a loss for words, except for believing that something did not want those graves to be disturbed. Our new friend found this rather difficult to believe that his friends had made much more noise when trying to brace up the entrance. Either way; we agreed that was strange, and that it should not have occurred. My sister then said we were lucky that neither one of us was killed, since we could still see the dust coming out of the now tiny entrance to this third cave. I currently asked the new owner if my cousin had told him about any other legends in this area. He reported that he was told about another house in his front yard by his driveway in which the owner, who supposedly had money on hand, was killed, and his house burned down. Accordingly, I asked him what he meant by another house. Subsequently; he told me about a Ben Hendershot, whose house was burned, with him inside with all his money missing. Ben had a reputation of saving a lot of his money, although foolishly bragging about the amount of his savings.

Moreover; I agreed that I had heard both stories. Our new acquaintance; told me that he had dug up the area around his house, and discover the foundation of a previous house, a few pans and two metal plates accompanied by a few forks and spoons. The remainder of that area was picked clean, thereby; he simply reburied it. I asked him if he would have any objections to us nosing around Coon Hollow some more. He got our phone numbers and promised to keep an eye out in case any state employees were looming in the area. Additionally; he offered another adventure, he would introduce me to visit a few houses on Coon Run Road and some new neighbors who were on Blair Hollow Road, considering that they may have some stories and events to share. He also suggested that we walked to these places, considering that they were near, and the neighbors tended to frown on anyone who drove into their driveways. Therefore, we followed him to his first neighbor on Coon Run Road and waited behind him as he approached the door to knock upon it. An elderly lady answered the door, in which he introduced us. She claimed to have gone to school for part of her fourth-grade was a young Hendershot boy who stayed with Gail and Freda for a few weeks. I confessed to her that it was me, and asked her if she was the tall dark-haired, extremely shy girl who got on the bus at this stop. She verified that I was her. I asked her how she could remember me, in which she replied that since I was the only other kid to get on the bus from Coon Run Road, it was easy to remember. She said the only other kids to ever get on a bus were from Blair Hollow Road. So, I asked her what she had done in all the years since my departure. She said that her whole life had been here on this farm, especially since both of her parents died when she was in her late 20s.

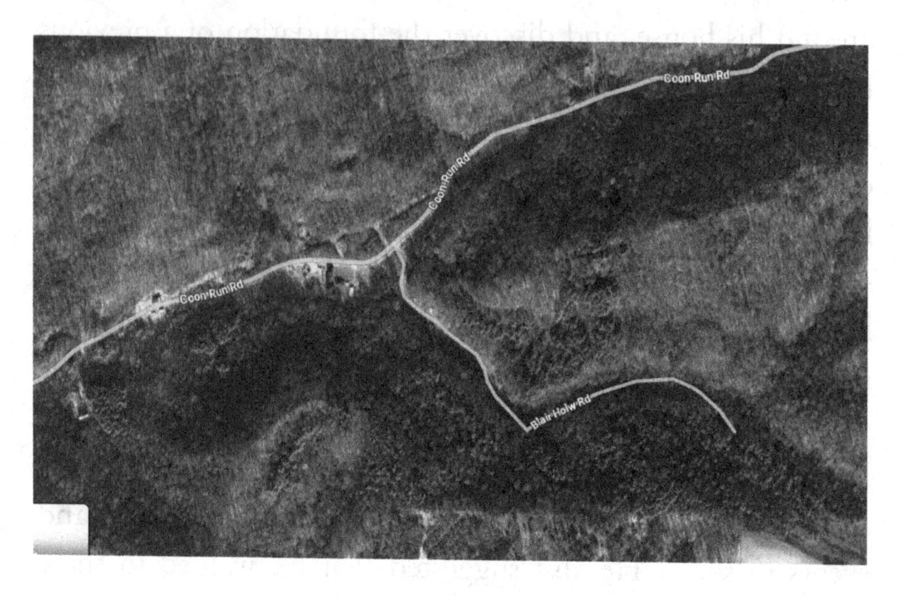

After that, she claims to remain reclusive, not wanting to socialize with the people whom she knew lived in this area. I confessed to her that neither would I have wanted to socialize with them, at which we both chuckled. I thought to myself; it was so sad that what I considered to be a pretty girl had lived such a lonely life. She asked what brought me back to this area after so many years? Before I answered; she confessed to having seen me twice at the Whipple Tavern with my Uncle John. She verified who I was through my aunt Tina, who also worked as a bartender there. She claimed to ask my aunt Tina to match us up a few times; however, with me being in the Air Force stationed so far away and not returning home as often as I once had, this invitation sort of fell through the cracks. Furthermore, she also learned later that Tina's sister also liked me, and decided to forgo our introduction in order to maintain their family tranquility. I explained to her that we were here because we felt there were some unanswered questions from Coon Hollow that ran beside my grandmother's house.

Her name was Beverly Johnson, and even though not a classmate of mine at Salem-Liberty, she was one grade below me. She verified that she experienced so many strange things on this road and in this area during her life that she just now ignored them. She learned for her survival that when she ignored it, it ignored her. My sister then asked her what sort of things had she ignored. She said the first thing was that she ignored was the strange lights that would walk on the road below her house on Coon Run Road each October 18. Her father once went out to investigate the lights and had a heart attack in the process. That was enough to convince her mother and her to ignore those lights. However, on October 18 years later her mother being drunk on some wine they made that summer foolishly elected to go out and investigate these annual lights, only to herself have a heart attack. Beverly continued that she had accepted that those lights were deadly and were not to be messed with. She heard a few tales from some old people who still existed on this road. The tales were told by different people and seemed to offer a lot of contradictions, causing her to totally discount them. Be that as it may, the lights still continue to shine up and down this road no less than three times each October 18. My sister and I look at each other, realizing that today was October 17. I, therefore, asked Beverly if we were secure for this evening. She said we were protected anytime except for the evening of October 18.

Therefore: I asked her if she noticed anything else unusual at times. She claimed that she had not, yet some of the logging workers who were working on my grandfather's farm claimed to have seen and heard a lot of strange events and warned her to stay away from the farm. Accordingly, she stayed away, believing that if you do not look for trouble, then trouble would not look for you. She asked what I intended to do if I were to find something strange. I told her to ask it as many questions that it might have and why it wanted me to come here, apparently with my sister. Beverly wished me luck in finding the answers to my questions and told me not to be a stranger and that when I came back on this road, I had better stop and visit her, and that she would prepare a good country meal for us to enjoy. We found out from our guide the next day in a text to our phones the Beverly had died in her sleep. The following stop was to discover what was on the Blair Hollow Road, which finalize only a few years earlier. And by a few, I mean around 20 years earlier. It was at most animal paths, when I was a kid. Our guide, or actually Bob, the man who bought Uncle John's house, confessed to having lost a dog on one October 18 who was barking as some lights he saw in the road. This probably would not have been an issue, except that they forgot to chain him up that night. He did not believe in chaining the dog up during the day because this was the country.

The Sheriff's office, had received many assorted complaints about lights and trouble on Coon Run Road, on October 18, they began closing this road off on that day each year. That had been closing it off for about 10 years now. At least, we had some more information in order to begin to form some potentially outlandish theories. My sister recommended that we will visit my father tomorrow morning, as he most likely would be in bed, by the time we returned this evening. Bob now said that we would visit the people on Blair Hollow Road, the first being the Biglies and the second being the Millers. I told him that there used to be some Biglies that lived on a path across a creek beside his garage. This was when Bob told us that this path had been leveled out in the actual Blair Hollow Road created, which had a natural bridge that crossed over two streams on the way to its end. Since the streams were little, so were the bridges. I remembered that the two streams met just before the path that people used to use to drive over it.

We first went to the Biglies, with only his wife and two sons being home. She agreed to discuss these issues with us once again, claiming that as long as they did not bother it, the peculiar events did not bother them. I asked her if similar curious events were bothering them. She recommended that it might be a good idea to discover why they were bothering me and wished me luck in doing so, plus offered to be of any secret service that she could be. She was very adamant about making sure that these events did not discover that she was attempting to undermine them, fearing great danger for her family and her.

Afterwards; we went to visit the Millers as they also welcomed us and claimed it was nice to meet any descendants from Gail and Freda. They further added that my grandparents had helped them on many occasions. The Millers were in their mid-70s, so had been around the area for a lot of years. They agreed with the Biglies that there was no danger if whatever was there was not provoked, such as the lumber people had done.

They further claim that the lumber people were given many warnings and changes to leave without problems. I asked the Millers, if I were wanting to meet with these tranquil forces, how would I go about that? They recommended that continue to do like I did today and go there walking around and maybe even speaking out in a calm, smooth, and peaceful non-threatening voice that they might respond eventually, once they knew they could trust me. I felt they had to know me, and that they trusted me, or why else would have they attempted to summon me here. Mr. Miller told me he did not know the answer to that question, that would be a good question for me to ask them. We thank them for their time and walked back with Bob to our car, making sure we had each other's phone numbers and email addresses in the event we needed to talk to each other about something we may have forgotten, or some other issue not discussed today. I was glad we exchanged these numbers, because it allowed Bob to inform me of Beverly's passing on. Currently, my sister and I decided to return to her house, as we both were somewhat hungry now and look for to get something to eat and a good night's rest before another day of investigating tomorrow. By the way, my sister asked me how my elbow felt today. She knew about my elbow not feeling okay today. This, initially, the off guard until she continued to explain. She told me that twice last night I fell off of their sofa twice, while I was sleeping, and hit the floor. The second time, they gave me a sleeping bag so that I could spend the remainder of the night sleeping on the floor. I never detected that I had gone to bed not in that sleeping bag; therefore, and thus was not alerted when waking up in it. This would be another mysterious force to discuss tomorrow, considering that this is starting to get a tad bit spooky now, and something that we really shouldn't talk about prior to going to sleep. Prior to going to sleep, we decided to upload the pictures we took from our cell phones on to their laptop. We were in shock to discover that none of the photographs were visible, yet were only solid black images. Ouch.

CHAPTER 03

Thirteen Stones (Part 1)

Dawn is approaching stirring up my eagerness to do some more exploring and investigating today in search of some answers. Suddenly, a sharp pain is flashing into my leg, and now the other leg, both of my arms, and then my back! I called out to my sister, who was an RN prior to retiring. I tell her that I am in great pain, and must now go to a hospital. Unfortunately, we are about 20 miles from the nearest hospital. With no time to wait for an ambulance, my sister tells me to get in the back of her van and away we go.

I'm just now screaming, is as if I'm being pounded by 1,000 nails. What in the world is causing this? I've never had this kind of pain in my life. My sister had called ahead to the hospital and asked to have the staff waiting for me. As we pull in, I'm immediately transferred to a hospital bed and taken to the emergency room. They notice that my body is currently red and swelling. The doctors are confused; however, decide at least now to give me some morphine. It is evident and a terrifying pain. Since the doctors bought themselves sometimes, they begin running every test, they can think that could possibly be related to this. They also gave me some powerful sleep medication. And very quickly, I am asleep. Conversely, I thought was, because now I'm fully awake and pain-free. Nevertheless, I do not recognize where I am. I do realize that I am in a round tepee. Now how did I get inside a tepee? I am wearing my same clothing; on the other hand, am I, as my shirt just changed and now my pants are changing, and now I have moccasins for shoes. This was rather a quick form of gradual. I could see this doing it but also see how it took its time, for as to make sure that maybe I noticed it. Whatever is going on, I am willing to play along. The alternative is those thousand nails pounding themselves through my body. Now two very beautiful Indian girls come in and start setting up some bowls, and they start a fire, plus give me a cup with some water in it and motion for me to drink it.

Therefore; I sniff it, smells clean, then take a drink. It tastes plane, and it hit the spot although not as good of a spot, that a bottle of Jim Beam, could have hit. Alternatively, maybe a shot of morphine if I had a way, that I could motion those doctors who are well below me now. That I can be good, for why are they below me? Subsequently, an elderly Indian man comes walking into this tepee. He looks at me and says, "How are you doing James?" Now a voice spoke here. How does someone whom I have never met in my life, know my name? At least, I know he speaks English. Therefore; I asked him how he knew my name? He tells me not to worry about such a trivial thing. Accordingly; I asked him what his name is? He tells me that he is the Creator, and is called Apistotookii. Therefore; I asked him what did he create? He looks at me and smiles saying to his two girls beside me that the white man knows extremely little about the very big things. They both laugh. It does not matter to me what they laugh about. I asked this Indian Creator why I'm here? He says to kill the Coon Run Ghost, which he says will be a mighty challenging task for me. For in order to do that, I must first get the special 13 stones, and place that where time flows into times.

Moreover, once I do that, I must kill the Dreizehn Häuser or the 13 houses that once flooded Coon Hollow. Once I've done this then I will have the powers needed to kill the Coon Hollow Ghost. Now I asked the Creator how am I supposed to be able to do this. He tells me not to worry, because he will explain each step to me. The first step is that I must collect the 13 stones and replace each one with an egg. He will provide me with the task, and that I must walk to each stone. Each stone will be guarded by a tribe. He now hands me a bag of magic powder. He tells me that this powder will help make the tribe weaker, at which time I can defeat them with my Golden sword. I feel in my left hand a light large Golden sword. I took a few practice swings and in doing so, I could feel the skill of sword fighting develop within me. I then asked the Creator what do I do with the 13 stones once I collected them. The Creator tells me to continue walking on the path that is provided, and I would soon reach a place where the path turns into three paths. At this place, I will see a giant altar and place to care for a place for each stone. Once the stones are placed, one of the paths will turn white. I will then proceed on that path. While on this path the Creator will once again walk with me and explain the next task that I must complete. I asked the Creator why he is helping me. He explains that I am the chosen one to do this great mission for the spirits of good. That helps explain one thing in my mind, and that is the reason why I was called back here.

Accordingly, he further explains that I am not to fear for what I see, because that which was and that which will be is as I was thereby is. All things are or are now. To say it another way would be that tomorrow is today as today is also tomorrow and therefore, all things are today. Talk about something confusing; however, I do have a feeling that this has something to do with time travel; consequently, I ask him if this does have something to do with time travel. The Creator answered yes, because on the path that you walk, time does not exist, as a result, you will travel deep into the past and even into the future in order to find the stones. He, furthermore, explains that this was necessary to prevent the wrong spirit or person from collecting the stones. Consequently; he further adds that all the time I spend on this path will be less than one second in my physical world. However, for in here, some of the stones are many days walk from each other. I was still really confused as to what was going to happen to me and why it was going to happen. The Creator mentioned that I would be visiting a lot of different tribes. I, therefore, asked him what did this have to do with Coon Run Road?

He then pointed to the ground and moved his hand. When he did this, I saw a big crack that ran the length of Coon Hollow. The crack was at least 50 feet wide and the length from grandpa's fence to Coon Run Road. When I saw this, asked him why nothing had fallen in there. He said because they put a temporary shield to separate the two dimensions, however, that shield was getting slighter and weaker. It was soon sucked in all that was around it. I looked down into this light; I could see nothing below it. I asked the Creator what was beneath it. He said all of time from four million years earlier to now. The Creator said he could place me exactly where he wanted me in time. The Creator, sensing my confusion, told me that the path he would provide was a very strong fiberglass tunnel, in which I would be safe at all times. I asked him if I was in a tunnel. How would I get stones? He told me that the point of getting the stone he would provide me with an opening. He also reminded me that time stopped all while I was on these trips and to take my time. Most important; do the job correctly? Therefore, I wondered what was the difference between correctly and wrongly, if I did not know what accurately was? Then the Creator said that he would give unto me his two maidens that were in the tepee with me earlier. They speak my language and would help me, even if I didn't think I needed help. I figured I would put up with some of their shenanigans just have somebody in a tunnel with me. The tunnel appeared, looking more or less like a portal with a vision of the land we would be heading towards. My two maidens that I will continue to call maidens because I cannot pronounce their names; they entered the portal. The Creator told me to rush in beside them now. I did as he said, being able to grab on to one of the maiden's dresses. The three of us landed in an open field. My maidens told me that we were on the lost continent of Lemuria in what is in my time the Pacific Ocean. We would need to locate the Bahrelphazai the main city in the center of this continent and to take the stone Kulta.

The Bahrelphazai was striving on this continent, which had many grass fields. Over a process of a few hundred years, they adjusted to living mostly off the grass and thus no longer had to hide among the trees. They were among the most short-lived of all the human species. I noticed some strange what looked like spaceships zipping around the sky. I asked my maidens about these spaceships, which they informed me that all species had been genetically engineered my aliens from sister galaxies. This is one reason why the Creator wanted to start us as such an early year, so as not to interfere with the genetic engineering of species who would be laying the foundation for another evolution. There really was no such thing as evolution, but successful genetic engineering from sister galaxies. The maidens explained to me that the Creator wanted me to learn much about these places, since modern science had completely misrepresented the history of mankind. They would always try to explain how these people migrated over the Earth.

They never took into account that aliens were the ones responsible on placing the humanoids in areas that were safer than others plus had more compatible food supplies.

The maidens vanished, leaving me alone in this tunnel that extended in front of me and up to the sky and the light opening. I could feel my heart racing, realizing that I was alone and did not know why I was alone. The maidens returned and told me they found a safe place for me to explore these people and their lands. Then we flashed into a small hut made from animal bones, animal skins, and dried grass. This wasn't too far off from what our current science was claiming. Notwithstanding; they were claiming from guessing, and I was claiming from what I saw.

When I looked around this almost empty hut, I discovered two elderly women. One woman had a leg missing, but had a wood stick that she could use as a crutch. The maidens explained to me that we could understand each other in that the Creator had established a method which I understand them, and they could understand me. Naturally, I asked him why they did not live with the other members of their tribes. The crippled lady claimed her tribe had banished them fearing that they would affect their defenses. I looked at them, and asked how could you hinder their defenses?

They looked at each other and chuckled, claiming it was the thinking of men and not the logical thinking of women. I thought to myself that this competition between the superiority among the sexes had already started four million years earlier. No wonder modern women had this down to a fine-tuned art. I noticed they had no food in their hut. Therefore, I asked him what they did for food? They claim that they only eat once every four days, as is a custom among all the tribes. I, therefore, asked them what was life like in the tribes? They claim that they had many sicknesses and deaths over the last few years. Their elders believe that the sky people may be doing this to them. Her tribe has always had difficulty with the sky people, which had made life much worse for them. The sky people would kill large animals, leaving their bodies on the grounds for scavengers and her tribes to compete for their meat. Those hunted were conducted randomly and usually when the tribes were showing signs of starvation. I asked our two hosts if they could guide me to the temple to get the stone. They knew of the stone, and that it had been used in many religious ceremonies. Although no power was attributed to the stones, they believed the spirits like it better when present. They also warned that there were many priests who existed around the stone, and that it might be difficult to get past the priests.

Another problem that we had was how to get the handicapped woman across the wide-open area, and the river, and up into the mountains where the tribe kept this stone. It would be impossible or extremely dangerous to bring the disabled woman with us. The other woman would not leave the crippled woman alone in this house. Notwithstanding; neither were any good. I did not want to chance it without them. We accept our path back up into the sky, so we can spend some time with these two women and learn about their culture. Now I thought that we needed for the study larger groups of this tribe in order to get feeling for how they lived. The main thing that these two women were telling me was that the aliens were actively involved with these tribes, something our history books completely denied or discounted. Furthermore, this tribe was I think were from all members of the species, in that they were spread throughout the other continents that existed during this timeframe. One of my maidens had the perfect solution, she would catch their heads and read in their minds the directions to the temple area that held the stone. I had no idea that she could do this, but she did it; she could guide us perfect for such a degree that we avoided some of the danger spots. Although I did not worry about the danger spots with my sword, I just did not want to do anything to alert the aliens and cause them to retaliate against us.

The path that we were walking on had high bushes on each side. As we were walking, I noticed a little stream beside us and the sound of the running water. Then like in an instant three Bahrelphazai jumped out of it, with small sticks started hitting my maidens. I swung my sword frantically many times and cut off the heads of the two of them who are attacking my maidens. As the third one was attempting to escape, he tripped over the body of one of the recently beheaded man. This gave me enough time to strike his feet with my sword. Once it has been cut off, the rest is easy. I chopped off his head. Following this; I wiped my sword off on vegetation along our path. Next, I took the three heads into the field beside room, so they were not visible. After this, I simply left their bodies beside road where they could be seen. I still wanted to get our message out, do not attack us. By removing the heads, I hoped to remove anyway for identifying that in the individual. I also thought since these were such perfect straight cuts, they may suspect that it was the aliens that had committed these killings. My maidens were both okay, and I think this will be a bonding experience through this. I wanted them to realize that if they were in danger, I would fight for them. The rest of our walk on this path was without incident. The path was on to this, then a short distance into the mountain I would say about 100 feet up than a straight level walk. I figured they felt safer in the mountain rather than walking across the field below. I was just guessing on this.

When we walked around 300 feet, four Bahrelphazai came out with their spears and rushed towards me. I thought oh my goodness, how can a sword defend against the spear. They said I just feared the spear moving into my personal zone. A spear with its tip cut was worthless. Within minutes, I chopped the tips of all four spears. The last man, after cutting his spear tip, then up on his tip a few feet, to my sword and cut off his head. When I cut off his head, I immediately longed for the guy beside him and got his head as well. Two down and two remaining. The two remaining attempted to escape, providing me a chance to get behind them and chop off their heads. As we turn around on this bend will continue down a small straight stretch. This path was extremely curvy and right on the edge of a 30-foot drop into the ocean. It started to rain making the path sticky and muddy. To be safe, I proceed at a slow pace, wanting to make sure that my maidens are protected. They seem not to be worried, whereas I tell them to pay attention to this as it was dangerous. As I'm speaking one of my maidens slips over the side of the cliff. I drop down and extend my hand trying to catch hers. She reaches to grab my hand, but slips sliding down this Cliff into a raging sea below. She actually falls about 20 feet from the shoreline.

This tells me that if I were trying to get down to the sea level and would swim about 20 feet to get her, that is if she can last that long. I decided to jump, and I land about two feet from her which was dangerously close; however, sometimes we just don't have the choice but at least I did not hit her. As I catch my breath, I grab hold of her and start swimming towards the shoreline. I get out of water and verify that she is bringing. I think she is more like in a state of shock. Not to see some way to get back up there. I asked my maiden if she can see a path proceeding back up to our destination path? She smiles, snaps her fingers, and we are once again on our path. I must sit down with these girls and find out what powers they actually had, in case in an event of serious fighting they could save our lives. Since it is raining and this road path is dangerous, I elect to sit on some rocks waiting for the rain to slow down. Subsequently, I asked my maidens, what powers do they have? They told me that they cannot really explain except when they need it, it is there. One of the maidens tells me that they can make people go to sleep. I asked them what size group, and she tells me the sizes all matter in larger groups may take a little longer. I thought that if this stone is heavily guarded by priests; I will ask my maidens to put them to sleep. As I don't care what religion those priests are from, I do not like killing priests. The maidens agree, and we continue our walk towards the stone.

Oh, if it can only it be could be that easy. As a swing around the bend about 20 minutes later, we run into another set of four guards. I swung my sword out and, while frantically swinging at every way that I could, every once in a while, chopping off one of their heads. I finally got all four, although it was not an organized attack. Furthermore, I have to work on this. It looked like to be that these are just routine guards making their rounds. We finally sneak up to the temple area where they kept the stone. I asked my maidens to put the priests to sleep now. They warned me that this only take the ones who were outside and anyone who was inside would still be awake and cautioned me to beware of buildings. Before they start spraying, I point at three of the largest buildings and tell them to also spray in those buildings and when they start spraying, I on the other hand will be at the center flame which burns above the stone. They spray the outside, as one heads to a building and the other heads towards another building. They would leave one building open for just a few minutes, so I just sit back and wait for them to spray the three buildings. Furthermore, they both converge on the third building and spray. Each building, they opened the front door and looked inside. The buildings were eerily empty for the most part. Nevertheless, the outside they got a lot of people or priests. I have my backpack and took out a little jar of dramatic powder that I must sprinkle on top of the stone before touching it.

Accordingly; I sprinkle it on the stone, which is small enough to fit in my hand. I wrap it up, put it in my backpack and then take out one of the eggs the Creator gave me a set that where the stone was. Miraculously, the egg turns into the stone that I just took. I guess this way they will not readily know that the stone is gone. I motion for my two maidens to come to me, and then we exit back to the path. Furthermore, I then say to the maidens that now would be a good time for the tunnel to arrive and take us away from Lemuria and over four million years in the past. Sure, enough, the tunnel arrives, as all three of us rush to get back inside of it. A person would think that we missed this tunnel, which of course we did. Unfortunately, we merely came forward roughly 300,000 years. We will however travel to another continent called Pangea, where we could locate the Afarensis tribes that may have the stone Anataasi. Meanwhile; I unload my first stone and put it into the special storage device that our tunnel has. One down and twelve go. Prior to walking the path, tunnel is going to brief me on the ancient continent Pangea. Supposedly, this continent breaks apart forming giant portions the continents that we have today. Some portions will be Laurasia, Eurasia, North America, South America, Africa, India, Australia and a Gondwana which merged with Eurasia to form Pangea. Gondwana brought to Pangaea South America, Africa, India, Madagascar, Australia, and Antarctica. But you know, in reality, I don't care what continents form into what. I just want to get my stones and go back to Coon Run and do my missions back there. There does appear to be a lot of wildlife on this continent, whereas Lemuria, contained some; however, they tried to remain hidden. Most likely from the aliens who were shooting the animals and dividing the meat among the assorted tribes. The tunnel has a special monitor to track and identify aliens in this area.

She has done the same thing for Lemuria. I guess the Creator will use this as evidence against the Creators of the aliens. I tell the Creator that he should destroy the aliens that are here now, because bodies on this planet is evidence that they were here. If we let them leave, then we had no evidence that they were here, however they will be able to sneak back in. The good thing about a dead alien is that the alien would not be any trouble in the future. The main thing that we are discovering is that mankind did not involve into other species. Each species was created for a certain function in order to survive during that period of time. As the environment and the Earth changed, so did the Homo species. To be honest, I don't care because I will not be a spokesperson for things that happened up to four million years ago. As I look at the tunnel's maps and diagrams of the so-called evolution of mankind, I'm starting to get a bird's eye view of this process; however, that is not what I need for this mission. The Creator congratulates me on my sword fights for the first but warns me that these will continue on each mission henceforth. He thanked me for saving the maidens. Since he now knows that I will be responsible for them, he would allow them to continue on future missions. He also told me that they begged him to allow them to go with me on the future missions. That told the Creator we were bonding and functioning as a team, which will be vitally important. I asked the Creator if he had any type of swords for the maidens. He immediately gave them each a lighter yet stronger silver sword. I thought this would be good because if we got ambushed, at least there would be a sword to begin the fighting while the other two would reinforce the fighter that was engaged.

Within minutes, we reached our debarkation spot. The Creator explained to me that the stones demanded that if anyone were to touch them, they had to walk among the people in the land before it. The Creator and tunnel would determine the minimum amount of space needed to walk for each stone. Moreover, I always hate it when they come up with these new little tangled up requirements that required more fighting and chance of death on my part. This continent has a rich abundance of vegetation, which in turn gives it a rich and large animal supply. And almost everything here is much larger than what I'm used to during my time. The elephants, deer varieties, and some strange creatures that I don't recognize but am told that they do, extinct. From what I see of these large creatures, it is to mankind's benefit that they went extinct. I can just hope that they don't pass my path, and that if they do, hopefully there be some locals to use the meat. Within minutes of walking on a path the maidens and I witnessed a 10-foot-tall woman with red skin, two large horns come out of her for head, and two extremely strange looking wings, that also appear like giant saw blades. She was dressed in a red bikini with tattoos over her body.

Her face looked somewhat normal. If this is a demon it sure lacked an aroma of evil. Therefore, I asked the maidens to contact the Creator and ask him what this was that was standing in front of us. The Creator quickly answered his beloved maidens telling them this is not a demon but was a product of breeding human species from the aliens. She had no special powers, yet did have some physical powers that she had developed. As I approached her, I said hello. She began to tell me her name as I completely blocked this out because I do not want to know names of things that have no bearing on Coon Hollow. Plus, names tend to personalize your opponent, making it harder to kill them. She looked at me and asked why I was there. I told her we were traveling through this land to the sea on the other side. She looked confused, and as she wanted to know what I meant by the sea on the other side. I told her that this continent had seas on every side. She confessed that she would not know these things because she only lived in this small area here on this path. If she departed from it, she would be in great pain, and soon face death. I asked her if she would allow us to pass through. I mean I told her to look at us, two young Indian girls and one old man. I asked her if she can determine the function of the two very young Indian girls? She laughed and said most likely to care for me. I told her that she is very wise and how can we appear to be dangerous. She cited our three swords. I asked her if she knew about the large beasts that roamed these lands? She said still that no one could pass on this path. I felt saddened that she said this wanting so much to avoid violence in the situation because her appearance may not have been her fault, being the product of alien genetic engineering. Her voice was calm and peaceful, so why did she had to be so stern about not allowing us to pass this path.

I pleaded was her one more time to please allow us peace going travelers to continue on our travels. She then said that if we attempt to pass her, she would have to kill us. That was when I looked at my maidens, and asked them if we should teach her a very valuable lesson? They nodded their heads yes, and we immediately drew their swords and begin swinging. Our initial swings had some impact, but not the impact that I had expected. She was bleeding but the cuts were not that deep, they should have removed or dislocated parts of her body like her arms and legs. I told my maidens we must continue as we did for almost one hour. You think all we had knocked her off her balance and she could not counterattack us while we were still swinging at her. After about two hours of continuous swinging our three swords she finally bled out and died. We quickly retrieved our things and continued on the path. We continue walking for about an hour or a safe distance to dissociate ourselves from killing the path blocker. We did pass a few families while walking. These people do not look like the Afarensis as reported in our current analysis of the development of the ancient people. One of my maidens told me that this was because the aliens would plant false bones and just a few in certain areas that would confuse the modern archaeologists. It was for one day for a minute that was the Earth having tribes of the species, why would there be only a few skeletons surface. The lands should have been filled with skeletons. Notwithstanding; these new bodies had bones that dissolved into dust upon death.

They were buried uncovered in the ground, and not in any form of coffin. When I thought about it, they didn't make sense, because why had they not discovered many more skeletons? To take one bone, and create an entire species that roamed the Earth for hundreds of thousands of years, and only come up with a handful of skeletons is enough to make you wonder what kind of logic these people were using. I do confess that they were not like me being able to see, but I was not prepared for what we were about to see. We passed through the first town, or should I say city. It had well over 10,000 homes, and these are not huts, but were multiroom structures combined with running water. I noticed that they did not have any police departments. My maidens told me this is because here no one commits crimes, because if you did the aliens would catch you and torment you, making you beg to meet death. I asked the maidens if the tribes used the aliens to monitor their population with this much detail, could they be monitoring us. My maidens then showed me some necklaces that they were wearing that I did not even notice. They said that this concealed us. I asked them how could it conceal us if I did not have one as well. They said that I had a Golden sword which concealed me. I then said we need to find the stone Anataasi. My maidens told me that it was only a three-day walk to get there; however, one day that would be through the grasslands. I asked them why that would be a problem. They told me that the grasslands have many wild beasts, who hated any form of humanity and were dedicated to destroying humanity. In fact, the aliens were so occupied with killing and reengineering these beasts that it took up most of their time. They therefore, except for monitoring crime, could no longer continue to provide technological advances for the tribes.

Subsequently; I asked my maidens if we needed any special weapons to defeat these beasts. They said no, except for no sleep and going straight through because if we slept, they would absolutely kill us. We walked along the path, having no contact with the natives, which was a pleasant surprise. They just simply ignored us as being inferior and no threat. We did however have a massive attack from the beasts. Fortunately, each swing removed one of their limbs or head if that was where we swung. It got so bad that we could not move because of all these carcasses and soon all the vultures who were there to eat these carcasses. This told me that the aliens had set up a system to help prevent the spread of diseases, which do manifest themselves within large amounts of dead carcasses. We had only fought for one hour before some alien ships appeared, and they began emitting a sound that only the beasts could hear. This forced the beasts to retreat. The aliens ignored us and when the beasts disbanded and retreated. We arrived at the temple that housed the stone Anataasi. There were no Afarensis there to protect it. I simply walked up, applied the dust, and swap the stone for one of my eggs. Oddly; the second the egg had completely involved in the stone; we were alone in this temple. Once the egg had evolved, a family and some soldiers came into view it. They looked at it and moved on. When we were safe from the swap, soon it was time to find a tunnel. My maidens were quite efficient at finding the tunnel, even though they love these adventures, there was a point where they wanted to rest. I told him I agreed 100%. We walked for six hours into a forest where the tunnel appeared and off, we went. Accordingly; I submitted the stone to our collection of two. Next; I asked the Creator where we would go next; he told me that now I can choose, because with the alien interventions, our actions would have minimal impact, if any impact at all.

CHAPTER 04

Thirteen Stones (Part 2)

While reviewing the information through the portal about my upcoming stones, our two maidens came into the room and each one selected one of my arms to escort me to another room which also had a portal. I learned that it is wise to just follow their lead when being escorted by the maidens. They seem to always have a good handle on the situation at hand. Where ever they were taking me, it had to be more important than reviewing for upcoming missions. I marvel how each time they take me somewhere, it is a place that I do not recognize.

Consequently; I'm beginning to wonder how many portals this place has, considering it also has numerous monitors. Either way, their number cannot be important, considering that it is primarily for my benefit. The maidens appear to always know what is going on. The maidens sat me on the middle seat of three seats, as they each selected a seat on my sides. They motion for me to look at the portal as it begins to start displaying images. The first image that it displays is one of my hometown newspapers with a date that reads July 12, 2026. I wonder if this date being my birthday has any significance. After having been four million years in the past, two years in the future is not something to knock me off my tracks. A nurse opens the door and what I see inside is disturbing. I see my sister, two brothers, father, and some of their families somewhere around a bed that has me in it. They began by singing happy birthday to me. This is when I asked maidens to stop the portal, as I have a very important question that I needed answers to now. I asked them how my body is two years in the future, when they told me that my total departure would I be a matter of seconds. The maidens explain that time does continue; however, this time is in a temporary alternate dimension. Once I've completed collecting the stones, I would have the power to remove this alternate dimension and have everything return to the way it was prior to my departure. I asked him what would happen if I failed to collect all the stones?

Accordingly; my maidens tell me that time dimensions would be the least of my worries, as so many other terrifying events would occur, creating a paradigm shift unlike ever before and existence of this dimension. I do not really understand what they just said, except to know that it cannot be good. Logically, I asked them if they believe that we would successfully collect all the stones? They both told me that their lives also are dependent upon this, and that they would gladly give their lives to ensure my success. I told them that it was up to their advanced powers to make sure they did not have to forfeit their lives, because to me that would not be an option. I felt our room shaken as much as a real small earthquake. The maidens smiled while looking each other, and then replied that they thought the Creator was pleased with my answer. I motioned for the portal to resume, as I saw the nurse review her notes. I decided to take the easy way, and asked my maidens. Even though I know they are not my maidens, although they have just been with me through two stones, with 11 to go, so to me, it just as easy to the concept of teamwork to call them my maidens. Additionally, I think the Creator likes it when I say my maidens.

Be that as it may, I asked my maidens if they can tell me what has happened to my body since I have been with them. They explained that I am currently in a coma, and my vital signs are all good. They have been giving me extensive physical treatment and therapy to prevent my muscles from atrophying. I asked my maidens if there was the danger of my muscles deteriorating, if I were to return within seconds of my departure. They verify that upon my return, my body will be restored pain-free. Remembering the 1,000 pounding nails, the pain-free term is very pleasing to my ears. I then verify that everyone will have no memory of this alternate dimension. They said all, including my sister. Having learned to question each little detail in their responses, I asked him what did he mean by including my sister. They reveal to me, that the creator has been sending my sister visions of my accomplishments through her dreams. He thought this necessary, since she is linked to this Coon Hollow Paradigm, and wanted to add some stability in our underlying assumptions about what was happening. More or less, the concept that two heads are better than one. Actually, I'm glad that someone knows the great things that I am doing, plus one less person to worry about me can only be a good thing.

Next, I invite my two maidens to return with me to the portal that I was looking at and help me in my decision as to which of my ancestors to visit first. I told them that I was leaning towards the Neanderthal, since they were the most recent to go extinct and closely related to my species, with even varying degrees of their DNA appearing in our European and Asian descendants.

They advised me that the Neanderthal would be one of our most challenging missions, and that they were so close to our current day, with us only going back between 30 and 40,000 years. The stone that we would retrieve is the Obsidiaani. Moreover, we be going to a continent that currently exists in my time, and that being Europe. I explained to them that I had never made it to Europe yet, nevertheless wanted to visit it. Maybe I can kill two birds with one stone on this encounter. Additionally, I asked my maidens why they were coming back around 40,000 years previously, whereas the Neanderthal allegedly existed as early as 800,000 years previously. The maidens explained that when we take the stone from the Neanderthal, it would be a species extinction event. I then asked my maidens if I would be the one responsible for the extinction of the Neanderthal.

Subsequently; they reassured me that I was not the one responsible, yet we were taking the stone at this time to prevent those who were responsible from capturing the stone as they had during the previous extension event; which, was vaguely recorded in our current history. We would actually sneak in a few days prior to their arrival. This would give us enough time to get back in the Tunnel to secure the stone with the Creator. The maidens now excused themselves to work with the Creator and Tunnel to make our final arrangements, and collect any special powers that might be needed. The creator came out now to speak with us. He revealed that for this mission, we had to go to 10 caves that the Neanderthal were known to have existed. From each of these 10 caves, we would have to collect a sample of dirt. Once we had all 10 samples, the location of the Obsidiaani stone would be revealed. The maidens each handed me a backpack, as they also kept one each, for a total of four backpacks. I asked them why we needed so many backpacks, in which they replied that the Creator and Tunnel believed that we needed these tools and powers. That was a perfect answer for me, except for one we need for me tools and powers. Some things may be better to remain a mystery until they needed to be revealed. The maidens also revealed that there were no walking requirements on this mission, therefore as we collected the dirt in each cave, we would store it in the Tunnel and proceed to the next cave. The first day would be located in southern England, not far from the channel.

The Tunnel dropped the three of us into this cave, approximately ½ mile inside. The maidens told me the distance inside, considering I would have no way of measuring this. We took out our container kit for this cave and I began chiseling at the ground, to no avail. Subsequently; I began chiseling at the wall and was making some progress. However; the maidens told me I was not getting that much dirt and that I had to continue chiseling at the wall. They would take and collect what I chiseled and filter out in the dirt. We continued like this until I probably chiseled in about six inches, at which time the maidens told me we had a verified sample of dirt from this cave. One down, and nine to go. I was thinking that with no transportation time between the caves, we might very well be able to accomplish this before the real exterminators appeared. Our next cave was in France, in which the Tunnel handed us our second container kit. I could only dread, how hard this would have been if I had to do it all alone. This wall was not as harsh as the one in southern England, and was in 30 minutes I had a verifiable dirt sample. As we entered into Tunnel, I surrendered this second kit, it was Tunnel who was storing the dirt samples separately. And off we went to a mountainous area in Spain. For this cave, we went in almost 2 miles. I asked my maidens why we went in so deep?

Nevertheless; they explained that the Neanderthal use this location for protection against freezing, for when the ice age began to start freezing them. For this wall, my chisel was completely ineffective. My maiden gave me what appeared to be a laser drill. She warned that I should stand back when firing this drill. I took the steps back, even to her recommendation, asking that this is far enough back.

She nodded her head yes, at which time I began firing, and firing, until I can start to see a small hand sized hole appearing. The maidens looked in the hole and told me to continue firing and this time make the hole wider and deeper. I continue firing for another 30 minutes, at which time the maidens motioned for me to stop. They now took out another section of device was a long hose and inserted it into the hole. They monitored the debris that was coming out to sort any dirt from it. Fortunately; we had a verifiable sample. I handed this sample to Tunnel as we prepared to go to our next cave, which would be cave number three, with merely seven more remaining. This stop was in Portugal, which also had walls as hard as concrete. I asked the maidens if all the caves that we were going to would have walls this hard. They looked at me rather confused and answered, "How would they know?" They once again handed me a drill, subsequently this drill was much larger. I began drilling, every once in a while, looking at my maidens to receive verification if I should continue. Finally; they nodded for me to stop; thus, we once again collected our verifiable dirt sample. We now had four, was only one more until halfway mark. Once again, I handed Tunnel my verified dirt sample, which was stored neatly and securely with the other dirt samples. We see it in as we proceeded to our next cave. This cave was in Italy, in their northern mountains, which I believe were called the Alps. For this cave, we only entered a few hundred feet. I could actually see the sun coming in the entrance.

The maidens handed me my freshly sharpened chisel as I began scraping along the wall. This went rather quickly, in that within 20 minutes we had a verifiable sample. I handed our fifth verified dirt sample to Tunnel as we prepared for the next stop. This stop was in Switzerland, on top of one of their high mountains. For this stop, I asked the maidens if I could see the entrance, wanting to see what this area looked like before my species chopped it up. They told me that I could as long as I stayed inside the cave, because we did not want to take any chance in the actual exterminators discovering our location. I was able to see what I wanted to see rather quickly, and having forgotten there was nothing more than covered with snow. Additionally, it was cold. I can only marvel at how the Neanderthal were able to withstand this much cold. This sort of made me feel sorry for the human wives that they had with them.

The maidens now escorted me three miles inside this cave, citing that since it got so much colder here, the Neanderthal had to go deeper inside it. Once again, I can only marvel at the guts it took to venture so deep inside a cave, considering that many predators would also venture this deep inside. For this extraction, both maidens also had a large laser drill, while handing me my extremely large laser drill. I always marveled how as a man I was required to confess that the women were so much stronger, while automatically accepting the harder assignments, which was expected from a gentleman. For this wall, we merged all three laser beams on to one point and drilled for approximately two hours. Once again, they asserted their section hose and filtered out the debris from the dirt, obtaining a verifiable dirt sample. We now, merely had four more samples to collect. Now we headed for Uzbekistan, which was located at least 200 miles east of the Caspian Sea and bordered north of Afghanistan. Naturally, Afghanistan did not exist at this time. This cave proved to be our easiest cave thus far, with me being able to scrape the dirt with my hand from the cave floor and obtain a verifiable dirt sample within a few minutes. The maidens verified the dirt sample and handed it to Tunnel for its verification.

They looked at me and said that it was better to take these extra cautions, than to have to go through this entire process once more. Of course, I agreed and told him to verify away. Subsequently; we headed for the Altai Mountains or Golden mountains in Mongolia. I was starting to think that considering the Neanderthal had no mechanical transportation, unless some aliens had snuck in there somehow, they really got around covering large areas. My maidens reassured me that the Neanderthal had no alien intervention, except for their extermination event that fortunately for them they would miss. Their absence would be excused considering they would have already been exterminated. My maidens recommended that I attempt to use my chisel, even though the walls were somewhat hard, they crumble easily forming a verifiable dirt. I therefore chiseled for about one hour and after my maidens separated the dirt from the rock remains obtained a verifiable dirt sample. I also was thinking that this semi spiritual existence was good for my arms considering the amount of chiseling I did today would have put a lot of strain on my physical arms. We now had merely two more stops before submitting our dirt samples. The next stop was Crimea, which nationally looked much better in this time era than it did in my war-torn era. For this stop, my maidens recommended I take a break and allow them to collect this sample. They warned me to stay close so as not to invite any unnecessary trouble.

They got out their laser beams and fired away and within approximately 20 minutes, had obtained a verifiable dirt sample. They gave this sample to Tunnel to include with the other eight collected thus far, bringing our total to nine, with solely one more stop. Our final stop was in southern Turkey. For this stop, Tunnel released a large laser beam weapon. My maidens helped me push this large weapon out onto the cave floor. My maidens told me that we were seven miles deep inside this cave, the reason being to ensure that we had not been detected. I began shooting this large laser beam for almost two hours at which time my maidens waved for me to stop. They each to the small chisel and began scraping at the sides of the hole that I had just created. They placed their scrapings inside a container and into another container. Next, they emptied a container into a screen device that they had and with both containers were able to collect a verifiable dirt sample. I will confess that I was certain to worry about this last one, since my luck always ran out on the last of any series. We now had our 10 dirt samples. Tunnel notified the stone temple that we had the 10 verified dirt samples. The temple was the location to deposit the 10 samples and once they were verified would notify us where to pick up the stone.

Meanwhile; Tunnel took us to the location and gave the temple officials the 10 dirt samples. I asked these temple officials when they will be done with the verification. The one priest told me that they were almost finished, and asked if we would remain and take them with us to retrieve the stone. Tunnel readily agreed and told them to make themselves comfortable while we waited. Within one minute the verifications were complete, we had passed. It was at this time I thanked my maidens for their extreme diligence in this process. Subsequently, I could see their beautiful faces turned into a shy blush. Accordingly; I winked at them, at which time Tunnel told me to behave. The priests gave Tunnel our destination, and we were there in one minute. The priest escorted my maidens and I into their temple, in which a Golden altar had the Obsidiaani stone sitting on it. As I approached, I sprinkled my dust upon it. Next, I took out a special container to put it in. Meanwhile; I took out in an egg and put on top of the altar, in which it turned into the stone. The priests looked confused, asking me if we did not need this stone. My maidens looked at them and told them that the stone was for them and their long, prosperous future. At this time; the maidens in I, with the Obsidiaani stone, entered into the Tunnel bidding our farewell.

Accordingly; I congratulated my maidens for wishing them a long and prosperous future. They asked me why I did not correct them for not knowing that the stone from the egg was not real. I explained that they were Neanderthal and thus not much intelligence was expected. At this time, I noticed a lot of round missile-like projectiles, filing the open space that once surrounded us. I asked Tunnel what was happening. Tunnel explained that in the next four hours we would be launching the Neanderthal extinction event, erasing their existence from the Earth. Tunnel would launch over 10,000 of these projectiles that would seek out individuals and vaporize them. Meanwhile; Tunnel would launch major attacks against every cave and tribal settlement that they had. The attacks against the caves would be a heat vaporizing force that will turn the remains into a powder that would blend into the cave walls. I asked Tunnel why so much detail, which time replied to conceal our operations from history and the Extermination Event Force that was prepared to launch the next day. There could be no remaining evidence of any kind. This also meant the total vaporization of all the tribal settlements, leaving history only to hypothesize that they were cave dwellers.

Throughout the next four hours, we could hear faint screams, because the vaporizers would vaporize their sound waves that were making the sounds from their lungs. Even my maidens were now looking somewhat depressed. I wondered if my search for the Coon Run Road Ghost was worth this much death. Tunnel reminded me that all I did was take one day from their existence, and also reminded me or should I say informed me that the exterminators were using much more inhumane methods for their executions. This troubling situation soon ended, although not as soon as I would have wished. As Tunnel was preparing to return to the Creator, I handed him the most recent stone. I commented that hoped, to know the remaining ones would not be as difficult as this one was. We would now visit the Heidelbergensis and obtain the stone Verna, which was reported to be on Lemuria. The Land of Mu was beginning to sink during our visit of one million years previously. This was the first time that Lemuria sank, reemerging around 300,000 years ago before their sinking approximately 100,000 years ago. The reason for this initial sinking is somewhat vague and beyond the mission of Tunnel to determine. This ancient continent took up most of the Pacific Ocean, ranging from Easter Island to well above Hawaii to east of Australia to the south of Japan. Our initial visit around four million years earlier found the continent to be at the early stages of turning into a desert. We returned to this continent three million years after our first visit and found it to be rich in vegetation and having many established settlements.

There were signs of extensive alien activity. This activity was because they concentrated on relocation purposes needed to establish this bustling civilization that would soon be flooded with the initial sinking of Lumaria. Once again, our available information concerning the Heidelbergensis was completely off track. This is to say that the Heidelbergensis who lived elsewhere on the Earth without alien support matched the conclusions presented by modern archaeologists. The Heidelbergensis that we were visiting were the much more advanced society with established territories and governments. It was sad to think that all this would be sunk deep into the minds of the ocean beds, which are secrets hidden from modern mankind for eternity. For this visit, since this will be a four stone continental visit, Tunnel decided to give us a good tour of this land. We see wide rivers with bridges, as these bridges were not made from wood, and were coated in white marble, which made them glamorous to see from above. Considering that there were some small mountain ranges on this continent, these bridges may very well have provided an entertainment for those who viewed them from these mountains. The roads were covered in some sort of well crushed gravel. The horse was the primary, except for boats, form of transportation. The boats were actually combat ships and were used to destroy any invasions from Asia or the Americas. Lemuria practiced total exclusion.

Consequently; there was one thing that would bring down this total exclusion policy, and that was a civil war that was currently being fought throughout this continent. There were four major governments established in Lemuria. All four were fighting each other, with no signs of any allies fighting together, against the other remaining tribes. This was enough over the five-year war to reduce its population by 70%. They had built it up and destroyed leaving only a remnant, which surprisingly came to a complete compromise on all issues. The aliens had decided to withdraw and began their reengineering attempts with the Heidelbergensis that existed elsewhere on Earth. Tunnel reported to me they were having trouble locating the stone Verna, believing that some priest had safeguarded it against the raging wars. Be that as it may, both the Creator and Tunnel were searching for the stone. While we were waiting, Tunnel prepared for us some masks and ancient clothing, so we could walk out and visit some of the buildings. Tunnel cautioned us not to talk with anyone, because if they did not recognize us, they believed we were there to cause them harm. Our investigation of their housing, revealed that those who had died in the war, had their doors left open, allowing anyone to come in and view them. We actually went in and checked out a few of these houses, determining certain things that were standard.

They all had running water, beds in their bedrooms with storage devices to store their clothing. They also had a large, I guess family room which had a large fireplace in the center of this large room. There was also a mysterious fan like device above this workplace, which most likely sucked out the smoke that would have come from this fireplace. My maidens and I discovered what appeared to be a restaurant. We went in and sat down. A woman gave us a menu, which was a flat piece of stone with pictures painted on it. We made our selections, and one of my maidens snapped into her hand some form of coins appeared, which we used to pay for a meal. The meat was well cooked actually has some seasoning taste to it, but had a couple vegetables with it, neither of which I recognized attributed to some platform that became am extinct wilderness a million years. We did find it difficult to eat with these masks on, therefore paid the left. Apparently, this restaurant got angry at us for not finishing our food. Therefore; I took some food from my plate and put in my pocket, as also did my maidens. This sort of calmed down the restaurant owner since there was no food left on the plate. I would think most likely the reason for the owner's frustration was that Heidelbergensis came with hefty appetites, therefore there is nothing ever left on their plates, I guess.

We decided now to look at a few more houses before going back to Tunnel. While looking inside the southern house, I noticed a couple of Heidelbergensis watching us. Therefore, I tapped my maidens and motioned for us to leave. Once we were outside, I whispered to them that I believe we are being followed. As he walked down the street back towards Tunnel, the two men continue to follow us. They are slowly gaining on us. Then we were about 150 feet from the Tunnel, they walked around us. I was as close as I ever wanted to come to confrontation with these bulky and stocky, almost ape things. When they passed us, we began to walk slowly directly towards the Tunnel. Tunnel that is in, telling us they located the location for stone Verna. It was being kept inside a temple, and then drop into a large deep well that the aliens had dug for them. The problem was that the well was filled with a form of a lead acid that anything that was dropped into would dissolve unless placed in a certain container. I asked him how he knew that the stone had not been dissolved. Tunnel told me because it was in one of those protective containers. I then asked if we had something to connect today as a container to pull it up. Tunnel said that there were six guards in and that they would have to be killed in order to have enough time to fish for this container. I looked at my maidens and asked them if they still had their swords. Their swords appeared in their hands. I then walked over to where I had placed my coat and pulled out my sword that I had tucked under my coat. Moreover; I asked my maidens if they still had their sleeping dust. They showed me that they still had it.

Meanwhile, I asked Tunnel if he had that connecting rope or whatever force officially for my container. Tunnel put the connecting wire on the floor beside my foot. I tell my maidens, let's go fishing. Tunnel had found a side entrance that he recommended we use. As we entered the side entrance, we simply had to walk about 30 feet to the temple which had its doors closed. We opened the door, entered immediately, then close those doors. The guards came towards us, in which I began swinging actually getting a head per swing. Therefore, like almost instantly I knocked down two of them by beheading them. By now the sleeping dust had kicked in on the four remaining guards. Once they hit the floor, off with their head. I did not want anything to disturb my fishing. I placed my two maidens on the front door, one each the side. Hopefully, if anyone entered, we would get them. We did have three people enter, one at a time, and each time my maidens got them and tossed all the bodies into this well figuring it would eat them.

After one hour, my connecting rod started to light up. I didn't know it could do this. Apparently; it is telling me it has a connection to the rock. Sure, enough, it brought up the container box. Now existed there looking at this container box I did not know it was safe to touch and so ask my maidens if they knew how I could open this container box. One of my maidens walked over to the priest's table and brought back a container that liquid in it. She then poured the liquid on the outside of the container. We can hear its sizzling sound and see some light smoke. After it looked like it had cooled down, she poured some more liquid on it. This time, there was no sizzling nor any smoke. My maiden told me that it was safe to open the container, after I applied my dust. Therefore, I applied my dust and opened the container, then removed the stone. I placed the stone in my pocket. The egg had now evolved into the stone shape. I lowered this container using the rope that Tunnel gave me to the bottom of this well. I tried to feel around and get it as close to where it was, as possible. Furthermore, I put the Verna stone in my pocket. Likewise, I then summoned my maidens, and asked which one wanted to keep our stone until we returned inside the Tunnel. Not only that, but I was projecting some sort of trouble on our way back. As the man, I figured they would attack me first. As we were walking back to the Tunnel, we were attacked by four men. The girls sprayed their sleeping dust on the remaining two men. My Golden sword was working with me now, I was able to slice and dice with ease, as the first two of these four were executed. My maidens finished off the remaining two that they put to sleep. They also helped me move the bodies to some low trees that were close by, I mean within a couple feet. You made it back to Tunnel with no more interruptions. I put the stone, or had my maidens put the stone in the container designated by Tunnel.

After receiving approval from the Creator, we went forward one million years will remain on Lemuria. Lemuria had survived its first sinking. The grass was much greener, trees taller, the people were starting to look more human, especially with their flatter faces. They would be extinct before 110,000 BC. The stone Turkooi held by the Erectus. They had tribes in Eurasia, and even Indonesia, plus Africa. Naturally, the only way they could be on Lemuria was by the aliens. This species would be instrumental in the steps towards my species. Tunnel claims the aliens are fine tuning these species toward getting what they wanted, and that was a slave race. I wonder why they have not taken mankind as slaves. They do have millions of years invested. I ask Tunnel what I must do to get the Turkooi stone. Tunnel explains that the priests had split their temple into two faiths. The faiths were bitter enemies. One priest decided if he did not get the stone, then no one would get the stone. Allegedly, the priest was terrified of the wilderness and never left the city although he had been known it to take the stage coach when visiting the other tribes. I checked with the stage coach company, asking them if they can remember tribes that this priest had visited.

They claimed to have no records. We can do these two ways: one asked him directly, however in order to do that we name some power that he is afraid of and tell him that he will be forgiven when he has the revealed location of the stone. The second way is to question his coworkers. This has to be done in secret, and questions need to be mixed up with many other job-related subjects. We can even question this priest, omitting questions concerning the stone. Hopefully this will prevent him from running scared. Actually, the results surfaced of three visits to smaller towns. We began questioning the next day. Fortunately, we came up with four strong possibilities. Throughout this day, my maidens were scanning this town with their portable scanners that can reach out two miles in one direction. Therefore, they stood back-to-back and were able to grab four miles or two miles each side, and they in turn scanned all the temple area and everything that this tribe had plus a scan of some caves that Tunnel told them about. Even though we came up empty on this first day, I felt that we had made progress through eliminating certain areas and by eliminating this linked tribe and all this tribe's area we knew he had to have left and tried to travel elsewhere since the priests did not have horses.

Horses are the only alternative with the exception of the stagecoach. I figured that he would take a lot of trips and confuse anyone that could be following him. I knew that he was smart enough that the place he dropped off the stone he would only make one trip. He would make multiple trips to the other areas again to create confusion for anyone trying to find the stone. I did have one person there who remembered vaguely the priest taking a short trip, 11 hours round-trip to a small tribe North of his temple. Upon reviewing his doctrine, I discovered that North was extremely important to these people. You might be asking why we doing all this hard work when Tunnel could find this in the matter of hours. One unfortunately, some strong device the creator cannot locate is jamming Tunnels scans. For his protection, he powered down all his systems. He also sent missile probes all throughout Lemuria with the sole purpose of confusing whoever was jamming him. Early the next morning we head for the tribe that I suspect. My maidens were able to get some horses for the three of us when galloping across the now beautiful Lemuria. Once we arrived at the tribe, we secured our horses at a stable. This tribe was a commercial trading tribe, therefore they had contact with foreigners. This basically meant we were not in danger. We scanned this town twice but came up empty. Afterwards; we scanned a two-mile radius around the outside of this tribe and also came up empty.

Therefore, I looked on my little chart where I had assembled the places his coworkers said he went to;

therefore, I decided to check the places or place he went to twice. It was also North. While riding our horses to this new tribe, one of my maiden's alarms began sounding. The second maiden's scanner began alarming; the other maiden pointed her scanner in the same direction, and it also began alarming or sounding. I looked at my maidens and asked them why their scanners were making all that racket. They smiled at me and said they may have found my stone. Therefore; I got my horse as did my maidens, and the three of us with our horses tied to our belts, followed the scanners which led us to an old vacant house which also had a well. The scanners were indicating that the stone was in the well. I dropped a small rock into the well, quickly hearing it bounce off the well's bottom. Just making a guess, I figured that the stone was within 25 feet. Therefore; I began to search the well. I descended the well slowly, trying to feel for any human passages. Approximately 18 feet down, I found a small open passage. As I reached my hand into this hole, I felt some cloth, at which time I began slowly pulling the cloth towards me. Because I had to spray with the dust first so it would not kill me. I was able to get to this stone to within one foot from my body.

Subsequently; I sprinkled my dust on top of the stone. Then I picked it up and put it in my pocket. Next, I removed an egg and watched it transform into the stone. Now I tossed the fake rock, wrapped in the cloth, deeper into this little hole. After this, I climbed back up and out of the well. At this time, I began to search for my maidens. Our horses were still tied up to wherever they went, they went on foot. I waited for about two hours; at which time they came back to our small camp. When they saw me, one of them was excited and ran over to give me a big hug, while the other began yelling at me for hiding from them. I told him that was not I am hiding, and pulled out the stone to hand it to one of them, I was in the well getting our stone. I then said to them, go back and tell the Tunnel to power up so we can go back to the creator. Now they both became excited, kissing my cheeks nonstop. I hate to say this, but I do not like this. I think I was tired from the climbing a well, plus riding on a horse without a saddle. Either way, I gave them a strong hug and then told him it was time to go. I also told him to save some of those kisses for later. This is when they told me that they could not kiss me inside the Tunnel or around the Creator. He told me not to worry, they would select the opportune time for me to receive the remainder of my reward. I told them that was the best news I received since being around the Creator.

Meanwhile; we went back to the Tunnel, whereas my maidens gave the Tunnel our most recent stone. He placed it with the other stones as we began our trip back to the creator. Upon my return, I go straight to the creator to complain. I question how I was sent to get the stone, if the stone was knocked being and just by going back to basics, and I guess some miracle we were able to find the stone. I asked the creator what is going on here? The creator tells me that in the stones he knows very little, has no power. He was sent to help me prevent the crack in the sky that that will not only destroy Coon Hollow, but all that is in this dimension. The creator tells me that if he could, he would do this. Subsequently; it was me who was chosen as we must do this. Even my maidens, which the creator complains that I have not given them names yet, will be in situations where they can, I help, and even have their existence put in a risk, yet also there will be many situations where they cannot help. On those situations that they cannot, I must search for and find the answer. I cannot believe what is happening to me. I thought it was illegal to go back to Coon Hollow, and find some simple solution, returned to Washington in my life will continue. Now I have been in a coma for two years and must perform miracles, of which I cannot, in order to get my life back. To compound issues, I have my right and left arm wanting to kiss me, and telling me they will find a way for this to happen.

I believe they will, and I will have no power to resist, and even question why should I oppose, they have been loyal and placed their lives in danger for no apparent reward. I will need to have a long discussion with both; however, first things first tonight I will give them their names as strongly recommended by the Creator. Also, I must redefine the role of the Creator, accepting any small thing that he did as a very large gift. I can no longer expect only to receive and must believe that whatever he gave me threw out this horrifying mission, to have faith that I could do it. There comes a time when you must believe in yourself, even when every being of yourself calls you a fool for doing so. These will be issues that I must fight with and overcome. Because my middle name is Doubt. My two maidens have now destroyed in my room and full chamber. I cannot call it my room because my physical body is in an Ohio hospital in a coma. They're both dressed in very formal and highly decorated gowns, a beauty that never seen in my life. Their dress is better than even the greatest Queens to have ever ruled empires or launched thousands of ships.

As they sit down, I apologize for having called them my right, and what is right may maidens. I explained that did this in order to establish the Creator as their master or leader. Nevertheless; our extensive experiences have changed the very foundation of our now eternal relationships. Therefore; during my recent conversation with the Creator, he expressed disappointment that I had not assigned you your names. I did not know I had the power to do this, nor do I believe that I have the right to do this. Nevertheless; there comes a point where what I believe may not be not be what I believe. Subsequently; I now truly believe that I must give you your names. I hope you like them and give you the right to refuse the name I've given you and have me give you another name, of which I will gladly do. Understand, you have the power to have me pick a name that you want. If you do not accept this power, then I will not give you a name. I call forth the first of my two maidens. As her beauty, puts warmth in every fabric of my being I look into her eyes which are filled with rivers of pure love and said unto her, your name is Woape, which means hope, because it is my hope in you that shall bring us great success, as we overcome the mountains of challenges, which lie before us. I now call forth the second Queen of absolute beauty and grace and said unto her your name is Orenda, which means magic power.

Notwithstanding; for as the creator claims I have magic power, of which I do not, I declare that you have magic power, which I know you do, yet you also claim that they do not. I now invite you to discuss with me our next mission. When I say discuss, I mean discuss, because your wisdom is much greater than my foolishness, and I regret that you may permit my foolishness to destroy us all. I now sat down with Orenda and Woape as I explained we will remain in Lemuria and visit the Rudolfensis and retrieve the Ametisti stone. The Rudolfensis were from Africa, and as a species existed about one third of their tribes in the Erectus. Yet they did exist almost twice as long as the Neanderthals and three times as long as the Heidelbergensis. Accordingly, for the creator the group for tribe that we will be obtaining the stone from were transferred here by the aliens, who have been expressing great concern over the quick decline of their genetical advancements. This tribe of the Rudolfensis do not have a consistent mythological belief system concerning the spirits. That is why our Ametisti stone is hidden beneath one of the temples, created for them by the aliens, in an attempt to present themselves as great spirits. The aliens sealed any entrances to the stone; however, a mysterious Tunnel was created for entrance into the extremely small chamber that holds this stone. We can expect that warriors from this lizard-like species will attempt to prevent us from retrieving the stone. This is why we will have our swords at all times. We must watch each other's backs because these lizard-like creatures can drift through rock as if it were nothing.

Meanwhile; Tunnel has prepared for us some additional weapons and devices that we will need for this mission. One such device is an eye implant which will rest on the outside of our eyes and thus cause no harm to come up on our own eyes; notwithstanding, they will provide additional protection against any external object from penetrating our eyes. This device will allow us to see in the dark, thereby no creature that exists in the dark shall be able to harm us. We can expect that these lizard-like creatures to destroy some of the passageways that we will be going through. In these events, Tunnel has given us small portal devices that can repair damaged passageways. Shortly thereafter, Orenda, Woape, and I entered the Tunnel to prepare for our return to the Lemuria continent, which has become nothing more than a genetic engineering platform for the aliens whom I suspect were instrumental in the second and final sinking of this lost Land of Mu. Our first encounter with the Rudolfensis, caught is unprepared, and that their appearance presented a flat face, open nostrils, and extended jawbone. It was scary to think what would happen if one of these things bit us. Our masks were mandatory coupled with our hairy bodysuits. Orenda and Woape expressed concern over how their bodysuits emphasized the details of their breasts. I told them not to be concerned because no part of their actual skin from their breasts were exposed, consequently these were necessary so that they could blend in with the other females that we may come in contact with.

Subsequently; while we were walking to our underground passageway interest, we did pass many males and females. Once Orenda and Woape saw these other females, their concerns disappeared. We actually ended up walking about five miles. I asked Woape if she had contact with Tunnel. She did, and thereby I asked Tunnel why had he parked so far away from our entry point. Tunnel claimed that is spot was the safest from alien detection. That answer good enough for me. As we entered this passageway, we came upon our first obstacle within about 300 feet. The passageway was sealed; therefore, we unsealed it. A delay of about 30 minutes, yet unavoidable. Fortunately, the tools the Tunnel had prepared for us were extremely quiet, removing from me any fear of a lizard detection. We walked approximately 1 mile before our next passageway obstruction. This time our tools struggled to gain us entrance, considering they block this for almost 200 feet. Apparently, they did not want the aliens down here. I was thinking as a courtesy we might reseal this passageway upon our departure. This time we walked for about four more miles until another passageway obstruction. Luckily; this passageway obstruction with only about 10 feet, which we passed through with ease. In there was a force of 10 lizard warriors with their spears ready to attack.

Fortunately; Orenda had brought a small laser beam weapon, which I did not even know they had. She immediately executed the 10 quickly and with ease. She looked at me to explain their execution had to be quickly so they could not alert their other forces. I told her she did a great job and thank you. Also told both of them they should bring this weapon with them on all our missions. The Ametisti stone was in plain sight on another altar. I put the dust over the stone as I gave the stone to Orenda. I placed my egg over the available opening and watched it transform itself into the exact, identical copy of the stone I removed. Likewise, I told the girls it was time for us to head back to Tunnel. Our trip back was met was a constant limited flow of lizard warriors. My girls easily zapped him with their laser guns each step of the way. I would claim that in total, we wiped out about 100 lizard warriors. Needless to say, it took a while to make it back to the main entrance. I did seal each opening that we had created, mainly to prevent the lizards from following us. When we reached the main entrance, we were met with yet another big surprise. Before us stood 100 alien warriors, with five small battleships with their weapons fixed exactly upon us. I thought to myself, without a doubt, this was the end of us.

Consequently; an alien commander ordered us to surrender. While I prepared to drop my equipment, I witnessed a barrage of laser exploding projectiles, that completely destroyed the five small battleships and all the warriors who stood before us. For the reason that we looked around to determine what had done this on our behalf, I noticed that the Tunnel was there before us. Because his doors opened, my two girls rushed in ahead of me, as I very closely followed behind them. Once inside, Orenda and Woape called out for tunnel to provide them with their outfits. By their outfits manifesting themselves before them, they completely remove their Rudolfensis outfits. I asked him if it was wise that they undressed in front of me. They claimed that such activity was now warranted since I named them and thereby, they belonged to me. I was thinking that this could present problems with my wife later on. But then again, a thought hit me, this is from this dimension they could not enter my dimension, I hope. I gave the stone to tunnel who gave all the stones to the Creator. The Creator congratulated us for another challenging victory. I did not know how to tell him that this last mission was among the easiest that we had.

Then again, I was thinking maybe the reason it was easier was because we all acted as a team, with tunnel coming in for the final blow as the seeds of our lives had kept our freedom. I knew that we needed some personal time prior to our next mission, and therefore asked Orenda and Woape to join me in my chambers for a post-mission debriefing. Naturally, this would come after my meeting with the Creator. This meeting which went quickly as the creator congratulated me and my team for outstanding work, as he has decided to believe I might be able to get all the required stones, even though I still had a little way to go. I attributed any difficulties that we had thus far were simple team growing pains. I then asked the Creator what the boundaries were for my relationship with his previous maidens. The Creator informed me that Orenda and Woape belonged to me, that he no longer had any vested interests in them while I was still in this dimension. Therefore, I asked the creator that when I left this dimension was, I expected to take Orenda and Woape with me. The Creator said that they cannot pass over the dimension line without immediately dying. The Creator also told me that they would be greatly rewarded for their contribution in the saving of both dimensions. The creator also told me that once I returned to my dimension, I would never remember anything concerning Orenda and Woape. I was thinking to myself, "My what a tangled web we weave, when it first we practice to deceive." Orenda and Woape arrived in my chamber door for their debriefing.

They had with them each multiple storage units (large suitcases and trunks) and as they entered the immense arrangement of storage units with them. I asked them why they were bringing all these things into my small chambers. They motioned their fingers as my chamber immediately tripled in size. We now had a very nice briefing room, plus there were extended monitors center on my walls. I asked them what would happen if they could not store all their immense assortment of clothing. They raised their hands as a large stairway appeared. They waved their hands as most of their wardrobe vanished into the closets above us. Furthermore, they told me they were almost finished unpacking. I could only imagine what this meant. Curiosity caught me now, as I went upstairs to see what they unpacked. I noticed both of my babies followed me upstairs. Meanwhile, I explained that I was just curious, and was exploring. As I waded through this massive collection, I had to ask them their age. Orenda answered first that she was 8,445 years old, as Woape revealed she was 6,992 years old. I was stunned. My girls looked at me and said we can talk about this later.

CHAPTER 05

Thirteen Stones (Part 3)

Accordingly; the recent news from my two new roommates' and their ages tossed me for a big loop. Orenda is 8,445 and Woape is 6,992. I would have been shocked if they had told me their ages exceeded 30, as I was worried, they might have been under 18, which would not have been a problem considering that the Creator is the king of this dimension. I have always been a history buff, amazed at the developments of the early Empires such as the Egyptians. Nevertheless, to think that my girls were born before these great Empires boggles my mind to say the least. What the greatest mystery to my mind is how beautiful Orenda and Woape are. Their bodies are perfect, and not even one scar. How can someone live for nearly nine millennia and not have any form of a blemish, especially considering how close to danger they live. Subsequently, their culture is so much different from what I had originally believed, and thus are their social norms, I mean to be virtually 85 centuries old and sleeping with a man who is barely 2/3rd of one century is definitely robbing the cradle.

Fortunately for all involved, this cradle is not complaining. We have some stones to find, so I can go back and continue my fighting, so I do not really have time to worry about such trivial things such as my new mates being older than my recorded history. Any ways, it is time to plan the retrieval of my next stone. This would be my last stone that I will take from Lemuria; it will be the Safiireja stone from the Habilis who were also transferred here by the aliens who were somewhat concerned about their original smaller size, bringing them here as to add a foot and a half to their size. The aliens in addition prefer that they make couples, and not have the next hole available form of reproduction. It makes it easier for them to genetically engineer control of the input variables and DNA samples. Least ways, that is the way my girls are explaining it to me. I must confess, losing the last of my original hope of actually discovering something productive to our current understanding of prehistoric man. The main thing that I have discovered this far is a lot of genetic engineering.

Meanwhile; it makes me wonder how much of me is alien engineered or from mankind through mother nature. I always have this is one hope of mine, and that is that the aliens do not get my stones. As my Orenda and Woape enter our planning room inside the Tunnel since I want to get this moving a little quicker, I tell them I absolutely need more input from them during these planning stages, considering they had to pick up some things during their lifetimes. They eagerly agreed. Habilis are not established large game hunters, and for their meat prefer to scavenge or fish. This is why they settled along the rocky shorelines of the northern coast of Lemuria. They prefer jumping up a tree as compared to open field face-to-face fighting; therefore, they are not concerned about acquisition of territory. They live in tribes of around less than 50, to be able to fight off large predators that may want what appears to be an easy meal. Furthermore, they are much more spiritual than many of the tribes that we have met; as a result, I project some fighting in order to get the stone, which most likely have a higher spiritual significance in this group. Likewise, they tend to live in small huts in groups, without any walls to protect unauthorized entries. The difficulty that I can see is distinguishing between the huts for living in, the ones for spiritual needs. Tunnel has offered to identify, which had the stone that I need.

Consequently; this will be a 'Leave no survivors form of invasion,' considering we cannot risk the aliens discovering this. The aliens can communicate with their other forces and hamper any future attempts we may have to retrieve any stones, if they are able to determine we were there for the stones. I can only hope that my egg producing the false stones will help, until we can for the time on my next extraction. When we arrive at this camp, Tunnel provides me some surprising news. The huts are empty. Consequently, there are slight signs beneath the surface. These people are using their huts as a decoy, possibly safety from invaders. Another possibility, in that there are alien forces in the tunnels we guess the city is expecting hostile actions to be taken against the tribesmen. We just don't have enough information to make an accurate prediction. I never like going into a situation blindfolded. The positive news is that the stone appears to still be in its original hut. This appears to be scarily simple. We only walk to get the stone, call for tunnel, and go back to the Creator. Precisely to be on the safe side, I asked Tunnel to do some surface scans to make sure that there is no one on the surface in this tribe. Tunnel comes back reporting that the surface is clear. My girls acquired a small handheld laser pistol for me like the one they each have.

Likewise; this is somewhat like the same message Tunnel sent when we were exiting the tribe. Creator claims that the aliens must know, if you don't know who you are shooting, and don't shoot. At this time, four more maidens appear. Creator tells me it is important to get back into action since the aliens are regrouping from this massive unexpected attack. Additionally; he will keep Orenda and Woape here at the Medical Center tonight. He believes that Orenda will be able to return to action late tomorrow. Woape will provide moral support. The Creator tells me that the four female soldiers he is providing for me are among his best. Until you get to know their abilities, you should not interfere with them while in combat situations. They will do everything they can to bring me back safe. Our next stop is on the Gondwana ancient continent, a tribe of the Garhi, and the stone Helmi. This is my first and I hope final visit to Gondwana, which formed the southerly portion of Pangea, bringing with it our modern-day southerly continents. The Garhi did not last long on the evolution timeline, nevertheless, did at a lot for the Homo series per current archeological theory. We will not be in this area long enough to debate this.

Subsequently; Tunnel claims we have no signs of alien activity, which must explain why they appeared and disappeared rather quickly when compared to the other species who were struggling to exist. These 'people' are smaller than what we have previously encountered, and allegedly more peaceful. We walk into the entrance and down their main street to the temple. I can see the temple's door, when out of the blue, my lights go out. Approximately three hours later, I awaken, tied to a pole in the middle of this tribe. I look around in as many directions as I am able to; however, I cannot see my four new maidens. A few children come out towards me with knives. I think this is not a way to perish, to have the kids stab me. They pull out their knives and come towards me. My heart is doing its normal beating like heck. Surprisingly; they walk up to me and start to uncut my ropes that are strapping me to this pole. Soon, I find myself surrounded by the village people. They are waving at me; therefore, I wave back. They start smiling at me; thereby, I smile back. I subsequently point at one woman, and afterward to me, and I point to the woman four times, after that to me four times and then pretend like I am looking. Next, one man comes forward and points to a tree on the hill, and after that heads that way. I follow him. When we get to the top of the hill, he points to another tree on the next hill, then proceeds to it. I, once more, follow him. We continue this for six days, until I see another tribe. The man walks into the tribe and then comes out with my four girls.

Therefore; they come running to me, and we walk back to the first tribe, following the man who took me to them. We walk into the temple; I swap the stones, get my four maidens, then call for Tunnel. I gave Tunnel this stone as we prepared to jump just a few hundred thousand years ahead to Pangea and to look at humanities preparation to move out of Africa, with the Ergaster, looking for the stone Rubiini. I was beginning to show signs of tiring, not being able to take my eyes off my mission for a few seconds, only to experience near impossible challenges. Furthermore, I was puzzled how that one of the least harmful to the species I had yet encountered was able to get four maidens and moved them to a village for six days with such little resistance. However, to have children guide me to them made me wonder why I was the only one not to see this coming. The reason to have four maidens was not to create extra trouble for me, after all, somewhere in this equation, I had to do the impossible and to capture what should have been easy retrieval of these stones, yet, for some reason, I am being forced to collect dirt from practically all over the known world, to cite just one of many unnecessary hurdles. Another issue I was having was. How could a maiden which had been in battle for almost 9,000 years mysteriously finally catch an arrow?

Questionably; was I going to have to march millions of warriors into battle to get a little stone from a five-year-old? It was time to talk with the Creator and find out who my true enemies were? My first question was why four warrior maidens had fallen to such a peaceful species, and what did I need to get these last four stones. The Creator also cited a concern over the ease of defeat in this latest encounter. I told him, that I would have to wait for Orenda's recovery and for Woape's return before approaching the Ergaster or Erectus, with only enough difference to create confusion, who from my initial review did not look forward to presenting too much confusion. The Creator at the present time assigned my two maidens and the four additional maidens to my team; Orenda would have two, whereas Woape would have two. Our team would now have three Tunnels, with each going in its own direction. All three would share the same space wavelengths in order to prevent any consistent tracking. An additional six maidens would be assigned to each of the two supplementary Tunnels with Earth alien tracking missions. The three Tunnels would perform detailed mapping of Pangea prior to our search for the Rubiini stone, and study of the Ergaster with a comprehensive DNA makeup. We were detecting variations between what the Tunnel in Asia, and the Tunnel in Europe were reporting as compared to the Tunnel we were in here in Pangea. This led to our conclusion that the sample we had here been transferred by the aliens. Nevertheless; we had no evidence of the aliens here on the surface.

Therefore; Tunnel began to drill, attempting to remove some of the surface material. This, of course, created some excitement among the sample species we had been existing among us. Considering; this sample was not needed, but a continuation of humanity, Tunnel elected to start a localized extermination campaign. It soon became evident, that the aliens had attempted to conceal their activities within this area. Recognizing; we did not need to remove all the service area, but instead, only the pathway to my stone. Alarms began to report that the other two tunnels were engaged with hostile activities from approaching alien war craft. The Creator began to launch hundreds of more tunnels to encircle Europe, Asia, and Africa, concentrating on removal of the aliens, and safeguarding the dwindling humanity species still in existence. The Earth was once again engaged in a world war, one in which no evidence could remain had ever existed. We had to ensure that no damage came to the future evolving species, which included the Neanderthal, Denisovans, and the Homo Sapiens, even though none of these three currently contained stones that I needed, yet were important for my Coon Hollow Paradigm.

Initially; for the first time in what seemed to have been an eternity, Orenda and Woape began to speak to me, asking what they could do to help. I explained that we needed to get the Rubiini stone and head for Naledi tribe also here on Pangea in a time era approximately 250,000 years in the past, but well in the future from where we were currently. That upcoming task would be to retrieve the Opaali stone from the Naledi. Be that as it may, we now were digging and searching frantically for the Rubiini stone and leave the local Ergaster remains for the Tunnels to remove from history. Orenda and Woape grabbed my arms and led me into a deep, dark black hole. We soon landed into an open chamber, in which the middle sat a green altar. This was the first time I had seen a green altar, and pre-cautiously asked Orenda if that color was of any significance.

They claimed it was of no importance, but that it was time for me to apply my dust. I applied my dust, retrieved the stone, inserted the replacement egg, and motioned for us; it was time that we returned to the Tunnel. I noticed a rather disturbed look on their faces. Therefore; I asked them if we had any difficulties concerning our retreat? They had that rather yellowish tone on their faces; which, indicated to me; they were talking with the Creator. I could now hear two other Tunnels drilling beside us. Our cavern expanded its width enough to encompass both Tunnels. We thereby entered into one of the Tunnels, and soon escaped the rather strong gravitational pull of the hole that we were within.

Recovering; as my vital signs returned to normal, I found myself in front of the Creator, giving him my most recently acquired stone. The Creator informed me that there would be a short delay prior to heading for my next stone, in that all evidence of current alien existence on Pangea, was being erased from history. He recommended that I reacquaint myself with Orenda and Woape. We, therefore, took a long-awaited retreat to our expanded chambers. At first, we felt uncomfortable with each other, as this uncomfortableness soon vanished. They were subsequently re-examining their wardrobes, rearranging their makeup, and complaining about my lack of tidiness. In other words, things were returning to normal. I took this opportunity to examine Orenda's wound, which had completely been restored to its previous state of perfection. I asked her if she experiences any limited motion or pain in this area. She claimed it was as always, in which Woape told me the incident had been erased from her mind in order not to have any form of negative impact on forthcoming fights, and that it would be best if I forgot completely about this as well. Because, any form of hesitation on my part could hamper our impending success in retrieving these final three stones. The way she emphasized these three concluding stones brought another question to my mind, and that was if our missions together continued after these final three stones.

Consequently; when I asked her about this, they replied that I needed to speak with the Creator concerning this. Electing, to concentrate on our missions at hand, and eliminate any unnecessary confusion, I put this on a back burner. Therefore, it was time to sit down and analyze our next trip, still on Pangea, the Opaali stone from the Naledi tribe. By virtue of it being on Pangea indicated some form of alien intervention. As I continue to investigate this tribe, it quickly becomes evident that the aliens must have taken some Homo Sapiens and got some genetic engineering to create this branch. Notwithstanding; this branch did not produce their desired results, in that the brains were smaller, and they are not midgets; however, were far from giants. The aliens this time were in the process of continually transferring their colonies from this continent to those of a cave in South Africa. They were extra cautious not to allow this branch to intermingle and naturally produce, as their goal was to have a humanity with larger brains than those with the tinier brains. Even though this branch has smaller brains, they did have a large appetite for fighting. This of course was not something that I was looking forward to, nor did I want my girls' risk additional injuries. Be that as it may, we once again holstered our small laser guns, and retrieved our large swords. Fortunately, the Tunnel could get us within 100 feet of the altar we were searching for. Therefore; Orenda, Woape, and I departed from the exit door to the Tunnel and with our night-eyeglass began the 100-foot walk to our altar that rested on it the stone Opaali.

Mysteriously; the Naledi were much more creative fighters than many of the previous human ancestors we had fought. They had hands whom could grip tighter than our modern tools, thereby gripping their sharpened stones, forcing a lethal pounding cut when swung in making contact with its intended target. Fortunately for us, our lights could temporarily bind them, allowing us to use our swords to behead them. What proved to be disturbing was the fact that they were shouldered to shoulder on both sides of our cave entrance that we had created. This of course created concern for me in that how they mobilized so quickly. I asked my two partners, in that I could no longer call them maidens, to provide us with gas masks, and to release a toxic chemical in this temporary passage. They did so and to our delight, the bodies began to separate not only from the sides, but also from above us. Apparently, those who were above would be deployed upon our departure attempt. This kind of like gave me some additional concerns, and that this enemy had the main requirements for victory in their arsenal, that being patients, and accurate planning for supplemental contingencies. Furthermore; they had what I considered the most vital element in military fighting, and that was discipline. Discipline was an issue that I was still working on with my maidens, having actually given up on training the four who had deployed with me on my previous stone mission.

Victoriously; all was not lost with those maidens in that they were now covering my flanks which for this mission proved to be central considering this tribe had a powerful front on attack strategy. We could make this 100–feet within a one-half hour. Most of this 30-minute invasion was because of my extra precaution. I did not want to become trapped. I quickly developed an appreciation for this tribe's military and clandestine guerrilla fighting approach. As we approached this bright-red altar, I motioned for Orenda and Woape to stand back and study what appeared to be a type of altar we had yet to encounter. I wanted to know what the bright red still for, an answer that Orenda and Woape could not provide me. I patiently waited for a combined response from Tunnel and the Creator. We stood there for almost one hour before receiving a response and another unique form of a container. My instructions were to open this container and spray this specific blue powder until all red was covered. Therefore, Orenda, Woape, and I sprayed the special blue powder and slowly covered all the red. We were instructed to also spray all the ground around it until the blue turned into a yellow. The Naledi taught me the importance of patients in my battlefield philosophy, considering previously on I just swung my sword into a crazy manner hoping to eventually hit something.

Painfully; I learned the hard way that such a strategy could result in one of my team members becoming injured, as did Orenda. I now had to accept full responsibility for the injury, and that when a warrior flights for almost

10,000 years without an injury and then within a handful of missions with me, becomes injured the buck had to stop with me. The powder turned yellow; therefore, I applied my standard dust on top of the yellow, as it presented a white color, I retrieved the Opaali stone and handed it to Orenda for transfer back to the Tunnel. Ordinarily, I would have given this stone to Woape. I made an exception this time in order to make Orenda feel reunited with our team. I was quite impressed how I can feel Woape sharing the same desire, as I remembered how depressed she was with the absence of Orenda. For the return trip, we once again put on our gas masks, and sprayed the tunnel once more with our chemical compound. This time we kept our mobile laser pistols in our hands with the safeties turned off. We quickly returned through this Tunnel, stepping over the bodies of our enemies.

Therefore; when we approached Tunnel, he had his doors closed, as he began spraying another detoxifying chemical into our air. Approximately; 20 some hoses protruded from tunnel, sucking up this air. The hoses were soon retracted as another three hoses protruded through one for each of us. This hose shot out a spray that completely covered us. Once the spray had been deployed for approximately five minutes, it turned into an air blower blowing the dust from our battle uniforms. As we approached the door, tunnel ordered us to remove our uniforms. Tunnel torched our uniforms burning them into a powder outside on the drilled dirt. Immediately we were showered with water, and air dried us, as the inner doors opened simultaneously with the outer doors closing. We now stood in our birthday suits in front of our new casual uniforms. Prior to putting on our uniforms, I gave each of my girls a congratulations hug. When I saw Orenda completely naked; I asked her what she had done with our stone. She told me Tunnel took it from her before detoxification from the deployed chemicals. I therefore asked Tunnel if the stone had been detoxified. Tunnel said the stone was detoxified and already received by the Creator. Naturally; as inquisitiveness was over taking me, I asked Tunnel why this stone had already been transmitted to the Creator.

Excitedly; the Tunnel now revealed to me that all the flanking Tunnels were going to all make a unison exit away from this continent. Moreover: I asked Tunnel why so much force was needed to perform such a routine task. Tunnel replied that they were also fighting the aliens and the Earth as the Earth was getting ready to split up Pangea, since Lemuria had already been sunk. I was confused what the aliens had to do with this process. Tunnel replied that the aliens were taking their engineered human species back to their alien worlds for their future scientific projects. Basically, only that which was on some scattered islands and a massive chunk of the southern tip of Africa will remain untouched as new lands from Pangea would surface. This explained, to me, one of the reasons that the archaeologists were fighting so few skeletons. The land that these early humans had existed on, was now very deep in the ocean, most likely not to be uncovered until the fourth or fifth millennia. The massive release of Earth's gravitational force on its tectonic plates were colossal. Tunnel told me to go ahead and put my uniform on as we were getting ready to approach the Creator. We had not realized that these events had captivated us so much that we had forgotten to put our uniforms back on. Therefore; naturally, we put on these nice clean perfect fitting uniforms and prepared to meet with the Creator. Meanwhile, we looked at the monitors as they showed the establishment of the continents as I had always known them to be.

Meanwhile; for some comforting reason, North America remained intact, the only exception being the Alaska area forming a new couple of hundred-mile-wide bridge connecting the new Asia, which was connected to Africa, is solidly connected to Europe. Australia and a lot of islands remained separate. However, somehow my ancient ancestors would find a way to colonize them as well. For this meeting with the Creator, I invited Orenda and Woape to attend with me. I introduced them to the Creator as my right and left arms. The Creator congratulates us on our solid teamwork during this last. What could've been an extremely disastrous mission? We now had 11 of the 13 needed stones. The Creator told me that these last two tribes could be among the easiest retrievals that we had faced, especially since they did not place any value on these stones, and thus should not be willing to shed that much blood to retain them. We were to return to Pangea and retrieve the Smaragdi stone from the Africanus. I took my two girls back to our review room, as we studied the monitors the Creator was providing for us in our preparation. There appeared to be some debate as to it this tribe was a forerunner to my species. As far as I'm concerned, they can debate for eternity, as long as I got my Smaragdi stone. The tunnel was now taking us back a couple million years to where they suspected the tribe was keeping this stone. We were once again being forced to deal with aliens, which unfortunately had hidden the stone.

Therefore; it was time to sharpen our knives and make sure our laser beam guns were fully charged. As a precautionary measure, we also wore an extra layer of insulated protection uniform with a helmet. This was because the Africanus were notorious for throwing stones. With their still extra-long arms, they could propel these stones like bullets from a gun. Once again, the aliens had buried my stone and blocked all entrances. Unfortunately; we did not have the help of the lizard people, since they were not interested in this part of Africa. In fact, they were not interested in any area that the aliens had infiltrated, considering it to be a useless and futile confrontation. I could actually understand this logic. My dilemma was that I had no choice; you get the stone and move on, if I did not get the stone, I lost everything? The number of them that died in this process was up to them. For this mission, the Creator deployed our full force, as he did on our previous mission. The Creator had his full of this illegal alien intervention that was devoting or defiling his creation. This time, the Tunnels decided to drill in from one mile below and begin 20 miles to the south. They believed that the one-mile below would provide enough sound insulation and minimum ground vibration.

Impressively; I was mesmerized that they accomplished this within the matter of less than one hour. Unfortunately; as they came up, that one be ended in the floor of an alien combat station. The three tunnels each entered with their own opening. In unison, they deployed a sleeping agent who put the 40 some alien warriors to sleep. My girls and I were given the task of stabbing each one or removing their heads while they were still asleep. We were instructed to do this diligently and quickly. While we were doing this, like all my other missions, for comrade maidens retrieved the stone and delivered it to our Tunnel. This was a relief for me as I was finishing up my head chopping. I looked around and noticed another 10 maidens of course dressed in their appropriate uniforms for the tunnel that they were on assisting us in the beheading. I was shocked that we accomplished this in a matter of minutes. The comrade maidens also disabled the alarm systems and radar systems of the station. We all reboarded our appropriate Tunnel and returned to our entry point and went back up to the Creator. I immediately thanked the Creator for the massive additional support that he had provided. I also thanked them for instilling my confidence in the comrade maidens. Jokingly, I told him that would not begin to give them names because Orenda and Woape were plenty for me. The Creator said that was a very wise choice for me, and that with only one stone remaining, he would not be taking any chances.

Almost finished; we now had 12 of the 13 stones, we could see that they were beginning to establish their intended purposes. We had no time to waste. While still on Pangea, which meant a possible genetic reengineering by the aliens, to get the Timantti stone from the Aethiopicus. Aethiopicus branched off of the Africanus which had another branch that the homo descended from. I will confess not knowing why the Aethiopicus have one of the stones, unless to represent a failure in the alien's genetic engineering, whereas a sister branch formed the homo series, this branch kept on producing apes. Notwithstanding; these were pretty smart apes. I believe this is a reason that the Creator elected to go full force on this Timantti stone. We encounter a challenge on this stone that was what I consider an ordinary use for something that they did not see any value in. Tunnel and two other Tunnels, each staffed with the comrade maidens, began to search for the Timantti stone. It was now the standard waiting game. We did not detect any alien presence here, as this tribe was being left to go extinct, along with its sister tribes located elsewhere on Earth, at this time a couple million years in our past on Pangea. It was now a waiting game in which my girls started to reveal stories about their childhood and a few of their adult adventures. Neither one had been previously married. They told me that the maidens usually did not get married until they were at the least 12,000 years old. They just had too much work to do to become involved with the family until they reached the agreed-upon 12,000 years.

Surprisingly; this if this was the standard for all maidens, none would be frowned upon for remaining single. I decided to get nosy, and asked them about their socially acceptable sexual behavior before the marriage. They both said such matters were told to be kept private and were at the maiden's desires and needs. After all, there were so many men with desires to service them. They said you cannot put candy in the candy store and not allow the customers to sample the candy prior to purchase. I was mainly concerned that our activities were not against their social customs and later could backfire upon them. Because they took complete control of our home. They removed all beds except for a colossal king-size bed. I liked this gigantic bed, and that there was plenty of room to completely stretch out, something that we needed because of the extra stress we put on our bodies to accomplish the acquisition of these stones. Tunnel currently informed me that the Timantti stone was at the present time in view. Additionally, there were no Aethiopicus in the area and that rock barriers had been established at the entry gates to this temple area. In those, the temple area was not used for religious purposes, but instead for marriage and funeral.

Notwithstanding; the Aethiopicus evolved enough to become monogamous and select one partner for mating purposes, and for the burying of their dead. They actually only buried the charred remains from their cremation efforts. This, of course, erased their bones from history. These were not standard customs among the Aethiopicus tribes. Their stone was mixed in with other stones that been used to form a wall. Fortunately; they had not developed the ability to create cement, but instead had used a combination that they dug up from inside one of the caves. This mud had some stabilizing force, plus provided some insulating qualities. We were able to use some tools that Tunnel provided in separating the stones that surrounded my stone so we could have about a one $ft.^2$ section of stone slab to slowly chisel away at. Tunnel had created a mild dissolving agent that would weaken the mud, and at the same time not affect the stone. This compound worked quickly as within 10 minutes from being outside of the Tunnel, I was putting my special dust on top of this beautiful stone. Fortunately, for us the stone was covered in a dull mud, most likely from the aliens, making it appear like a regular stone. I handed the stone to Woape for transfer to Tunnel. Tunnel once again immediately released it to a very eager Creator who received it. My girls boarded our Tunnel, as our force returned to the Creator without any incident or interference. Upon arrival at the station, I grabbed Orenda and Woape and proceeded to meet the Creator. As we entered, we saw a beautiful arranged collection of the 13 rocks assembled.

Happily; they were in their full glory now receiving their united power from each other. The Creator said that none could touch it or use this power except for me. Even the Creator said he could not touch it nor move it. He recommended that it remained where it is because it would have all his forces to protect it. There was no greater power than the 13 rocks. Even though its Creator built in extensive safeguards for this awesome power, the ability of evil to eventually discover a way to steal can never be underestimated. The Creator said that any who touch it would die immediately, except for me. He told me to go out and touch my stones. When I touched my stones, a vision of blood flowing on Coon Hollow; furthermore, I saw 13 houses that housed demons and an evil River flow from the evil soaking the land. The next thing I witnessed was the sky cracking open. There was a bright shining white-light fighting to make the crack larger. After this, my vision turns black. I could speak now, so I asked him Creator what should I do because my vision has turned black. The Creator told me to release my hands, for the vision was finished. I then proceeded to tell the Creator what I saw. The Creator said that I must avenge the blood that was shed on this land. Except for this, the stones would take me back into time if I needed to. I would be under their full protection. I must also remove and defeat all evil in the 13 houses, by defeating each house one at a time.

Sadly; my maidens could only help me when I was here; however, they cannot cross over the dimensional line. The creature told me not to worry because my 13 stones would provide a way for me to come victorious. Once I cleaned the blood from Coon Hollow and defeated the 13 houses, the crack in the sky would seal up and save both dimensions. At this time, I would no longer be able to travel in this dimension. My stones would transfer themselves to a secure location in Coon Hollow. The Creator said that for tonight, and for five days, we were going to celebrate, with massive parades and many events. For these events, the Creator would do so in one of his physical bodies. However; for tonight, we shall rest.

CHAPTER 06

Wohpe

Morning arrived with sounds of festivities flooding the Creator's empire, as far as I could see. There must have been a solid lake and sky filled with maidens. I could never have had imagined this many could exist or were created. The joyous music had now awakened Orenda and Woape as I asked them about the maidens and their uniforms, which were at least 1,000 different styles and colors. They explained that these uniforms identified which tunnel, they served on. Nevertheless, they did not recognize the bright red uniformed maidens. Additionally, they claimed there were too many of them to serve on a Tunnel. I would ask the Creator later this day, since we had five days of festivities ahead of us. Orenda pushed the body cleaning button as our bodies were completely cleaned. My girls looked strange without their makeup. They, like all maidens would not permit a device to apply their makeup, and thus had to dedicate the hour to applying it.

An hour, which offered me some much-needed relaxation. We each had a new, fresh uniform to wear on this important day for the Creator. When they finished, finally, the way my two girls looked was well worth the wait. We opened our chamber doors and proceeded to go outside yet only to see his ocean of maidens including even the warriors who had their Spears. This is when it started to hit us. This was a great event, but why was it so big? And then I looked over, saw the Creator waving for us to join him. When I approached the Creator; I asked him why were there so many big festivities? The Creator look to me and said that within the next five days the most magnificent device to save the loss of the spirits and most of our dimensions, eventually ceiling the crack that appeared above Coon Hollow. The first, he handed me the stones and told me that were supposed to put them over the 13 gates or portals in order to activate the gates today. Once the stones were in place, they would scan the universe to retrieve their powers. Fortunately; for me, the portals appeared one at a time. In addition; these were nice big portals, appearing like an upside-down horseshoe that stood over 200 feet. When looking at it from this side, I could only see a hazy cloud. Nevertheless; when you voiced in a location, that location would appear. The first stone that I picked up was the Timantti, which I put over the Gate of Saints.

This is the gate in which all the previous Indian Saints would enter or depart from. The Creator told me that if

I needed help from my dimension, this would be the gate or portal that I would assess. The second stone that picked on the container was the Obisidianni which I put over the Gates of Pain. The Creator told me that this gate would show me the pain that has been suffered from the ones who had everything taken from them. What they freed was a liberated lost Indian spirit, it would separate the pain from the soul, cast that pain into this portal. I looked at the Creator and asked him how would I know which gate to use, as it was only two gates so far, I'm confused. The Creator told me not to worry because gates would guide me in the direction of justice. At this time, another beautiful, gigantic portal or gate appeared before me. For this, I picked up the stone Verna and placed it upon the base at the top of the portal. I noticed afterward that my feet were not on the ground. Moreover; when I placed Verna in his slot, the Gate of Harmonious activated. Now I proceeded to my fourth point and placed the stone Turkooi as this slot had activated the Gate of Love. I could feel the love flowing from this portal, combined with the spirit of harmony, created a peaceful experience I had never before enjoyed. The Creator told me that these two gates, among others, flowed into the future lakes that I would establish. In my next portal, I placed the stone Ametisti upon it, which activated the Gate of Blood. The Creator told me that this station would begin working instantaneously, and that all the dirt and dust ever to flow through Coon Run Road would have to be siphoned for any blood, because there would never be any peace in my Valley and even my Hollow until all blood that was shed upon this land was cast into the Gate of Blood.

Consequently; I could see small beams of light scanning Coon Run Road and Coon Hollow. Shockingly; I cannot believe the power that I was seeing from these stones.

What was even more surprising, or continues to confuse Me, is that only I can touch the stones? Why they trusted me with this much power I will never know? I don't like not knowing, especially when I have the answer standing beside me. I, therefore, asked the Creator, why do I have so much power. The Creator told me that the stones cried throughout history for me, knowing that I would liberate them as I am today. The Creator also told me that I could not question the knowledge of the spirits for they can see tomorrow at the same as yesterday; therefore, their choices were always immaculate. I then asked him why did he pick someone who was so not perfect as me and declared me to be perfect? I now had to realize that they gave me permission to do, I had to do what they needed it; Me to do. I must confess, once again and most likely not the last time, my total confusion. Be that as it may; I still have the stones to place. The next stone that appeared before me was the Safuureja in which I placed over the Gate of Time. The Creator told me that this was the gate that allowed me to travel through time to acquire stones. In addition; This gate would give me total access to tomorrow and yesterday. What this meant, was that the stones and myself were no over bound by the chains of time. I noticed that portal appeared, they had about 100 miles of solid 300-foot-high wall marble coated trimmed in gold with diamonds spread throughout the wall. When the sunlight hit it sparkled. I marveled at its size thus far.

I asked the Creator how wide this would be, which the Creator said that when it expanded, it could hold 100 Jupiter's inside of the walls. Accordingly; when extended the portals would have as much as 20,000 or more miles between them. The Creator also said that it could be in addition be the size of a mustard seed, and thus hide beside the dirt on the ground. It was not bound by material space; it could transfer easily among the 2,000 already known dimensions. Most of this time would be spent in a sister dimension, one which I could access in the Creator could also access. I also noticed some large buildings appearing inside these walls. I asked the Creator what these buildings were for. The Creator then informed me that he gave me 10,000 maidens, the once dressed in a bright-red uniform. They shall care for and protect all that is within these walls. The Creator now asked what this giant spirit should be called. I told him this place was called Wohpe or the Spirit of Peace. I believe that Wohpe was growing restless with our conversations, therefore, appearing before me was the Kulta stone for the Gate of Fertility. This fertility doesn't include the wombs of our maidens; additionally; the harvest of the seeds that we plant in the ground for fall harvests. For without an abundant harvest, hunger could kill. Moreover; the beauty of our flowers as they made our gardens appear heavenly. During the days of our Indian ancestors, this gate was in one in which so many fell before pleading for its mercy. The next stone that appeared to me was the Apafylliitti; which, bonded with the Gate of Life.

Me, is that only I can touch the stones? Why they trusted me with this much power I will never know? I don't like not knowing, especially when I have the answer standing beside me. I, therefore, asked the Creator, why do I have so much power. The Creator told me that the stones cried throughout history for me, knowing that I would liberate them as I am today. The Creator also told me that I could not question the knowledge of the spirits for they can see tomorrow at the same as yesterday; therefore, their choices were always immaculate. I then asked him why did he pick someone who was so not perfect as me and declared me to be perfect? I now had to realize that they gave me permission to do, I had to do what they needed it; Me to do. I must confess, once again and most likely not the last time, my total confusion. Be that as it may; I still have the stones to place. The next stone that appeared before me was the Safuureja in which I placed over the Gate of Time. The Creator told me that this was the gate that allowed me to travel through time to acquire stones. In addition; This gate would give me total access to tomorrow and yesterday. What this meant, was that the stones and myself were no over bound by the chains of time. I noticed that portal appeared, they had about 100 miles of solid 300-foot-high wall marble coated trimmed in gold with diamonds spread throughout the wall. When the sunlight hit it sparkled. I marveled at its size thus far.

I asked the Creator how wide this would be, which the Creator said that when it expanded, it could hold 100 Jupiter's inside of the walls. Accordingly; when extended the portals would have as much as 20,000 or more miles between them. The Creator also said that it could be in addition be the size of a mustard seed, and thus hide beside the dirt on the ground. It was not bound by material space; it could transfer easily among the 2,000 already known dimensions. Most of this time would be spent in a sister dimension, one which I could access in the Creator could also access. I also noticed some large buildings appearing inside these walls. I asked the Creator what these buildings were for. The Creator then informed me that he gave me 10,000 maidens, the once dressed in a bright-red uniform. They shall care for and protect all that is within these walls. The Creator now asked what this giant spirit should be called. I told him this place was called Wohpe or the Spirit of Peace. I believe that Wohpe was growing restless with our conversations, therefore, appearing before me was the Kulta stone for the Gate of Fertility. This fertility doesn't include the wombs of our maidens; additionally; the harvest of the seeds that we plant in the ground for fall harvests. For without an abundant harvest, hunger could kill. Moreover; the beauty of our flowers as they made our gardens appear heavenly. During the days of our Indian ancestors, this gate was in one in which so many fell before pleading for its mercy. The next stone that appeared to me was the Apafylliitti; which, bonded with the Gate of Life. Me, is that only I can touch the stones? Why they trusted me with this much power I will never know? I don't like not knowing, especially when I have the answer standing beside me. I, therefore, asked the Creator, why do I have so much power. The Creator told me that the stones cried throughout history for me, knowing that I would liberate them as I am today.

The Creator also told me that I could not question the knowledge of the spirits for they can see tomorrow at the same as yesterday; therefore, their choices were always immaculate. I then asked him why did he pick someone who was so not perfect as me and declared me to be perfect? I now had to realize that they gave me permission to do, I had to do what they needed it; Me to do. I must confess, once again and most likely not the last time, my total confusion. Be that as it may; I still have the stones to place. The next stone that appeared before me was the Safuureja in which I placed over the Gate of Time. The Creator told me that this was the gate that allowed me to travel through time to acquire stones. In addition; This gate would give me total access to tomorrow and yesterday. What this meant, was that the stones and myself were no over bound by the chains of time. I noticed that portal appeared, they had about 100 miles of solid 300-foot-high wall marble coated trimmed in gold with diamonds spread throughout the wall. When the sunlight hit it sparkled. I marveled at its size thus far.

I asked the Creator how wide this would be, which the Creator said that when it expanded, it could hold 100 Jupiter's inside of the walls. Accordingly; when extended the portals would have as much as 20,000 or more miles between them. The Creator also said that it could be in addition be the size of a mustard seed, and thus hide beside the dirt on the ground. It was not bound by material space; it could transfer easily among the 2,000 already known dimensions. Most of this time would be spent in a sister dimension, one which I could access in the Creator could also access.

I also noticed some large buildings appearing inside these walls. I asked the Creator what these buildings were for. The Creator then informed me that he gave me 10,000 maidens, the once dressed in a bright-red uniform. They shall care for and protect all that is within these walls. The Creator now asked what this giant spirit should be called. I told him this place was called Wohpe or the Spirit of Peace. I believe that Wohpe was growing restless with our conversations, therefore, appearing before me was the Kulta stone for the Gate of Fertility. This fertility doesn't include the wombs of our maidens; additionally; the harvest of the seeds that we plant in the ground for fall harvests. For without an abundant harvest, hunger could kill. Moreover; the beauty of our flowers as they made our gardens appear heavenly. During the days of our Indian ancestors, this gate was in one in which so many fell before pleading for its mercy. The next stone that appeared to me was the Apafylliitti; which, bonded with the Gate of Life.

I can see that they were itching to get out there and mingle with the other maidens. It was a chance for them to show off their unique uniform that matched mine. As we moved through the festival enjoying maidens, a path always opened as they also bowed much like the Europeans bowed to their royalty. We enjoyed our time mingling with them, because I did not want a living soul that could face her death on a battlefield on my behalf not to feel that they were not appreciated. Even though there was no way I can meet with the over 100,000 of them that were nowhere; however, Orenda and Woape told me that the maidens transmitted their impressions and feelings with each other. Whenever possible currently, due to simple logistics, Wohpe was gradually replacing the Creator's maidens with the newly produced maidens through the Gate of Angels. I also understand that the Gate of Angels would now become a primary producer of angels for my dimension and the Creator's dimension. I wanted to make sure that no maiden was being disposed of. Orenda and Woape assured me that no maiden was being replaced or removed who did not wish to be removed. So many of the maidens were well over 1,200 years old and wanting to begin their families, a fire that burned in every maiden. Now they could begin their selection process. The Gate of Love with analyzing all the maidens and warriors in an attempt to provide possible matches. This of course meant to complete psychological and social spiritual analysis. Once the Gate of Love has completed the possible candidates for a match up, they released the information to the maiden requiring the matchup. This was where the maiden could study and capture the spiritual generated summaries of the top 10 candidates. Usually, a maiden is completely occupied by her mission.

Consequently; when a maiden was in the selection process for a mate, she was completely free of all duties during this process. This dimension understood the importance of the family unit, and wanted to do everything to ensure success. The maiden would usually reduce this down to three, of which she would spend some time with determining which one she would select. Once they had mated or were married, they were sent to another portion of their dimension to raise their family to enjoy the rest of the lives. Now was just a waiting game, waiting for the stones to sync together as to multiply their powers. Eight Creators were in the area to provide military backup if needed. Naturally, we had thousands of tunnels searching through the universe to detect any potential danger. I was sort of concerned that everyone appeared to be on the edge.

The Creator calmly informed me that they captured a spy, sent from a different dimension. That dimension prepared or created their spies to a new level of protection. Nothing that this dimension could do would get this spy to talk. Wohpe wanted to know if I had any recommendations. I had one extremely simple recommendation, and that was that this spy spends a few hours in the Prison of Evil. I wanted a few hours to ensure that this spy's resistance level was fried to say the least. When we retrieved this from the Prison of Evil two hours later, the prisoner, she was ready to talk. Fortunately; we did not have to rely on her to talk, as our sensors could scan her mind. We now knew everything that she knew, and what she knew was disturbing. This was a total sabotage and destroy mission. Their first target stone was the Simaragdi in that he believed the command we had a tendency to stay away from death, if all possible. The one thing that no one wanted to do was make death angry. Therefore, without delay, we intensified or reinforced the forces at this gate. As an additional measure, I had the Gate of Death linked up with the Prison of Evil, revealing their linkup through an additional river flowing from this Lake to the Gate and to camouflage the entire outside the Gate of Death. This was created for purely psychological effect; however, the link was functional. I had no desire to negotiate. We're trying to use possibly fruitless methods to obtain the most up-to-date enemy status available. We already saw how a spy reacted in this prison, providing our needed information almost instantaneously. I also planned that after we retrieved the needed information, we would reprogram the spies to believe they successfully completed their portion of the battle. Because I knew they would be debriefed upon their return. In war, you cannot believe all sources of your information and updates. We quickly learned that their success depended upon this gate being nonfunctional. At that time; they would openly deploy their forces. Now the trouble was what to do. I based this on how to deactivate this one stone and even reactivated to have all the power base reestablished. One method was to mass-produce a backup inventory of energy, then when the stone reactivated, all the backup would be employed energy that would be employed, bringing the 13 stones back up to the power level they had prior to the stone's removal. Still, this question remained. How do we know that these first spies were not reprogrammed themselves?

Accordingly; I will moreover, as a result in that place, and you will show us the video of and consequently and that it was her as we now caught about 300 spies, who stories ran somewhat consistent, with a few variations here and there. I wanted the small variations completely analyzed and recommendation of what to do included in the report. We now had estimated that as many as 4, 000 of the spies were on Wohpe. We had to find a way to remove their cover. One method would be to redeploy 100% new maidens to the station, taking the previous ones to special screening stations in which the Tunnel would have to set procedures for this non-conventional approach. I was smart enough to know that if the enemy had lost the basis for its attack, there have two choices: choice number one would be to retreat. Choice number two was to move up their invasion and fly into this battle blindfolded. Retreat for them could produce certain defeat, and that for normal training purposes, tunnels had blocked every form of entry or departure from Wohpe. Reports started coming in from Tunnels of some success in retrieving information from the rogue maidens. They reacted to some of our routine on board cleaning chemicals. This reaction was such that they reverted back to the original appearance, which were from the species unknown in or from a distant dimension. Therefore, most of their information was based upon actions taken here in Earth in a deep dark past. Excitement filled the air as the maidens were monitoring monitors every little move plus the scanners was looking for any distortion in the dimensional balances, knowing that every time you cross the dimensional line a wave form is released.

Is it as night, it is on now? Although most invading forces had equipment to keep this an absolute minimum, there is no minimum for dimensional shift? Something bounces somewhere to make room for the entry. The tunnels did an outstanding job in discovering the infiltration agents and executing them. The executions in this manner had to be absolute and instantaneous, so as not to send back any signals that may have been established during the dimensional shift. I must confess that this is some serious high-tech activity. We finally got our first break in that we detected a minute dimensional shift in one of our outer parameters. The tunnels were there to follow this invading force, which would meet another defensive line of tunnels had entered. It is important to try to capture as much of the invading force as possible because any premature engagement could warn the bulk of the force to retreat, in which they would simply regroup and re-invade. We now knew approximately how large the invading force was going to be, and when they approached that number, we attacked from both sides front and back. Battle such as these did not last long because of the need for instantaneous annihilation. All the stones were naturally back in place and fully functional providing much-needed real-time battlefield information and updates. Currently the tunnels were scanning all available space looking for any potential escapees. It was now time for the counterattack in order to show the devastation that will come for any dimension attacking our dimensions. This counterattack had our most advanced destructive weapons and was actually launched in unmanned vehicles. Physical bodies were terrible for relaying the position and status information, many times leading force into a nice capable ambush. This force scoured the invading dimension for three days destroying everything they came in contact with creating massive confusion among its intended targets.

After three days, the equipment is called back and the dimensional link sealed. Wohpe had passed his first test, proving to all within this dimension that it could defend and punish any invaders without mercy, quickly, and absolutely. The original maidens were returned, and to replace their previous assignments. It was time to resume the Creator's festivities. The Creator, however, had to excuse himself for an important meeting with Wohpe concerning reaction times in defensive measures, there was a concern that with me returning to my dimension that it would not be able to get my approval needed to fight off invaders or even to take advantage of invasion opportunities.

All the Creators within this dimension attended the meeting. They asked me if I wanted to attend the meeting as well, in which I declined. I consider this to be a matter of their survival, and therefore, I wanted their absolute input. I figured the more we work together, the further they would be willing to defend my dimension if needed, so that long crack of light that appeared above Coon Hollow could be neutralized. Be that as this may be; the Creator wanted Orenda to attend in her uniform to represent me in my interest. In this dimension, a maiden which wears your same uniform represents you 100% considering that maidens do not lack the ability to betray their leader. If this was a custom, then I did not want to offend them by not showing respect for their ethnicities. My primary concern was that I never really had no intention of becoming too involved with this dimension, the exception being that they needed my help and I told them that up to and including the forfeiture of my life if need be. Nevertheless; We were way to intermingle now, and Wohpe was very wise to recognize this, and to accept me in the foundation of my life prior to their calling me to duty on their behalf.

There was no doubt that one of the absolute best of these people and the hundreds of thousands of absolutely gorgeous in divine maidens who were, in essence, true Angels. In the meanwhile; Woape and I decided to retire to our chambers and grab some much-needed rest. Even though my tasks today were not physically strenuous, they were mountains of stress, that flowed through this powerhouse today. An invisible enemy was destroyed, which I was left a future opportunity for a revenge. Wasp and I upon entering to our private chambers naturally removed our uniforms. It was customary in this dimension to always remain without clothing while in the chambers. This is a custom that could learn to appreciate, although I knew when I return to my dimension such a practice would be considered taboo. Nevertheless; when in Rome, do as the Romans. The chamber played our favorite music for relaxation. I am told that the Gate of Harmonious controls this, and I must add that they continue to do an amazing job. This device totally analyzes the body's reactions to the activities that were performed that day and creates an atmosphere that completely rebuilds the body, is astronomical to say the least. I also appreciate the heating mechanism within our chambers, which I feel would read your mind and your body to create the perfect temperature for each person.

Moreover; this way, if one of my girls is cold while the other is hot then each will receive the proper temperature to bring them back into a comfortable balance. As the bodies are reestablishing the energy needed to depart from this chamber and be mission ready is one of the millions wonders within the station and dimension. Our tranquility is interrupted by the arrival of Orenda who briefs us on the results of the defense and offense programs. They now will be prepared to react within a few seconds notice from any portion in this dimension. Today's invasion was a much-needed wake-up call, and with only me being available was our reaction time sufficient enough to defend this dimension. Even though our bodies could function without food, they could still process and appreciate good food. Naturally; Orenda and Woape wanted to enjoy some of the popular restaurants in this central station, while wearing the prestigious uniform. Personally; I enjoyed seeing them in this uniform as it revealed their ultimate bond with me. They had been with me as the three of us were one. And if two-heads are better than one, then it stands to reason that three-heads are much better than one. Another important biological function in this dimension is what would save me when I return to my wife in my dimension, and that is sexual activity. Every sexual activity here is mental and complete, leaving no room for any additional desires or fantasies. I enjoyed this especially because the thought of trying to "satisfy" two divine angels would clearly be beyond my abilities both physically and mentally. There were happening at all the time to set aside time for such a primitive, yet vitally important for survival, function. My girls were happy and so was I. The other really nice thing about the food that we here did not have calories nor any fat nor any chemical compound that could any way harm our bodies.

Accordingly; we actually received our vital vitamins and nourishment through the air that we inhaled. I worry so often now is this is not a dream or a wild off delusional fantasy. If it is a dream, then it is a dream that you never want to wake up from. After we went to three restaurants, my girls took me to a nightclub where we can dance. Without a doubt; I had no idea how to do these dances. My girls fixed this problem quickly, by simply touching my head and instantly knew every dance and was a master at each one of them. This made the night so enjoyable as I was impressed with how advanced their dances were; which, when you consider they did not have a long history of continually killing each other and the division as we divided into so many small nations that continue not to compromise or share in many of their cultural foundations.

Moreover; it would take a person a lifetime to learn the hundreds of thousands of dances created by these individual separate cultures. The question remains, how many times must you reinvent the wheel? We now realized that it was extremely late and would have to rush back to our chambers and have our revitalization processes expedited if we were able to function tomorrow for what would prove to be a day of the Creators festivities, which would be on the third day, yet we had missed the first two days. My girls also wanted to explore these fantastic gates with their portals, something that at no time I even imagined could have existed. Subsequently, without their help this may not at any time have manifested itself. That is a possibility we never want to there was no consider. We did it, and that's final and that is done.

Accordingly; another concern that I have is somehow, I Feel Coon Hollow is drifting past me. Orenda and Woape alleviate my fears by reminding me that the blood, and the gate of pain are working now harder to purify the bloodshed that soaked the dirt. Therefore, centuries had been stained by such ruthless and unmerciful killings. Once this dirt is cleansed, then I would be capable to proceed with my three major objectives: one to seal the crack in the sky and protect my dimension; two, capture and the destroy the Coon Run Road Ghost; three defeats the 13 houses that bred evil into my one-time pure Coon Hollow. Each task could prove challenging and that since they were in my dimension so many of the resources that Wohpe had been available would not be competent to function in my dimension.

The Creator also informed me that I would have to have a major conference with many of the Indian spirits in my dimension, and they may be able to provide me with the needed support I would need. These spirits were not going to negotiate until the bloodstained dirt was purified from Coon Run Road. That would be a mission that I would worry about in the future, because for the next two days, I was going to enjoy the festivities on Wohpe with my Orenda and Woape. Another problem, quite uncharacteristic for this dimension, Orenda and Woape began reporting to me about what they consider to be rude and inappropriate mistreated by some of the other maidens. This included pushing them into walls, physically hitting them when close enough to make mild contact. They, also being verbally abused and accused of betraying their dimension. They would also tear at their uniforms. Orenda and Woape were my maidens. When they would walk by one would stick out their foot and trip them. They were always pushing when walking down the steps.

Additionally; as they told me this, I became extremely upset. I took them with me to see the Creator. The Creator could verify this through their identification sensors. It could identify 13 offenders, many of which were repeats, and wait for another opportunity to harass Orenda and Woape. The creator summoned the 13 offenders and their leaders. He played the video recordings of harassments. The harassing maidens did not realize that my girls had these identification sensors. Since they had access to critical classified information, these types of sensors were necessary, if not security essential. Naturally; the leaders of these offending maidens immediately detached them from their unit and surrendered them to the Creator. The creator reduced these leaders ranks to maidens to replace the ones whom they just detached. The creator declared that the leaders were responsible for the actions of the maidens; therefore, they should have had intensive training programs established to prevent such infractions. The infraction upon the chosen leadership of Wohpe was extremely serious and ranked among the highest among criminal activities. The leaders of this initial group were grandfathered from the future punishment, which was one week in the Prison of Evil. Nevertheless; these offenders would spend one month in the Prison of Evil, the remaining one on a prison planet for the remainder of their lives. This entire judgment was published for all who were in this dimension to witness. A new law was also established, any who wore Wohpe's highest leadership uniform could never be within 8 feet when they passed by, unless granted permission for one who wore a highest leadership uniform. His uniform would now have a 2 inch bright shining yellow star.

Subsequently; the star would identify any who was in the 8-foot pathway. An additional highest form of salute was also initiated. Any maiden that was watching this highest leadership uniform pass by were to immediately drop their pants. These pants will remain down on the ground until the leadership passed them by 25 feet. This was to show the absolute power that Wohpe had over-all maidens. When I heard this, I was definitely shocked, because if we simply strolled through a group of maidens, they would reveal their exceptional privates. And it would definitely be the three of us, as my angels would not let me pass through without them safeguarding their lover. The Creator said that no maiden had any special privates, their sole purpose was to defend to the death Wohpe and those whom he appointed to represent his interests and power. Orenda and Woape wanted me to test this new law by strolling through the multitudes of maidens who would be celebrating today's third day of the festival. I can see that this meant so much to them, and their need for both revenge and the confidence that they would no longer be harassed. For a maiden to reveal her privates in public was a show of reverence to a power greater than their honor. Actually; by revealing their privates for this purpose was indeed a pronounced honor. We, therefore, strolled through the multitudes that day, in which the maidens adhered to this law with pronounced precision, honor, and excitement. This kind of surprised Orenda, Woape, and myself. This also showed me that these maidens had the confidence in this force and had the discipline and desire to serve above any personal inhibitions.

Moreover; they all appeared so excited about this fresh intimate service requirement, because it displayed a desire to serve Wohpe greater than the desire to place one higher than the Empire who ruled them. Orenda and Woape were so proud to display their new yellow star where they each attached to their right breasts, and pinned mine also to my right breast. They wanted to make sure that mistake they had a yellow star, and they want to make sure that was easily visible. We noticed that when we entered a restaurant for lunch, a 25-foot parameter was established around us, in which only the restaurant employees could enter. That entry was contingent upon our approval, which we can grant by simply waiting our hand for them to approach. We also noticed that approximately 20 law enforcement officers appeared to protect the perimeter. It appeared to me that this society was so eager to abide not only by the letter of the law, but also the true spirit. In that, the spirit was simple, "defend Wohpe with all your honor, might, and life."

I asked the creator about the maidens having to drop the pants required, since although a man's dream, it can also be a man's nightmare. The Creator told me that was Wohpe's requirement, in that he wanted only those who would serve that were willing to surrender all themselves. Furthermore, the Creator added that by all doing this, there was no shame, the exception being if one did not comply. He further added that was the reason for the cheers and excitement, that the maidens exhibited while complying with this. He also noted that they were slow in retrieving the bottom portion of their uniforms. This is like a great experience that had ended, with no other form of authority ever to receive this great of a, “SALUTE.” I could see their great sense of pride in serving such an extreme power. We witnessed this power has recently as the previous day when a large invasion force from another dimension attempted an invasion and was destroyed.

Furthermore; not only were they destroyed also a large portion of their homelands destroyed. All believed that Wohpe was serious about his dedication to protecting his people. Therefore; there was no argument against showing this great leader their ultimate support and willingness to serve at all costs. Nevertheless; I often wished that I could share the same degree of dedication and service at all costs, with the only honor since of service to Wohpe. Orenda and Woape asked that I thanked Wohpe for the new protection he gave them. I told them to snap their fingers and take us to Wohpe.

They told me that their snaps did not have enough power to penetrate his awesome force protection field. I told him to look at the yellow star and to snap their fingers now. They instantaneously, without thinking, snap their fingers, we course appeared before Wohpe, who joyfully asked what was the honor of this very special visit. I am touring first, I wanted to thank him for saving our dimension from the most-recent invasion. And secondly that Orenda and Woape wanted to thank him for the additional protection that he gave them against the brutal harassment they had recently suffered. Wohpe looked at them and apologized for not detecting that earlier, citing that he had been so busy trying to build a new better, stronger world for them to their descendants to flourish in. He also looked at me and chuckled, saying that it was me and not him who saved this dimension yesterday; Nevertheless, the hard work in a very successful meeting yesterday they devised plans to ensure a rapid and solid use of the offensive and the defensive strategies to repel forthcoming invasions, and equally important future invading campaigns. Wohpe in addition revealed something new to us, and that was he had rewired her minds to where I can communicate with Orenda and Woape across the dimensional lines, as well that they could equally importantly communicate with me. This included instantaneous thought transmittal and receptions. This way if he needed to speak to me, he would speak through my maidens.

Naturally; Wohpe also granted through written law that only Orenda, Woape, myself, and any other who wore the yellow star, had instantaneous access to him or his throne. My maidens and made them promise they would visit him regularly, if not only to eat a special meal or to watch a stupid movie. They were on their knees in a bowing position, raise their heads and agreed to his command. Wohpe also told them never to bow before him again, in that this would be a great testament to others of their union with him. He also gave us each a new red star for our left breast. This star showed all of our unlimited access to him. He further added that any whoever disrespected them again would meet his extreme wrath. Orenda and Woape now walked with great pride. There was a new ruler in town, and they were part of the Royal family. Additionally; they were concerned about their inability to speak with me when I departed to my home dimension. That concern had been addressed; they would always be able to talk to me. That of course gave me some concern, which I would have to speak with Wohpe prior to my return to my dimension. There was no reason to stress out my girls at this point. We still have a lot to do, is not at the minimum to be the visible face of Wohpe. Our fearless leader invited us to play with the gates and get a feel for their abilities and powers, hopefully getting enough understanding to make recommendations for your future uses if needed. Therefore; I asked my girls which gate to go to first, they replied the Gate of Saints. They wanted to meet some of the saints who were their heroes during their childhood.

Consequently; they also wanted to share this knowledge with me. They agreed not to burden me with their complex names, most of them written during their ancient days. As we approach this portal, I was once again mesmerized by his awesome beauty. Wohpe had standardized all the portals in an attempt to confuse any enemy invasions. The new enhanced portals did much taller and wider. They can only be accessed by steps, with required detailed security measures. Our stars allowed us to bypass these majors as we walked up the 13 steps, the standard number of steps for all the portals. For some reason, Wohpe was fascinated with the number 13, attempting to remove any previous reservations about its use. Each portal now stood the height of five men, was a giant arch in the middle which added another height of two men. Each side has support structures, which were 50 feet in width and the height of six men. They were adorned in diamonds and marble, beautiful statues embedded within them around the side rose a thick, dark blue and white cloud. As we walked across the steps, the portal opened with a giant statue of an Angel appearing maybe 5 miles before us. My girls told me that was a statue of the highest Angel ever to serve the Creators. As we looked inside, we saw hundreds of temples, each surrounded by beautiful gardens. My girls wanted to see inside one of the temples, which is truly beautiful.

Amazingly; they had the spirits of Saints sitting around tables joyfully discussing the various theologies and were extremely happy and gainfully employed. My girls could sense the power being inflicted by his powerful Saints and stressed the importance of such a gate. There will still be able to make their precious contributions, while the same time offering motivation for others to follow in their footprints. The next gate was the Gate of Pain, which my girls wanted to know nothing about, and quickly rushed me to the Gate of Harmony.

Here they began to shine a growth total synchronization was all that existed. They sang so many songs and danced on so many streets as we walked for hours, without the girls tiring. Unfortunately; I was tired; I think it's because I did not fully appreciate the true harmony that was flowing from this structure. These songs and music were the fundamental basis for my girls in a structure of their lives, as so many challenges were met easily with the spirit conveyed by many of their songs. It was that they were a living medicine. I wondered how greatly beneficial such a structure would be in my dimension. Sadly, such endeavors could never be accomplished on such a divided world. Maybe someday? We now went to the Gate of Blood. My girls were not interested in this gate; however, I was very much interested, especially with the results of cleaning up Coon Run Road. As I entered, several of their leadership spirits appeared before me and began to give me status updates on the work so far completed. They made it down at least 18 inches throughout the entire roadsides, neighboring hills and of course Coon Hollow. The estimated at least another 10 feet, since they were dealing not only were the Indians, the Vikings, and Civil War soldiers, plus a wide assortment of lawbreakers and evildoers. They also had to deal with the 13 houses. They hoped to give me detailed reports for my future meeting with the Indian spirit chiefs Kosh Kosh Kung. I told them I did not know such a place. They told me that I would know at the appropriate time.

However; the importance was that all blood spilled by Indians had to be removed before that meeting. This is why they were giving priority in their search for Indian blood, which unfortunately accounted for most of the blood shed here. They have been given a high priority from Wohpe and provided additional resources from the other gates in order to accomplish this as rapidly as possible. I returned to my girls, appeared so excited to see me. I told him I had undergone for a few minutes, was a replied that was a few minutes too long. They now guided me to the Gate of Time. I knew that this could be a very important tool in among our success in handling many of the future challenges we could face. To be in a place where yesterday was today as well as tomorrow being today still boggled my mind. I understood this concept, always believing that our Almighty had this ability. As long as it was protected and not have used it can provide a lot of benefits for our dimension. The next gate was a favorite for my girls, and that is the Gate of Fertility. Considering that Orenda had less than 3,000 years before she could marry and start a family, she took this place extremely serious. Woape also took this as serious but not with the same degree of urgency as her sister-wife did. The ultimate goal in a maiden's life was to reproduce and have her family. They wanted to meet as many spirits here as possible. I personally think that this was to make sure they saw the red and yellow stars in front of their breasts. I believe this gave them extra confidence that they would someday have their families, having the blessings from the Gate of Fertility. I was smart enough to recognize how important this was my two living angels, thereby followed offering them all the support that I could.

Shockingly; the amazing thing was that the spirits did not worry about me, but instead worried about their shining stars, there were appearing in front of them. This made me feel good, and that when I did leave these girls would receive the respect and support that they would as if I were here among them. We now went to the Gate of Life. Orenda and Woape stressed to me the importance of this gate, and that was our life is nothing but empty death. This gate actively fought to protect everyone from death. Additionally; this life included eternal life. This is something which complex subject they needed time for me appreciate it. Such an appreciation must be cultivated and cared for: not rushed while filling in these empty holes with assumptions, but instead of more properly filling them in with answers. We, currently, all agreed to bypass the Gate of Unknown Spirits, considering this gate would be used only in certain mysterious situations when dealing with the anonymous. This gate also reminded me of an image of a god that Paul spoke of in our Bible. He used this image of the unknown to introduce his Savior and God to those whom he was preaching to. Therefore; However, I definitely appreciated the need for such a gate. I was also informed that this gate continued to search for unknown spirits in the event such as knowledge would be needed someday. I was very adamant in acknowledging my support for this gate to Wohpe, reminding him that until recently he was unknown. The unknown can be made known as fast as the known can be made unknown.

Speedily; we now had to go quicker in that the Creator was wanting us to join him in his festivities, considering that they were almost halfway through, and we have avoided this for two and ½ days of their scheduled five days; it may not be a good idea to continue this avoidance, if not for anything but to share in his great excitement. Actually; of the remaining four days, only two appealed to me. The first one was the Gate of Angels, in which my girls totally flabbergasted by the magnificence of this pure well of love, peace, and joy.

I jumped to them that this was my birthplace. They looked at me with serious eyes, and very calmly replied, "We know." I was smart enough not to touch this one with a 10-foot pole. Everything in every part of this humongous world was absolutely magnificent and beyond anyone's wildest dreams. Therefore, it was important to me that Orenda and Woape believe that I acknowledged this as their rightful birthplace. The next portal was the Gate of Eternity. To think that someone could be in eternity for over 10,000 years and still have no fewer days remaining than when he first arrived, the finality of the concept of eternity. It just never ends. There would be no difference in the number of days remaining for those who have been there for a long time than those who were only now arriving. We had two remaining gates, I too had many negative connotations for me to conceptualize their true value currently; however, I would never be foolish enough to claim they had no value whatsoever. These are the Gate of Hate and the Gate of Death. I always believed that hate is the absence of love, where his death is the absence of life. It was now time for us to rush back to join the creator's festivities, hoping to sneak out for the next few days to visit the awesome lakes that adorned the lands within this powerful dimension saving force. So, let us let the festivities begin.

CHAPTER 07

Creator's Festival

Orenda and Woape wanted so much to enjoy this festival. We missed the first complete two days, and I too wanted to see why this atmosphere was filled with so much joy and happiness, and a flood of non-stop cheers. What is remarkable considering that just within the last few days we faced the great dimensional destructive event. I knew my days, here, were quickly coming to an end because I had some serious issues I had to face. I must clean the bloodstained grounds that laid below Coon Hollow, I had to defeat the 13 houses, silence forever the ghost of Coon Run Road, plus now attend a summit that was called Kosh Kosh Kung. Likewise, I had no idea what this was; therefore, I would approach the Creator and ask him what this meant. Furthermore, I seem to enjoy how each day the things I must do increase, as if I should have known this all along. Much to my surprise, the Creator was here to greet us. I apologize for having missed the initial two days. He said that since we were at war, the initial day did not count. Moreover; as I looked like a chicken with its head cut off, the second day was also easy excusable.

In addition; I thanked the Creator for the excusing me, and asked him what Kosh Kosh Kung meant. He had no idea, and recommended that since it appeared to be Indian-related that I ask Wohpe the next time I saw him. He did not know when that would be. I pointed to my red star and said it would be very soon he smiled. He then said he recommended I joined the crowds now. I explained that sometimes it was difficult to join the crowds when they all stood at attention with their pants on the ground. I wondered if this was embarrassing for them. The Creator told me it was not in any way ignominious because the maidens viewed their bodies different from what we did. He recommended that I speak with Orenda and Woape concerning this issue. I, therefore, asked Orenda and Woape what the creator meant by me asking them. They smiled at me, as both began chuckling, and asked me if I did not notice anything from our chamber environment. Had I not noticed anything when looking at them?

I was quite puzzled and asked them to please explain what they were talking about. They explained, that the bodies of all maidens were created equally from the waist down, this was to ensure their ability to reproduce after their long centuries of dedicated service. They further explained that from the waist up, there are slight modifications.

Therefore; to expose from the waist down was redundant, and only showed to verify that they were not deformed or abnormal. To expose the waist up would be so humiliating that many would immediately resort to possible suicides. Then they challenged me to identify which of them; I preferred from the waist up. I was smart enough not to answer this question, notwithstanding, I said that they both were so magnificent that to make a choice could haunt me for the remainder of my days. Would they want me to spend the rest of my life in pain and agony? They both rapidly answered that would be what they would never ever want. As I looked among the crowds, and all the parents were on the ground, I hurriedly recognized what Orenda and Woape had just told me, to be true. Therefore; it was my lack of understanding and personal dimensional biases that were the incantations that were the abnormal processes being exhibited in this, "cultural deep understanding," there was a stumbling block here. I can understand why they did not present any major concerns for me, as my concern was for these beautiful maidens or angels. I could tell by the joy on their faces, this was not disturbing them that much. So once again, when in Rome, do as the Romans.

Moreover; we quickly moved through this very receptive crowd to a sitting area the creator had prepared for us. Except about 25-feet above the festival ground as it was a perfect view. The festival began today with the release of maybe 500 color balloons. Next, the Spirit of Harmony flooded the area with solid peaceful party music, I saw as the hands waved with excitement throughout the entire area. The party was on. These maidens had worked so hard, and as such they played hard as well, accepting the great gift that the Creator was providing for them. This was so far the greatest party I've ever attended, and to sit in a booth above it was another joy in itself. I'm so impressed with how the crowd bounces up and down and shifts in perfect unison with the songs that harmony is playing. Unfortunately, I will have to wait until our chambers before I practice or fine-tune such movements, as the Creator feels that is more important for me to be visible as it creates an appearance of strong leadership. Such are the trials and tribulations of a leader, the burden that I will soon have to forfeit when I return to Coon Hollow. At home I will be Mr. Nobody, a title I'm looking forward to once more. The important thing for me now is to enjoy this day with Orenda and Woape, a reward for their dedicated service that they so richly deserve. It is so rewarding to see the entire culture enjoying this festivity to this high degree. It cannot help but to allow it to soak in my bones. I am now receiving a telepathic message from Wohpe explaining what Kosh Kosh Kung means. He explains that it will be a meeting with many Indian chief spirits throughout the ages and a chance for them to voice their concerns. He will split it into two parts as he tells me not to worry for his spirit will be with me, even though the second part is in my sister dimension.

Nevertheless; he has received the authority to attend with me. He guarantees me that they will leave with a modified attitude, as many secrets will be revealed on that day, many which will surprise them. For now, enjoy the next two days with the angels they have given me. I usually understand that when Wohpe tells me not to worry, that I am worry free for this event. Actually, I am now looking forward to this event. I had the guards move our safety parameter to our legally mandated 25 feet, so our maidens can pull their pants back up and enjoy this festival. I feel this will help create the proper environment that the Creator intended. Orenda and Woape just made me a request to visit their hometown prior to me returning to my dimension. They're both from the same hometown and the planet, which would make a visit take one-half of the original time. They claim that many of their friends and family do not believe them when they tell them they belong to me. It is important for the maidens to belong to something, which I guess is somewhat the same for my home planet. Belonging to Creator provided a sense of achievement and security. I really look forward to this visit, and that I always enjoyed doing things that elevate them. For I would never again have such loyalty and beauty at my complete disposal. This kind of support arrives once in a lifetime. We see now so many of the balloons are actually changing colors and flashing. I asked my maidens if this meant anything? They claim it is a part of the show. I must submit that does something to the show. At this time, the maidens are raising the color flashing wands as the excitement intensifies.

Additionally; the background at the present time changes into a series of flashing lights, with many different colors, flashing up and down as a large yellow with assorted gold squares, ball begins to float among and just above the crowd, eliciting a cheer that literally rattles the walls. The ball currently changes into square multicolored rows and columns. This time the lights on the ball were a big ball of flashing in unison with the wall behind it, another extraordinary display of color magic. Now large white beams of white lights are strolling and flashing above it around the audience, adding another dimension to this excitement. The audience appears to be tranquilized by this experience as it continues to intensify. The strobe lights now appeared to be shooting out from the stage in a wide assortment of colors, with hundreds of smaller colored balls flooding the dance hall. Consequently; the colored balls disappear as the beams intensified their magnificent array of colors shooting out from all the walls that surround the structure. Green, purple, blue, yellow, and pink create an overpowering stream of light as with the strobe and flicker creating a random sense of continuous movement. At this time; the colors reduced to blue, green, and red solid beams projecting from the stage area as the audience now appeared paralyzed and absorbed by this continual wide assortment of light displays. Moreover; the lights at present appear with a candle base of a warm white, thousands of them covering the ceiling and reflecting from the limited space of the dance floor. The maidens and their selected guest all now concentrate on the floor's sidelines to appreciate the magnificence of this color display.

Amazingly; the warm white light contrasts with the chaotic display of assorted colors. Moreover; this now creates an appearance of solidity and unity, qualities that I'm sure the maidens appreciate intensely. In view of that; these amiable candle lights at the present time appear to be floating up to and through the structure's ceiling into the open sky above. Ironically; the sky peers to be a chestnut color shift due to the friendly white candles as their flame's flicker reaching into the heavens not far above. The floor now appears as a warm brown Lake of amiable water, capturing the reflections of the candles as they slowly drift away. Our attention now is drawn to the dome-shaped multicolored lights as they create a tunneling appearance reaching up on the floor and meandering at the ceiling to once again complete their semicircle series of multicolored flashing and strobe lights. The actual semicircle dome must create a sense of home for many of the maidens, who have spent years serving on the Tunnels. It also served to draw back in the audience's attention to the area they were dancing on, somewhat closing the open sky that just appeared and now disappeared. Continuing; currently multicolored to include green, purple, orange, and a few scattered white meteor lights began with a light display which covered the entire ceiling appearing in multiple rows. These lights appear to create a movement of up and down, practically as if they were actually meteors falling from the sky. They now switch to green, blue, yellow, red, white meteors with small white lights flashing among, creating almost an appearance of snow, which I'm sure would be a foreign and unfamiliar appearance for many of these maidens. This causes me to ask Orenda and Woape if they were familiar with snow. They confessed to have never seen snow except in many of their galaxy studies of planets, which were covered with the snow.

Appropriately; they confessed to a curiosity of someday hoping to witness snow. I tell them to relax, for the first time it snows when I'm back I will link their minds to my eyes.

They will not only be able to see it, but also to experience the cold that usually dampers the experience extensively. At this time, the lights take on a new appearance, now appearing like enormous butterfly wings, with blue and pink veins flashing through the while others appear orange with a dome-shaped in many flashing legs as will be seen on an octopus. These huge objects slowly float among the audience before escaping out and disappearing. The ceiling now begins to spray distinctive colors of paint on the audience, as they graciously cheer the paint that splashes on their bodies. Groups began spreading the paint in unlike patterns to decorate their fellow festival acquaintances. Orenda and Woape informed me that the maidens must really be enjoying this in that they seldom permit themselves to appear not totally disciplined, especially when in uniform. I tell them that since the creator created this festival and sense, Wohpe is also sponsoring it; they may accept this is a time for them to release them to enjoy many new experiences that they otherwise would not permit themselves. It almost makes me want to grab some paint and paint my girls. But then again; they were most likely to force me to clean them and the mess it would otherwise create.

Additionally; although, I know that in my life, I sometimes did not let such obstacles prevent me from redecorating a friend. I can understand why the creator added this element, creating a true display and appearance of uncontrollable joy for those who witness it afterward; crafting in them an intense desire to join in such activity when or if the situation were ever to introduce itself to them in the future, which most likely will be the subsequent day of the festival. The succeeding display had Wohpe written all over it, in that its first large square green silk blankets began to descend from the ceiling. They were followed by green long poles. When the blankets stopped falling, so did the poles. The poles then assemble themselves in groups of three forming a circular triangle, at which time the silk blankets wrapped themselves around it to form a tepee. Then strings of white lights began to weave themselves through the green silk of the tepees. This is followed by beautiful green and red circular bands appearing at the point where the three poles met, and formed their hoop-shaped triangle. One thing that I didn't know, and that was not see tepees this magnificent during my future meetings with my Indians. Subsequently; there appeared the stands and branches of crystal trees highlighted by strings of lights of assorted colors with groups of flashing meteor lights extending from their upper branches. This created a wintry ice-covered appearance, although these trees created a light bluish-green color. The trees were spread out among the dance floor, which offered the maidens an opportunity to get a feel for them.

Moreover; I also saw a wide assortment of transparent small pyramids, most of them appearing as the same color as the trees, with few exceptions. A few pink highlighted translucent pyramids floated between the trees. There were a few other odd-shaped triangles, most of them a warm white color, that floated throughout this display. Now the strangest display for this area appeared, and those were string lights that have a white base informed at the top, much like did the tepees. These, however, were to represent Christmas trees in my mind. I asked Orenda and Woape if they recognized these see-through color trees. They had never seen this before but had studied about them in the universities. Long ago on a few planets within this dimension, strange foreign groups would decorate the trees around our homes to celebrate a special winter holiday. They do not remember what the holiday was, but did remember the decorating of trees. I told them that someday they would see me decorate a tree for a holiday that we called Christmas, for the birth of our Christ. They both were eager for me to send this and thus see me do this. I just felt so sad that they could never physically help me decorate the Christmas tree in my future, considering my children had already grown up and no longer joined their parents in this activity. I guess that is the circle of life. For this next display, our ceilings once again opened up as thousands of the meteor lights of all colors began ascending upwards. They would occasionally stop to allow the numerous meteor lights to join their parade in the sky. I could never have dreamed that the lights could be used to form one simple display. Orenda and Woape told me not to worry about this abundance of lights, in that they were holograms and once completed would vanish into a small storage container that would be stored for their next use. I asked them why so many people, who had to know this, were still so excited to see it.

Therefore; they told me that the fact that they were holograms did not take away the magnificence of their display. As I once again looked at them, I found myself having to once again agree with my right and left arms. The next light display, matches this transition leaving us in awl as the previous trees reappear this time becoming much wider speckled white lights and adorned with so many bright orange meteors. The floor turned into brown dirt, as the green plants began to emerge. A nice sheeny red road went around the perimeter of the dance floor with a beautiful polished green that's just around the outside of the road. The fence had only one green rail. A cool breeze now ran across the bright orange meteors, as the composed breeze began to gently subside, as harmony provided the perfect peaceful sounds of nature to create an illusion and feeling of the birth of life as green plants began to grow slightly expeditiously, and flowers began to bloom. All who were in attendance, bowed their heads being reverence to a scene that was representing the birth of life. This scene continued for almost 20 minutes as not a soul in this building moved. Slowly, the lights and trees began to fade as the dirt returns to the dance floor. The world was now left in total darkness, as the leader lights began to reappear. Harmony stopped playing nature's music, and once again began to play the festival's music. I had to confess to myself and to all who heard me, that this was absolutely the greatest show of lights I have ever seen in my life. I truly had no idea that the creator had put this much effort into creating to the great festival for his people. People who always gave all that they had expected nothing in return.

Subsequently; the maidens were truly enjoying every aspect of today's festivities, as were my maidens and I. I noticed a couple of times that Orenda and Woape were moved to tears in their great joy. I could feel that there were hidden meanings to everything that I witnessed today. Consequently; without the deep cultural background that everyone here had, that I have not had the foundation to process these hidden meanings. Nevertheless; it was enough for me to know that two of the most important people in my life were enjoying this. I almost said the two most important human beings in my life; as a result, I had to think, were they in reality human beings. They looked, acted, and felt like human beings; however, were they actually human beings. This was an important question that I knew I had to ask the Creator, naturally, when away from my two angels. This question kept pounding on my mind, forcing me not to have the patience to wait to ask the Creator. There's only one trustworthy source that approached concerning this within the time limit that my inpatients allotted me, and that was to ask Wohpe, yet this created a dilemma for me. What if Wohpe took this to mean that I was unsatisfied with the performance that Orenda and Woape had given me. When approaching him, I will continue to emphasize my great love for my two angels. Fortunately; I use my mind link to ask Wohpe.

Therefore; I took the first step in this not able to return quest, and asked Wohpe if the maidens were human beings, considering that life spans were so much longer than those of the human beings on Earth. Wohpe could read to me like looking through a glass and casually answered that Orenda and Woape were not human beings, but the closest to human beings that one could ever find in any of the other dimensions, or for that matter, any dimension he had any knowledge of. Human beings, unfortunately, had way too many defects to survive anywhere in the universe, except for the very secluded Earth. This is why so many alien forces refused to have contact with Earth, and as I had witnessed those, had made contact with solely based upon efforts to improve their genetic imperfections. He further asked if Orenda and Woape had done anything to cause me to ask this question. I said the only problem, they caused me would be my eventual inability ever to find any living beings to match their perfection and concluding loyalty, and of course willingness to make any sacrifice to satisfy any request I ever gave them. Wohpe confessed that they all were this highest caliber, when they work, they work industriously with a play they play assiduously, as I witnessed during today's festivities. I further told Wohpe the Creator had surpassed any expectations thus far in the festivities today, and I felt his servants also appreciated this; nevertheless, worried that they were not entitled to even more. Wohpe told me that we still had almost two complete days before this small five-day festival concluded. He also added that there's never anything more worthy than the best that you can give.

Consequently; the intention of this festival was not for the reward of their service, as there were other vessels designed to provide this reward. This festival was established to introduce the spirit of the 13 gates as the ultimate monument for the accomplishments and goodwill of their people. They also told me to have no fear for falling arrive with Orenda and Woape, because they were worthy of the greatest love that you give them. Moreover; I asked how I could juggle this love with the love of my family and most notably my current wife. He told me not to worry because they were two separate kinds of loves. Such as a love, you have for a combat soldier you fight in wars with, and the love for your country that you fight for. He also assured me that my wife would soon figure that out. He also told me that he felt his empire needed a Queen, and if I had any recommendations. I told him personally, as he has should have more than one Queen. He agreed and once again asked me for my recommendations. I told him that I did not have extensive knowledge of the available maidens for such a high position, that I knew of only two who would without a doubt unconditionally satisfied that need, and they were Orenda and Woape. Wohpe unconditionally agreed, claiming to know all the minds of all his maidens and could not find anyone to be greater than Orenda and Woape. He also told me that the Gate of Time had also told him that Orenda and Woape were soon to invite me to their hometown for introductions to their family and friends, and of course a well-earned chance to flaunt their stars.

Happily; he told me to begin preparing a speech that would ring through their hearts for the next 2,000 years. Our supreme Emperor told me that he would crown them in front of those whom they love the most, to ensure they received the greatest honor possible for such a great day for his empire. He believed that they would epitomize the need for a loving face to represent his people. He believed in the power of love being the greatest power that a living being could ever possess. Orenda and Woape were now returning in from some lite shopping they had done. I sort of felt bad that they had returned so quickly, and asked them if they had seen everything that they wanted to see. I knew without a doubt they had not. Notwithstanding; they told me that they wanted to see nothing else. I realize that in one way to tactfully negotiate this hurdle. I said to them, "Darn, I was hoping that they would show me some things, considering that I would soon have to leave for a long time." Their faces glowed as they told me not to worry, they would make sure that they would show me anything that was vitally or remotely to my possible liking. I told him that we first had to go eat something, and then they could perform their usual magic on me. I heard Wohpe say in my mind, "Fast thinking there, buddy." I replied to him mentally, of course that it was the skill that any wedded man needed in order to remain married. Furthermore, I told my two future Queens to select a place for me to relax and enjoy some foods that they would select for me that would add some much-needed cultural knowledge. They look to the other, naturally speaking telepathically, and both agreed upon a place that was close. I recommended that they notified this establishment that we were on our way.

Subsequently; this way will not create that great of a disturbance, because those who enter were here for the festivities. Upon our entry, I notified everyone there that this was a festival, and thus we were excused from the normal legally mandated courtesies. I looked at the maidens and told them to put back on their pants. They smiled and complied with my what they perceived to be a command. This command, by the way, could keep them out of prison if any law enforcement people were to misunderstand our situation. I furthermore, told the restaurant management to put a sign-up inside their door that all command courtesies were temporarily postponed for this meal, or until we departed. Internally, I began to see some relief when speaking to my wife about my two maidens, in that I would refer to them as Emperor Queen Orenda and Emperor Queen Woape. I was sure that it would place my wife totally at ease, especially when we talked about any dimensional wars. I could also see her excusing me for having to speak with them, by simply saying we were talking about matters of the Empire. Furthermore, I could see future peace and tranquility in my small home back on Earth. As we began to sit down and order a meal, a large group of maidens for a solid line, three rows deep, around our 25-foot border, and began to cheer, "Orenda and Woape." At first, we could not understand why they were cheering, although I told my angels the cheering was so much better than being harassed. Then one of the maidens spoke up and offered thanks to them. Then it began to hit me, that my two angels represented a sense of worth for these maidens. They no longer had to walk around feeling lower were second-class, for they can cite Orenda and Woape's accomplishments as a true value for all maidens. I, therefore, telepathically, asked my two angels whom they would stand up and say thank you and to shake their hands of those who were in attendance.

Appropriately; I would also follow them and shake hands. I stressed that it was important that I followed them, an act, I felt would solidify the maiden's intense belief in their accomplishments. My bashful, yes for the initial time timid, maidens agreed and went over and began shaking hands and saying thank you. After the first handshaking, I telepathically told them to ask for their names and to thank them by adding their name. We stopped, calling back the first maidens that they shook hands with and asked them for their names and immediately thanked them my name. This is a personal touch that I felt was important in that it personalized the congratulation or thanks. I of course thank them by name, even though, some of them, I remembered their name when they told my angels. Either way, it was more important for me to thank them also by name. We ended up thanking everyone by name, to include the restaurant employees, who were in this restaurant for a festival meal. I explained to my maidens, telepathically of course since walls do have ears, this was important to thank them by name, if possible, because our stars represented Wohpe and we had to do everything feasible to bring glory to this Empire and to give its members a feeling that those who were in leadership positions truly cared for them. My maidens asked me, where have you been for our lives thus far. I told them that were trained by the best and gave them each a kiss on their cheeks. Although unintentionally, this sent another wave of cheers throughout this restaurant.

Therefore: I felt decent in that we were making them feel valid, because that someday they will want to lose their lives for this empire at least they would feel they had surrendered their lives for a good cause. Well, that's enough preaching for me now, it is time for me to enjoy this very tasty and delicious looking low-calorie meal. My waist size always forced me to emphasize low-calorie, although so far, I have lost 15 pounds since arriving here not from having scales, but that information is posted on my medical card, which is updated real-time. Accordingly; another 75 pounds would put me in real business. Maybe that is something that I can dream about when I regain consciousness back on Earth. The Creator currently entered the restaurant to ask us what our plans were for the remainder of the day. I told him that I would like to walk around some of the beautiful lakes, that were present in this beautiful city. He now chuckled, asking me if I realize that these lakes were currently over 400 miles in diameter. I told him I was just going on how big they were yesterday when I named them; therefore, I guess we will be only walking a few miles each, except for the Prison of Evil. The Creator told me that he established large groups of maidens to act as tourist guides for these lakes, considering that so many were here for the festival. I took this opportunity personally to thank him for the outstanding light display this morning. It was truly something so spectacular and was beyond my wildest imaginations of being possible. I feel that this brought great joy to this Creator. He of course, being in a physical body, gave both Orenda and Woape a kiss on their cheek, an action, which obviously brought more cheering among the bystanders who were nearby.

Jokingly; I asked the Creator if he was running for reelection? He gave a puzzled look, then he shook his head slightly as if to indicate that the light just came on inside it, telling me that he had already won his reelection. Smiling, we both shook hands as he said he would see us tonight for the entertainment events that he had scheduled. I shook my head in agreement and said that we would not miss it for anything, unless there being another dimensional war. He laughed, saying that in that event he might also you have to excuse himself. We now proceeded to walk through the beautiful landscape in route to the Lake of Peace. Notwithstanding; along the way, we approached a very wide River, called the River of Hope. I commented to my maidens that I hoped there was a way to cross this River. They winked their eyes and snapped their fingers, and naturally were soon standing on the other bank of this River. I keep forgetting that all they have to do is to snap those beautiful fingers. Feeling a sense of being ornery; I asked him if they ever thought about walking on the water. They looked at me seriously as if they had not, for why would they want to walk on water when you could simply snap your fingers and be on the inside. I had to pretend that this was such a stupid question, was totally based upon Earth's culture and would not be understood by anyone in this dimension.

Therefore, I shook my head and said that they were right as we moved on. To my surprise, Woape began laughing and told her sister-wife that I was joking about that person called Jesus in my Bible. I looked at her and asked how she learned about Jesus. They both smiled at me and said that they tried to study everything about me. I smiled, as they once again let me speechless to say the least. The front of this question for me was that I asked them if they had any deities or higher spirits that they worshiped. They shook their heads' no, claiming that they worshiped the Empire. I asked them if they were now the Empire did, they worship themselves? They both looked at me, and gave me that you are very stupid look, and said no. They then continued their movements. I looked around at the waterfalls, snow-covered peaks, the nearby mountains, and rocks that fell into small streams that flowed into the river, and told my angels that this reminds me so much of Earth. This is when they told me that the creator and Wohpe had used my mind for ideas on how to design the landscape here, wanting to create an interdimensional compatible appearance. Sort of a, "We have been around the universe," appearance. Moreover; the Lake of Peace easily lived up to its name. Many varieties of small animals, a few I recognize as being from Earth, like rabbits, squirrels, and birds were dancing around the lake's sanded beaches.

Consequently; there were many other groups of maidens also touring this Lake. This is where I appreciate the dedication to law that these maidens lived by, and that any who saw was immediately moved us close to 8 feet away that was possible and dropped their pants. I trained my angels well that the three of us eagerly shared our hands with them with respect to the data shown us. Then my angels gave me that there were also shopping places nearby that they would gladly share with me. I was kind of trying to think in my mind when they could have previously visited these places. However, then again, I realized that all maidens were pretty much on the same wavelength, and that if some visited; they all visited. We, therefore, visited a few of these establishments. My Angels selected some things and snapped her fingers, sending them back to our chambers. They asked me why I had not selected anything, which I explained that it was too much difficulty transferring them back to my dimension, and that most of these things were designed for the people and places in this dimension. They accepted this and continued to talk about other things. I asked them if they ever talked about warriors. They informed me that they were still way too juvenile to be thinking about such things. My goodness, it must take a lot of will power still to think you're too youthful when you're approaching one millennium of existence. I especially for my family on both sides would have been considered a miracle for them to make it out of high school without first feeling the need to reproduce. Once again, I'm so amazed at the wide selection of commercial products available for their people. However, then again, remembering all the packed wardrobes in our chamber, I quickly realized that this was not a new concept for this world.

I guess you become a human being in order to desire new products and new things to use in your life. Speaking of new products, I notice that nowhere in this dimension had I seen motor vehicles. Therefore; I asked my angels about motor transportation. They looked at me and told me that the ancient, and I mean really ancient ancestors depended upon transportation; however, the Empire simply snaps their fingers, and they go where they wanted to go immediately, so why would anyone want to waste time on such antiquated transportation methods. They also told me that tunnels were available to take them to distant planets if they needed to go there. Upon thinking about, I so no need to visit any planets here, since they were in a different dimension that would not be able to see the stars that these planets rotated around. At this point, Woape handed me a set of eye goggles and asked me if I want to go swimming in the lake with them. I thought why not; then immediately jumped in and saw a what must have been 300-foot gigantic fish, at which time I rushed to get out of the water. Orenda called me back demanding that I get back into the water, with them wanting to know why I rushed out of the water so quickly. I told her I just had seen a gigantic fish. They informed me that this was actually a small fish for this dimension, and that it would in no way hurt anyone, in fact, they grew up playing with this small fish. Therefore, I got me back into the water, and they told me not to be a scaredy-cat and to stay close to them. Therefore; we swam for a little while before getting out of the water. I then asked them what I was supposed to do with my clothing. Naturally; they snap their fingers and asked me, "What wet clothing." I should have known that they were not worried about it, then why should I? I afterward asked them if they wanted to go to the Lake of Love? That's when I realized that the lake was at least 400 miles away.

Following this; I then asked them if that was within their snapping range? They said it was not; however, the Empire would transfer us there within seconds, in that they did not want this to be outside their protection. That sounded good to me, as we were transferred to this wonderful Lake of Love. There was a mysterious arena that surrounded this Lake. Even though it was an invisible arena, it could still be easily felt. Even the air around soaked into our bones, filling our hearts with peace and love. My angels told me it was from this Lake that love was spread throughout their dimension. Even though love manifested itself internally, it many times needed jumpstarted where something was needed to excite and ignite it. Life has so many challenges and hurdles that an extra dose of love can overcome it. I had never thought that much about this previously. Nevertheless; it did make logical sense in that any emotion could run low of energy and at times made some extra fuel to move on. Love is not one of those things that you ever wanted to take a chance of being without. I asked my angels whom they thought they needed an extra boost of love. They casually look to me and replied that not all as I was with them. Chalk one up for my angels, great answer. I will have to remember that in case I need it someday. While we were here, I asked my maidens if there was any way that we could tour the endless landscape from this massive world. I wondered if this was a flat land or an actual ball made all the other celestial object populated the skies. Orenda could answer this for me; I mean, it wasn't the ball that was self-propelled throughout this dimension. It remained mobile so as not to provide other dimensions with a stable target.

Amazingly; even though it was hollow on the inside, it stored many of the much-needed offensive and protective military equipment needed for proper defensive and offensive campaigns. I keep hearing about offensive campaigns and asked Orenda and Woape if they knew of any upcoming invasion campaigns. They knew of no such campaigns. Accordingly; Afterward I asked why the Empire needed to store such weapons? Their reply was most likely in the event if another dimensional force were planning to invade us, we could, after that, not only stop them, but also defeat them making sure they would never try such a foolish endeavor again. One great way to gain this insurance when you completely removed from any sense of power the force that propelled that invasion, and to reestablish a new government that would protect our needs and by making them a part of the Empire helps provide the resources needed to ward off any future attempts from other dimensions, but also provide a replacement for the resources needed to subdue their threat. The best way to do this was to make them a so-called part of our family. I further asked them if they knew of any expansion plans? They did not know any, claiming that they held a deep belief that obtaining additional territory never warranted the loss of lives needed to acquire it.

Accordingly; I had to confess that I too shared this belief, noting how many senseless deaths occurred in my Earth's history because of a delusional expansionist madman which did not care about the loss of life, but only about potential gains in power, economic resources, and land. More times than not, they eventually lost quality, gained too much more. Once a life is lost, it is lost for eternity. At least one eternity of the realm that it was lost. I told them that since human beings existed more deeply in the physical around, such losses could affect the remainder of their lives, such as leaving them crippled or even emotionally damaged, and leave their families financially destroyed. Most times when killing is required, the costs drastically exceed the benefits. This is rather a morbid topic when sitting before the Lake of Love. Soon, a fleet of 75 smaller, yet extremely mobile tunnels arrived with a complete fighting force for our defense when we toured this magnificent world. After traveling for about 30 minutes, I saw a giant circular waterfall. The cliff had trees scattered among them, where the water appeared to go down it had nowhere to go back up. In the middle of, this waterfall crater appeared islands surrounded by yet another series of gigantic forested cliffs with many smaller streams jetting water across them. I estimated that the distance from where the water began to fall and where it formed lakes to be at least two miles. This raised another, of my millions of questions since arriving here, where did this water go? Woape informed me that it was stored inside this word and recycled back to the surface as needed. Their lives without water would cease to exist. I wondered about this in that I seldom witnessed them drinking water. Orenda told me that most of their hydration were through the air that they breathed.

Logically; that seemed like a logical method to me. I had never seen such pure water in all my days. I believe that this added to the dark green of the vegetation. At this time, something else hit me as strange, and that was I could never remember seeing a sun. I asked Orenda and Woape if they knew where the sun was. They asked me what a sun was? I attempted to explain this to them. They explained that this dimension, like most dimensions, did not have suns, and instead this power source was generated and supplied by the dimension itself through a complex energy atomic level generation process that was unconditionally invisible and was absolutely at the atomic level. I asked them how such a thing was possible, in which they asked me how a heat source could send heat through millions of miles of cold space and yet not heat the space that it traveled through. Furthermore; how could plants use this source to feed themselves? They both laughed at such a concept. The more I thought about this, the harder it was for me to rationalize it. I simply told them that it worked, in which they pointed at the trees and land surrounding me and said that this also worked. They were not going to accept what I said, nor was I going to accept what they said. The sole compromise here was that they both worked, and to claim that they did not work would be to deny what was before our eyes. I must confess that both methods appear to be impossible, yet all the lives on both of our dimensions depended upon this.

Nevertheless; this waterfall continued as far as my eyes could see, with even rainbows appearing above the water that was flowing from the deep surface far below. I finally saw something that looked familiar, and those were leaves of different colors. I asked my girls if the leaves changed colors and fell from the trees each year, and then grew new ones the following season. They said that they did in certain worlds that had limited heat sources. I guess that Earth would meet that criterion. We were now approaching what Woape called the flower lands. These were low slopping hills covered with endless flowers of every type, shape, and color that blanked the landscape. This was my first taste of the reality of not being on Earth, and of being up there somewhere. I did not recognize these flowers or any of the plants. However; I did appreciate their awesome beauty and such a wide variety. Orenda claimed that Wohpe brought them in from throughout this dimension. I asked Orenda if she knew how substantial a dimension was, in which she replied; it is as large as the universe, since it is the universe. She further explained that dimensions coexisted in the same space. She jokingly claimed that we could actually be standing in my living room. Back to this landscape, it was spotted with sizeable rocks, sort of like the glacier remains from the ice age. As we continued our flyover, I spotted a large bluish rock that resembled a pyramid. The primary difference was that this was a solid rock, with large flat rocks providing, it supports from the back.

Naturally; it was spotted on its front and right side by sizeable purple flowers. The remainder was a large green field with small darker green bushes. What I found truly amazing was the low slopping snow-covered mountain series. Even though the peaks looked high, it appeared to have passable pathways rolling across it. This range was towering enough to have a tree line. I also saw two additional ranges running behind it. This was actually making me feel homesick for either the Rockies or Appalachian (Allegheny) mountains back home. After retiring from the Army, I lived in the Allegheny for 10 years and the Rockies (in Washington State) for 20 years. Therefore; suffice it to say, this view brought back some special memories and was making me homesick. Although I know that someday I will be returning home, I still do not have a feel for when. Sometimes it feels like I must run 100 miles a minute to get caught up enough to go, yet other times I feel as if I have forever to do what I feel I should do. I am aware that every day I stay here; it will be harder to leave, and some innocent people such as Orenda and Woape will pay a high price for my procrastinating. I will have to take Orenda and Woape feelings seriously since they will soon be Queens and men who make Queens angry tend to lose their heads. Woape reminds me about tonight's festival, and that we should be heading back. Accordingly; since she noticed my interest in mountains, she will have our combat Tunnel pilot's crossover, some of the best peaks and fly parallel with the River of Hope back to the Throne. I told them that this worked for me. I presently can see field after field covered with an extremely wide variety of beautiful white flowers that created a snowdrop effect. Furthermore, I was very much impressed with these mountains; thus, I now focused on the River of Hope.

Therefore; I could easily identify the massive recent construction that it took to carve out this water pathway, with fresh trees planted on both sides. It also had a wide variety of beaches, which most likely were put there for the public to enjoy. Things of this nature always make me feel good, in that I still consider myself as a member of the public, that I will be for the remainder of my life in Ohio. My belief is that if you take the bottom out of a trash can, then everything in it will fall out as well. I believe that is one reason I try to shake as many hands as imaginable, got to keep the bottom of the trash can as full as possible. Woape shows me the Throne, which now is in sight. As we prepared to land, Orenda told me not to worry, because the first part of tonight's entertainment was a very popular cultural play covering the birth of the Creator's kingdom. When we landed, the Creator rushed up to me and told me that Wohpe needed me to appear before him. The warriors escorted me to his throne. When I appeared before him, he told me that there was a problem with making Orenda and Woape Queens. I remained quiet, waiting for him to continue. He maintained that he could not have Queens without at least one King. That King would own his Queens. He further inquired if I knew of any possible candidates for a King, and that should be careful in who I recommended, in that they could have the Queens immediately beheaded so he would not have to share power with them. This candidate must be willing to share power with Orenda and Woape. I asked him if knew of anyone? He then became extremely serious and while looking at me offered the kingship to me. I asked him about my returning to Earth, would that still be possible, or would I have to remain here for the remainder of my life. Wohpe told me that I could leave anytime I wanted and simply declare my Queens as Sovern for life.

Next: I asked him when would this occur? He told me as soon as today, and that this would glorify Orenda and Woape when I crowned them. He told me that he already built the coronation hall, which would seat 500,000 warriors, maidens, and citizens. He also added that the festival activities for tonight would take place after I returned with my Queens. I asked him what my name would be, and he said we would keep it simple and call me King James. My next question was how this would change my life. He then told me that King and Queen's titles were for the people and fell below yellow and red stars. At this time, Orenda and Woape arrived in their new ceremony uniforms. I asked them to explain what they were wearing? They told me the official clothing for my coronation, which was about to start, so I needed to put on my uniform. They handed it to me and helped get me dressed. They now told me to follow them. When we went outside, there were around one million warriors and maidens. The maidens remained at attention with their pants still on. Orenda and Woape told me that the pants dropping were suspended for this ceremony because it was being televised throughout the dimension, and no one wanted to shame the maidens with their home worlds. I saw what appeared to be thousands of golden motorized carriages, as everything was decorated to the 9s or to absolute perfection. The Spirit of Harmony flooded the area with triumphant music. When the ceremony was to begin in the new massive stadium, the warriors escorted me onto the stage.

Therefore; Wohpe appeared as a bright white light, unleashing his famous continuous display of lightning and thunder. Wohpe's role in this event was limited in that he merely showed his support and selection. He just said, "Behold King James, your new King." Then his lights vanished. The crowed, arose and cheered. Now began the important endorsements, including their speeches. I was actually feeling cheated out of the festival tonight, regretting my original reluctance in attending. Nevertheless, anything for Orenda and Woape. I was trying to imagine the look on their faces when they were to receive their crowns. Then again, when will I get my crown. I will most likely die from the boredom of these extremely long speeches. I guess even the politicians in this dimension could not pass up an audience of this size. With so many wearing expensive heavy highly decorated robes and royal customs, the long speeches were causing physical reactions. Be that as it may; the Empire had so much information to relay, and knowing that the masses would never miss a coronation, used this vehicle to get the needed information out to its citizens. For me, I had some upcoming events I would not miss. I was going to attend the remaining Festivals, attend Orenda and Woape coronations, and both parts of Kosh Kosh Kung. Part 1 would be in this dimension, sort of wake-up call, and Part 2 would be in my dimension, part of an opportunity for me to set the record straight and exact in some revenge, subsequently I would have to clean up the 13 houses, and afterward stop the Coon Run Road Ghost, and finally attend a picnic at my sister's house.

CHAPTER 08

The Queens

Day five of the festival was to begin soon, in which my maidens and I agreed that we would try hard to have as much fun as possible today. The conclusion of yesterday's festivities was postponed to a future date because of my coronation. I was rather curious about how the public will respond to their new king. Even though I'm not all that comfortable with this fresh title, I understood my need to keep it in order to protect my right and left arms. Orenda and Woape already completed all the travel arrangements for our two-week vacation back on their home planet. We will travel during the late hours of this evening by Tunnel. The entire trip would take less than two hours. We were not permitted to sleep in their parent's homes, because we wore stars, we had to sleep in the maximum security offered by a small fleet of Tunnels.

This entire section of this dimension was placed under extreme maximum security, with the deployment of approximately 300 combat divisions. Their home planet was only about 200,000 light-years away from the Throne, which for this dimension was practically in their back door. And in case there is any doubt, Orenda and Woape had their entire wardrobes stored in one of the Tunnels. The maidens had a custom of giving away their used clothing to their friends and families. This clothing would take on an added appeal in that they came from the holders of the Stars. They were actually already beginning to shop for the replacement clothing, in which today's festivities would offer them a rich resource of potential vendors. Nevertheless; I will be actively involved with these selections, even though I felt bad that I would not be there as these selections were worn after my return to my dimension. Be that as it may; they can see in me if I was not offering my absolute, unbiased selections. Therefore; I had to tell them truthfully, if I really liked it or not. I guess this is fair in relationships, especially when there is an intense desire to please and satisfy. There is no doubt in my mind that they would look absolutely gorgeous in any outfit they selected. These outfits were usually long, highly decorated robes.

Maidens traditionally only showed their legs while working, and when they played, they wore the long robes to conceal their legs. Since some of their work had to be geared towards potential combat operations, it stood to reason that they would want the extra maneuverability offered by wearing shorts. I'm sure that will have the time to talk about their work through rehabilitation and re-modernization later in our adventure. For now, this festival should actually be called the King's orientation because it absolutely increases my awareness in this massive kingdom. I don't know if I should say my kingdom or not because it is Wohpe's empire, as soon will be actively involved by their new Queens. I will speak to them by working with Wohpe and taking an active role. Furthermore, I had no idea how many planets we were really talking about until I witnessed this. Accordingly; the Creator with limited in what he could display today. I believe we tried to do was represent as many of the maiden's home planets as he could, although we actually saw maybe 500 planets. What he did was to display the planets that some of these people had maidens that were from there. We also could see I would say a square with 25 displays, showing some of the popular dances and holidays. I sometimes wonder what was I involved with. I've been kept voluntarily and in a very protective shell. Likewise, I'm here to fight for maybe to fight for a Hollow that can be no more than 1,000 feet, and that is stretching it. Notwithstanding; Orenda and Woape explained to me that there could be as many as 500,000 planets that submit maidens for the emperor.

Subsequently; I am from a world that has yet to find life on another planet. We can also safely say that it takes months to reach the nearest planet which does not show an atmosphere that we could breathe. That is a truly scary thought went through my mind, questioning how this throne is maintaining the government that is keeping his people satisfied. Now I wonder if the Creator is simply showing the magnitude of this cooperation, which within itself is a great feeling of unification and of belonging. Simple logic would say that if everyone else likes it and supports it, then must be right so I too should also support it. Now the Creator social display of some previous military campaigns to eliminate internal threats. This Empire does not mess around with squashing rebellions; they go in and do a complete wipe out and then leave, allowing the local planet and their militaries to do the cleanup and reestablish their order. I would surmise that this is what helps establish the, "It is us." This must be an important element in maintaining this peace. I should probably watch how I analyze and comment on these issues, because I am a Mr. nobody from Mr. nowhere. I still have trouble mentally grasping what is happening here. I think a couple of weeks on Orenda, and Woape's planet should help to give me a view from the outside and not from the very deep and secluded top.

Even trying to conceptualize this throne and the 13 gates that help build, work at the correct stone in the precise place created. The maidens, who are the subject of this festival's display today, truly to go through a transformation process. What I see is them in their perfect fitting battle uniforms; nevertheless, I see them change from their planet's uniforms or outfits into this unified throne. Even their maiden uniforms change as they transfer to his throne. The Creator also shows this transformation stage and processes, which is massive cheers from our maidens. It is equally important representative of a recognition of this process and the difficulty of the challenges that are interleaved into this process. Orenda and Woape explain to me that each maiden, here was doing an elimination process that runs out to for each 3,000 perfectly qualified maiden, one was finally commissioned into the throne's super elite forces. I can honestly say that to have Orenda and Woape always at my sides is a degree of security and protection still beyond my ability to comprehend. It is their positive and strong attitudes and pride in this service that tends to toss me for a loop. They have yet to question any of my requests and to without any, or I should say very limited, hesitation. Most times that hesitation is from them trying to determine what I'm really saying as to what they are understanding. I can never underestimate the fact that I'm a simple old hillbilly from a very primitive planet, and they're worlds that are based in discipline and confirmatory. I shudder to think what it would be like here without them. Furthermore, I trust and support them like they fully trust and support without question me. Likewise, I hope that our two weeks off their planet will help convince them that we also dedicated fully appreciative of their efforts. Each time a maiden or group of maidens watched them pass by with a yellow and red star, as well instills in them this stone's dedication to the warrior maidens. Every time I think about one thing another concern arises and that is if our male warriors are feeling neglected.

As they were again reading my mind, Orenda and Woape explain that the male warriors have received the highest honors and respect since the beginning of this Empire. It also appears that the male warriors are enjoying this recognition being bestowed upon the maidens as an important element in the fighting force. Simple logic is that the stronger these maidens are, the more likelihood of the male warriors surviving future combat. No one wants an idiot to be covering their back in combat. The maidens, simply due to the male superiority complex, do not present that great of a threat when initially encountered. However, when they, "whop the crap out of you" your view is quickly readjusted, while in chains being taken to the appropriate military war prison. Now back to our festival, the massive crowds continue to cheer each planetary presentation. To my egotistical conceited thrill after each planet presentation and was a half-minute video showing me receiving my crown and its phrase, "long live King James". The massive large crowds pause and bow during this video. Being the man of a million questions; I ask Orenda and Woape why so many people, or should I say Empire subjects, are paying this much respect to me since they don't even know me? They look to me and laugh saying, "they know you" while they wink at me. I asked them how much of that understanding was provided by them. Once again, they reminded me that all maidens are linked telepathically. I asked him if all of our chamber activities were also linked.

As they slightly blush, they answered no. The activities of husband and wife are unfailingly screened, considering that they must wait for many thousands of years before they gain this experience, knowledge, and emotional enrichment. Notwithstanding; they're perfectly allowed to develop their intimate skills with the massive inventory of male warriors consistently present. I guess it also provides insight into the males' complete support of their maidens, not wanting to lose this valuable and available component of their fighting force. My maidens moreover revealed to me that my new image is the Inter-dimensional King, or the King from our sister dimension. When the empire subjects see me, they see one from the unknown and the other side here to help them create a peace that everyone craves. Again, I asked her about emotional security and seeing not one, but two maidens on my side. They recognize that they know everything I'm doing and have access to my, "filtered and censored" thoughts. This is in the feeling that I am theirs, and therefore, they can safely be mine. Wohpe did an amazing job spinning this from a potential obstacle into a sword in the empire's military arsenal. The safer the people feel, the weaker their fear will become. Maybe, when I go back home, I can find some kindergarten somewhere to command. That would almost be like marching cats. It appears now that today's festivals activities are concluding with a massive display of fireworks, with the Spirit of Harmony intensifying the emotional impact of this festival. I can see the Empire subjects really feeling moved by the power that is protecting them and their home worlds.

Even though I was here for the entire day, it feels like it was only a few minutes, with me eagerly awaiting the next planet's presentation. I asked Orenda and Woape how many planet's presentations we saw today? They told me that we saw 2432 presentations today, which is only the tip of the iceberg. What proved that these two angels have worked so hard for me to communicate with me is their excellent command of idioms. I guess if you are going to speak to an idiot like myself, then you should speak with idioms. They also tell me this time for me, or us, to do a walk-through between the crowd. Tunnel has verified that this is secure. We now began to walk around the crowd. Perceiving this is a mixed family cell festival audience, I suspend all commands protocols. I don't want my maidens standing around with their pants on the floor in front of children and other married men and sex-starved male warriors. The suspension of protocols is posted as a Spirit of Harmony begins to drum up the audience for my walk-through. We walk through slowly, the three of us shaking as many hands as possible. The excitement and thrill in so many of my maidens faces that had tears of joy flowing down their body. That is an experience I should take with me to my grave. How will I ever, or we always, live up to the expectations that these people put through faith in us. Accordingly; our Empire must enjoy this great faith and confidence they have in us if we wish to keep our government strong.

Consequently; we are only as strong as our dedicated fighting force has in us. I can sense Wohpe's great satisfaction in what he is witnessing. This is personally and personal recognition of the value of each one of our subjects. I'm not standing on the top of some mountain somewhere directly the Tunnels to mass exterminate; however, instead, one-on-one looking at them into their eyes and saying, "thank you." This walk-through has already taken about four hours, and could be making us late for a scheduled arrival at my maiden's home planet. At this time, the Creator announces that today's festival activities are now concluding and that the King must travel to visit another planet. The crowd prepares their exits, as I can feel the disappointment in those who left without my handshake and thank you. After verifying with me telepathically, the Creator announces that there will be one more day of festival activities upon the King's return from visiting the other planet in two weeks. Because this day was originally had only four hours of entertainment remaining, the King and his royal assistants will shake hands for eight additional hours. Even though we know that this will create an increase in attendance, I completely agree and even offer to shake hands until physically not being able to on that day of subject recognition and appreciation. I have to know that will have two new Queens to help on that day. This will also be a day of maiden's Renaissance in the beginning of the special element of the Empire moving from their dark ages to their enlightenment age and rebirth into the life at the command and empire's highest levels of power. The emperor's warriors now escorted us to the fleet of Tunnels that will zap us 200,000 light-years to my maiden's home planet. Otherwise, according to my maidens, a small trip in the local neighborhood. As we limp love to our space vessel and take our seats, the fleet begins our mission. The excitement and thrill that I currently see in Orenda, and Woape's tear filled eyes begins positively to affect me, as I am becoming very excited. These killing machines would now review and re-examine the foundation to put them where they are today. While traveling through this universe, I watched as we leave our galaxy and proceed into another galaxy, which was not far away from my maidens who tell me that their galaxy is the closest one to the throne's galaxies.

Therefore; naturally, I asked her what she meant by throne's galaxies. They told me that the throne was sandwiched in between three tight galaxies and would have a rotation that moved through all three of his galaxies. This was for security reasons, of course. While enroute and on my first major trip in a Tunnel that is not drilling inside the ground somewhere, I noticed the monitors that were displaying the space it was going through. I also noticed that we were going past large Suns, and asked Orenda and Woape about these Suns and the sources of heat that they were providing for their nearby planets. They both agreed that some suns provided energy for their adjoining planets, but not the throne since it rotated around and within galaxies, thereby were not subject to the gravitative pull of any single star. The throne generated its own gravitative pulls, which it did not really set a gravitational pull nothing could escape or enter its space. That is why it had to release our tunnels today for the trip to their home planet. They told me now that their home planet had three Suns and over 100 moons. Subsequently; it was three times larger than the Jupiter in my solar system. Additionally; its population was around 30 trillion citizens. Unlike my Earth, their home planet had only one central government. One central government per planet or small group of planets were standard for the throne. The throne had seven major military forts on their home planet. They also said that throughout history, they had contributed 19 maidens to the throne. Moreover; they were two of the seven who are active maiden duty at this time. Next, I asked why so few. She said that was the throne's approval rate, which was considered average for their planets with this population size. If only my little angels knew the surprise that was waiting for them. When viewing the planet from orbit, it looked like it was totally devoid of life.

Consequently; my maidens told me that this was a defensive mechanism established in all the inhabited planets. It was called a Planet Protection Disguise. As we began to descend, I still did not notice a surface. This is when they told me that the surface area was actually 200 miles below the upper burning gas layers. As we continue to descend a beautiful surface began to appear. My Angels commented that there was a fresh gigantic structure that they had not seen previously. Apparently; it had to be new. The pilots asked them if they would like to visit it first, that it would only take a few minutes. Having always a sense of adventure, they tried to make it quick. As Tunnel entered the inside dark, the dark changed into multi-colored lasers shooting light beams everywhere and the Spirit of Harmony playing the Royal welcome music. Orenda and Woape both commented simultaneously that their homeland welcomed me before them. I looked at him puzzled, saying I did not recognize that as a King Royal welcome. Tunnel landed in the lights came back on and as his doors opened as my angels' parents entered. Orenda and Woape asked their parents why they were here and not a home. Both fathers told their daughters that if they wanted to know the answer to this question, then they should follow them as they proceeded to exit the tunnel. Once these girls exited the tunnel they were met and hugged by their mothers.

Subsequently; my girls look out among the visible audience and see all their friends and relatives, who began to clap. My girls looked at me and asked why they were clapping; it was; I replied must be because of the red and yellow stars. They seemed to buy this answer and proceeded to exit. When they exited, all the lights appeared and giant signs, which said welcome Queen Orenda and Queen Woape. In total shock, they both look at me and asked what this was, because if it was a joke in front of their friends and family, it was not funny. I pointed at the two gigantic statues of them wearing the crowns and said that those who do not look like jokes to me. And that I recommended they proceed to that large stage in front of us. Given that they always do what I tell them without question, they proceeded to the stage. I followed until we reached the stage, at which point, I stood in front of them holding two crowns. I then told them to hold their crowns, that someone special had something to tell them. The lights in this gigantic place turned a warm yellow as a Spirit of Harmony played Wohpe's Royal welcome. The lights immediately began to flash many colors as a bright white ball began to appear above us. subsequently a voice of thunder declared, "Behold my two Queens, long live the Queens of my mighty and enduring Empire." And next their crowns were lifted from their hands and ascended upon their heads. Now having my crown on my head, I proceeded to give them each a hug and told that they had better take good care of my Kingdom when I left to go back to my home. I could feel an intense shock beginning to overtake them; therefore, I motioned for their parents to join them on the stage. We now took our seats, as four additional seats were included for the parents, and began the long charade of speeches. I motioned for their president to keep the speeches short and to the point, or I would have some heads to join with my current collection.

Joyfully; as my Queens began to take their seats, I motioned for them to stop, and for their robes to be given to the parents to put on their daughters. I believe this was when my girls realized that this was true, because anytime new clothes were involved, it had to be reality. Orenda motioned for me to put my ear to her mouth, in which I did. I believe the shock of this event made her forget she had telepathic abilities. She asked me, "Why them?" As I kissed her check, I told them we could not find any better. Warm tears flowed down those royal cheeks. It is always rewarding to see the oceans of pride flow from the parents as they witness a level of achievement beyond their wildest dreams. Their daughters were now Emperor Queens. As the local speeches concluded, the president motioned for me to take the stage. This would be my excel or fail moment. As I walked towards the podium, the Spirit of Harmony played the Royal King's welcome. The audience began to cheer, as I suppose most of our Empires, in that none saw me speech previously.

Naturally, in carrying on my tradition, I shook the hands of all who were on stage with me. I waved in all directions, realizing that this was being broadcasted throughout this vast empire. My speech was as follows:

Today, I stand before all who serve Wohpe, who searched not only this dimension, but many others to bring me here. The harder I struggled not to come, the harder he continued to recruit me. I could never determine why he wanted me; nevertheless, am so glad that he did. He saw in me what not even I saw. Together, we built the 13 gates which adorn our magnificent throne. For me to say, the 13 gates are the greatest gift to our throne would be false, because our throne today has received even two greater gifts, gifts that will bring great peace and joy to your wonderful Empire and agony with defeat to all who challenge it. Wohpe saw that I was lost when I came here, and thus searched for the support that he knew I needed. When he discovered Orenda and Woape, he knew his search was over. What was to be my greatest gift turned into a great challenge, as Orenda and Woape struggled hard to answer every question and find every answer that I needed to ensure that what Wohpe saw in me became a reality. Orenda and Woape and I have thought and acted as one literally since our initial meeting. Such a unity is only created by the heavens. For all who are here today and those who are watching from throughout our Empire, you can tell your descendants that you witnessed the true birth of our empire in the day that Emperor Queen Orenda and Emperor Queen Woape accepted the Empires Crown. This great day of joy for our Empire shall be a terrifying day of pain and agony for our enemies. It would have been better than they were never born. We have a Prison of Evil *for them and a* Lake of Love *for you. I can only hope to live up to the faith they have always had in me. I will strive hard to do so. Any who would harm them, harm me and harm Wohpe, who will exact his greatest revenge on them. Wohpe and I also today declare our Queens as* Sovern for Life. *They shall remain Queens until their deaths. They are not bound by the mating requirements of the maidens, and shall immediately work on providing your Empire its future Kings and Queens. Furthermore, they are why I am here, and they are why you will always have freedom and an Empire for your descendants. My words of praise could continue for days, yet you have two Queens who want to show me* Dionysus, *for which they have such great pride. We have extreme pride in your world, and thank you for giving us Two Queens.*

Orenda and Woape asked me if we could stay in their parents' homes tonight. I asked them which parent's home. They told me not to worry, they would all stay in the same home for tonight. I agreed as the warriors began scanning the entire neighborhood for possible security issues. I reminded my Queens that we had a lot of hands to shake, and therefore, the warriors would escort her family and friends to their homes. We strolled the audience, shaking hands and thanking them for attending. It was so rare to see a group this large with no maidens. My Queens were telling the truth when they claimed very few maidens came from this world. There was an overabundance of warriors, which most likely means they serve in the remote areas and away from the throne. I must confess that the two gigantic statues of my Queens were an excellent touch by Wohpe. I am told that he also created this humongous stadium.

Moreover, I must discover how he is doing this. Still able to read my Orenda explains that he uses the Gate of Time to create them and then bring them back here. That made perfect logic to me, and was a wise use of this gate. This building would forever hold the statues of our Queens, as a show of the great honor and power that they now had. Woape had some warriors tell their parents that our welcome home celebrations would be postponed until tomorrow, because they were all too exhausted this evening. I looked at them and asked if they were exhausted. They confessed that they were not; nevertheless, wanted some special alone time with me. They needed some time to make the proper adjustments. This really touched me in that they wanted us together over the reunions with their friends and family. We soon entered our special Royal chamber in our command warrior Tunnel. The Queens were happy that their wardrobes had been delivered and setup. I reminded them that those outfits would be stored in a museum somewhere and that the command's public relations departments would select their royal outfits, naturally with their input. The three of us had an extremely busy day and as such snuggled up together in our bed to enjoy the first night of our two-week vacation. As we prepared to rest, I asked my Queens why there were not any maidens in attendance today. I mean, maidens were being crowned as Queens. They explained that unless visiting their home worlds we were not allowed to travel openly through space, mostly for security reasons since many either had or had access to sensitive information. Then, out of curiosity, I asked how a girl could become a maiden. They said the first requirement was they had to graduate within the top three students of their graduating class.

After this; they then had to attend a university that was ranked in the highest five percent of those on that planet. From this university, they had to graduate within the leading five students. They then could apply for the maiden academy, after getting a perfect score on a warrior's physical fitness test. Their academy lasted for six years. Every day started with three hours of physical training, followed by an additional three hours of combat training. Subsequently; only the top 50 percent graduated into the advanced maiden academy. The remaining 50 percent is assigned to the reserve commands in case of a major war. The advanced academy was for four years. This was the final stage and upon graduating, they were given their first assignment. I was absolutely flabbergasted when I heard what it took to become a maiden. They in reality were in school longer than the doctors on Earth were, actually twice as long, excluding residency. I wondered if the reason they had served me so well was because they had no thought of not doing so had been driven into their deep subconscious. Woape told me that was not the reason, the reason was a much more powerful force, and that was love. This was the first time the word love had appeared in a conversation to describe a feeling between us. Now things could get hairy, to say the least. We would not deal with this at present, because this was their special time on their home world, and I just wanted to know everything possible about my two Queens.

CHAPTER 09

Lost Spirits

Having traveled back to their home planet only to long for the comfort of this chamber, my two new Queens and I lie here snuggled really tight. I can feel the security they believe I provide. It is true or not I have no idea yet I also feel the security. Our monitors begin to flash, listing our Royal duties for this day which is mostly having our faces seen while wearing our crowns and shaking hands. It will be a long day but a happy day as we will to soak in our subject's enthusiasm that now is on in the face or faces, they can attached to the power of this thrown. I began to lightly shake Orenda and Woape who are still sleeping in order to attempt to wake them. I feel rather guilty in breaking the tranquility and peace that appear to be flowing from their faces, nevertheless it is time for us to get up and get moving.

Accordingly; our chamber delivers to us our robes and crowns. As Orenda and Woape see their robes, a glow reappears on those faces that just moved from the dream world to reality. They leap out of our bed and quickly put on the robes which fortunately fit too perfectly to their combat physically conditioned bodies. The robes are decorated with diamonds that are sparkling gems among the best that Wohpe had been available, which is actually his reproductions, they discovered to our dimension. Fortunately, our crowns are made of a very lite material. As I began to put on my robe, I can feel my legs as they are filled with a numbing pain. It has been so since I have felt any form of discomfort in my body. This numbing pain is taking away the control of my legs, forcing me to drop to the floor. Orenda and Woape began to scream as they are grabbing hold of me trying to lift me back into our bed. Somehow, they are able to get me back into our bed, as they can no longer see my legs. Now my arms take on this same numbing pain as a vanish as well.

Alarmingly; This is scaring my two Queens, as currently my head takes on a more excruciating pain, and I can no longer see Orenda and Woape, as I at present see a fuzzy hospital room, with tubes running from my arms. I am absolutely confused, yet I can hear the voices of Orenda and Woape telling me that I'm going back to my dimension. How they know this I do not know; however, I can smell the distasteful environment that I am in at the moment. My whole body is now in this apparently hospital room as I can hear some monitors start beeping loudly, as a couple of nurses come rushing into my room. I hear one of the nurses tell the other one that she thinks I'm coming out my comma. I can feel my body totally wet with sweat now, soaking my bed. I can also feel air coming into my body and leaving out my mouth. I must have been used to this previously. I've been here for less than one minute; notwithstanding, wish I was back in my chambers. I can look over and see the time, which is 2 AM. The nurses call for aids to come in and help them this me out of this bed. They want to test if I can walk, a test that I immediately fail, in which the nurses with the help of their aides, put me back in my bed. I can feel a discomforting pain flow through my entire body. To be honest, if this is what my dimension has to offer me, then I want to go back to the Throne. I call out for Orenda and Woape, asking them if they can take me back. They claim that this is a dimensional pull, and that they have no ability to bring me back. I should have realized, that it was all too good to be true. My question now is. Why did it decide to bring me back now? I can see one of the nurses swapping out one of the bags that has a tube running into my arm. She looks at me and tells me she has given me a mild tranquilizer to help me go back to sleep, as the doctors want to control my transition from my coma. She also tells me they will be transferring me to a hospital. She smiles at me and says that I surprised them, having been in a coma for two years now.

Shockingly; I am confused because I believe I was told that my return would be instantaneous from when I departed. Woape now tells me that Wohpe will be giving her the information concerning my current transition, so she can answer any questions. It is so strange to have her voice in my mind, yet not be able to see her. I already miss their beautiful faces, and wonder if I actually could handle this transition. Still the question is why am I coming back? My Angels, which is the only appropriate term I can use to define them in this dimension, tell me that I have a great mission that I must accomplish. I can now see what appear to be miles deep of tangled up spirits. I am to reach up and grab one and after hearing their story tried to pull them and any other fellow, "tribe's members." I will then if it is a good spirit tossed them into the throne's Lake of Peace, or if they are bad spirit tossed them into the Prison of Evil. I asked why I am the one that must do this in that I do know my Earth has a supreme deity. My Angel tells me that this was a condition that Wohpe had to agree to in order to use me for a short time. I guess I must be thankful to have had this wonderful experience while in the Throne.

Moreover; Now comes the scary part, I must reach up and grab someone hear their story, then decide where to go. I'm smart enough to realize that an evil spirit will not tell the truth. I asked my angels how I can decide? They tell me that the evil ones will have a black spirit; nevertheless, I must hear some of their stories so that the Prison of Evil can adjust their torment level. Now the fear comes over me, knowing that many of these spirits, will probably be capable to overpower me so quickly. Orenda and Woape, whose voices are now faint, tell me that I will be able to control any spirit that I pulled down and of all their tribesmen who follow them. Unfortunately, with the voices now trembling, they tell me that they will no longer be with me but that Wohpe has been able to get my dimension to agree to give me an assistant to help me. Now a new stronger female voice and body appear beside me. She introduces herself as Devika and tells me not to fear for she will help me, even if she must summon some legions of angels to assistance us. Devika also explains that at most I can see her and that when I am speaking to her, as long as I say her name first only, she can hear me and that those around me will not be able to hear me speak to her. I now am in an ambulance, I guess heading for my hospital. I don't remember them taking me out of the comma center's bed. Devika explains that once she was talking to me, they moved my body.

Happily; I looked at Devika and complimented her beauty, saying that she will make this transition a little easier for me, as I'm leaving behind too extreme and wonderful Empire Queens. Devika tells me that she's had a long and comprehensive conversation with Orenda and Woape, who explained to her that they had a great love for me and if anything, bad happens to me, they would get her first. Devika assures me that she will provide me the same love and dedicated service, although the love may not be as intimate as it was with my Queens considering that my wife is also in this dimension; nevertheless, she will submit to all my commands, considering her relationship with me is spiritual and not physical; therefore, the rules of the physical realm do not apply. Devika asked me if I want to know what will happen today. Naturally; I am a creature of curiosity; I say absolutely if possible and not an inconvenience. Devika tells me that no request or command from me would ever be an inconvenience, and I can expect the same level of support from her that Orenda and Woape provided me in our sister dimension. Subsequently; I asked her what she means by sister dimension. She tells me that the dimensions that have cracks between them are called sister dimensions. She's already impressing me with a detailed knowledge, I feel that this could be the support I will need to tangle through the web of, "lost spirits," that are hovering above Ohio. I asked her if I must clean up all Ohio, whereas she tells me that I must only clean the southeastern part, mostly above Washington County.

Consequently; The trouble is that as I open the hole others will slide into it, so I could be dealing with some archaic Indians, Kickapoo tribes, and even Eerie Indians. However; these will be limited, as the majority spirits up or down will be Delaware, Wyandot, Cherokee and Shawnee. I will also be dealing with murderers from the Vikings, French, British, and Civil War. I asked her how someone who murders under the command of their government or king can be held accountable? Devika explains that it is the heart that determines the punishment if indeed a punishment is warranted. Those who kill other white men will be excused and released back into this realm for their final transition into the afterworld. Most were poor and already have their information recorded into the Book of Life. The reason they are still in transition is because they may not have been subjected to the laws of this dimension at the time of their death. Their judgment will be fair, and they will be transferred back into the throne. Devika informed me that getting ready to receive my first visitor, and that I will discover another surprise during this visit. I told her that I was not in the mood to be waiting for surprises. With this being said, a vaguely familiar face enters my room, yet as she gets closer to me, I recognize her as my sister. She says hello Michael. My family has called me Mike, as I always went by James everywhere else. I then went to say hi back to her Devika stopped me, tells me never to mention her by name because evil spirits could try to latch onto her. Now my big surprise came when my sister looked over at Devika and said good morning Devika. I looked at Devika and asked her to explain why my sister could see her since she told me that only I could see her?

Accordingly; Devika explains that my sister will be helping us in our battles against the 13 houses. My sister explains that she has received the visions in her dreams about my adventures as King James. Naturally; she had to keep this a secret. She revealed that by seeing me in a coma had put great stress on her and while doing this would harm her while being. Therefore, by seeing these visions, she knew that was okay could regain her physical well-being. I can tell that she had contact with the spiritual realm in the way to that she was clarifying physical. Devika now tells me that she's will witness the first one, and then depart for the majority of today as she must inspect the warrior legions that we will need. I, therefore, asked her why we need warrior legions, which she naturally answered to subdue the wicked spirits and transfer them to the Prison of the Evil. They expect great resistance from the evil ones, and will take no chances in them escaping their doom and rightful punishments. They were judged by our Book of Life, our review, and the throne's Gate of Death, prior to being received by the Prison of Evil. Devika explains that we will witness enough of their evil deeds to be comforted to know that they deserve their rightful punishment. Moreover; I asked her why they are being transmitted to another throne's evil placement area and not the ones available to Earth. Devika further explains that she does not know except there was an agreement reached between our two dimensions.

Apparently, Earth was overwhelmed with too many evildoers. She further asked me if there were any additional questions, I asked her when she returns. She told me within a few days, in order to give me some time to readjust to the physical realm. Nevertheless; if I needed her for any reason, I could call her, and she will immediately appear. With this, she disappeared. Even though I've seen the appearances and disappearances and the moving here to there ever since my relocation or should I say temporary relocation to the throne, I'm still surprised. I recognize this even more now by seeing the surprise in my sister's eyes. I say to her that it does take some time to get used to this. Even she now confesses confusion in deciding what is real and what is not actual. She was really impressed with the 13 gates that I put the 13 stones on. She was also amazed when she first saw Dianysus, not realizing that the place to be that big and has so many other living beings that so closely represented we were living in the stars. I reminded her that it was another dimension, and although we can see the star, we could not see life on it although life could exist on it and other dimensions. I told her that I too would like to return and visit Dianysus with Orenda and Woape, if we could sneak in and sneak out without their planet's public relations discovering us. My sister told me that my wife, two brothers, and father would visit today. Their visits will be short in order for me to regain my strength. I told her that my unexpected trip, here was filled with uncertainty and distress of not knowing what was happening. She asked me if I was of afraid of dealing with the lost spirits.

Accordingly; I told her absolutely, being afraid or not afraid would not change my destiny, considering there was no way that I could refuse this challenge. There was just too much at stake. She asked me if I knew much about the 13 houses. I told her that I did not know except that they had to be cast into the prison of evil; therefore, I can only expect a lot of fighting, in which I believe Devika will make sure we have everything that we need. I know that the first I must clean up these lost spirits before I must go to Kosh Kosh Kung for an Indian chief's meeting, after that seal the crack between the throne's dimensions. Then my final mission will be to capture the Coon Run Road Ghost. These are the only missions that I know of that are ahead for me. Subsequently, my father and two brothers enter, with excitement written all over their faces. My father asked me how life in a coma was, in which I replied that it had some good days and bad days. And then he asked me how I felt? I asked him how he would feel if he had been in bed for two years? The father said he was glad that I finally woke up. Subsequently; I told my first white lie, and said that was glad to be back as well, and it was so nice to be able to respond to them when they spoke to me. Then my youngest brother approached and thanked me for the $1,000 in cash donation made to his church each week in my name. I told him to rest assured that my friends would continue making this weekly donation, as long as he's remained in the battle against evil and the protection of our Saints. Then my middle brother came up and shook my hand. He had been working out of state for the last 20 years, and as a result we lost touch with other. Although he is retired now, and according to my father has mellowed out a lot.

Accordingly; I believe he is raising one of his grandsons was keeping busy going to their ball games and such. I miss going to my son's and daughter's ball games. I was saddened to know that there would be no more although maybe someday I can go to some of my grandchildren's ball games. Only time will tell, something that keeps escaping me daily. We all started talking about some miscellaneous things that have happened over the last two years, none of which I am even remotely interested in; nevertheless, I nod my head yes. A nurse comes in room now and tells him that I need my rest that all need to leave except for my sister. One of my brothers asked why does she get to stay. The nurse replied because she is a retired RN and has a few questions for her. Once all were gone, except my sister, she tells her that they will keep me here for at least three more weeks. Most of my time will be in physical therapy to recondition my legs, so they can support my body weight. The terrible thing is my mind, I will once again be eating food that has calories it will make me fat. I will miss all my delicious calorie-free foods from the throne. Be that as it may, I can only think that to have the memories or to not have experienced this, and have no memories, I much would rather have the memories. My sister has a seat in a chair beside my bed and drifted off to sleep. I find myself also very sleepy and fall to sleep as well. Then suddenly, I'm awake when my sister beside me in the clouds somewhere as Devika came before us. My sister looks terrified, in which I tell her not to worry because our bodies are still in the hospital. I asked Devika about her being gone acquiring warriors. She tells me that they have already been acquired.

Moreover; she further verifies what I just said to my sister and tells me to reach my hand up to grab something up there and to pull it down. My sister asked why she is here? Devika tells her only so she can see them and better understand since she would have to explain to her family members why I am still so sleepy. She has a chair up here for her as she takes her seat and begins to watch as I pulled down my first leg, which we all breathe a sigh of relief in that it was white so hopefully we'll get a good story. I wanted to call them Indian because if I say their name, and any evil spirits are working around them could torture them. Therefore; I would not take that chance. I ask where were you raised from, he tells me he is from what we today call Harden Village in the Fort Ancient Culture. I asked him what he remembers while still alive. He tells me he had a family with nine children. I asked him why he needed nine kids. He tells me that a friend of his told them of a new white man with barrels that spit out death would soon be crossing the mountains and start stealing their lands and hunting their food leaving them to starve. I told him that what he said would come to pass, but I was more concerned about what happened the day he died, even if he remembers having died. He tells me that they are constantly reminded each day that they are dead and doomed.

Additionally; He claims that in the day that he entered the clouds, he was hunting a deer and when he was just about ready to shoot it, was hit in the back of the head with an ax. It was an advance scouting group that was preparing for their invasion and wanted to know what was available. Each of his body parts was thrown into a nearby river, so that no one from his tribe could discover his body. He claims to have lingered in the area for seven days, in which he returned to his tent only to find his wife and children crying because they knew he should have been back and that something was wrong in that the other scouts could not find him. He was one of three scouts missing, which disturbed their village's chief that ordered all the warriors to begin looking for them. You were to kill anyone whom they did not recognize. To his great delight, they found the three who had killed him. I asked him why he felt he was in the land of the lost spirits. He claims it happened so fast that by the time he saw the light came for him, he did not know what it was and ran away from it staying hidden until the light finally left. When the light left some other spirits came to drag him up into the sky dropping him into the land of lost spirits. I look at Devika and my sister and said that I did not see any evil wrongdoing in this man because of the confusion surrounding his death and believed that he should be placed into the Lake of Peace. They both agreed at which I asked Devika if there was any way that we can reunite his wife with him. I figured his children had remarried and had their own families, so they would not really be that interested. Devika speaking in my head told me that his wife had remarried, and thus as Indian had to travel on by himself.

In addition; I told him that the place I was sending him was wonderful, and that he would have an eternity of peace and rest. I further asked Devika if any who traveled with him could join, and she said yes so far, they had found 300 from his tribe and that their medicine man did not really know the spirits enough to guide them on their initial afterlife journeys. When this Indian man saw the other 300 coming, he told me that he recognized many of them. Moreover; they all were so excited about getting out of the land of the lost as our Indian friend explained to them that they were going to a much better place. At this time, Devika raised her hands, and they vanished. We could hear the joy and cheering in their voices as they sank into the Lake of Peace. Devika told me to reach up and pull down another leg. I pulled it down once again by luck in that I grabbed a white leg. I asked him what tribe he was from, and he said from where the white man called the Hopewell Interaction Sphere. Not far from Coon Run Road. I asked Devika how he knew about Coon Run Road. She explains that as they are being poured down, they show them information about me, and that I do have Cherokee Indian blood in my ancestry. This tends to calm them because many of the spirits have been harassed by evil spirits for way too long. I; therefore, asked this Indian what his story was. He tells us that one day they were on a hunt searching for some meat for their families for the upcoming winter. Totally surprising; they were attacked by northern Indians who were likely Eerie who were preparing for future war to drive them out of their lands.

Consequently; I asked him why were they after them. He claims that they also use this land for hunting so they could feed their families'. I looked at Devika and asked her what her judgement was. She said he is worthy of ascending and to call his friends. I; therefore, called for his friends and families, of which 311 appeared. Devika briefed them that they were going to the Lake of Peace, a place in my empire, as she pointed to me. I waved at them and yelled out for the Lake of Peace to receive them. I now asked Devika, who screened the additional ones that appear. She tells me that there were 744 who tried to join him, yet only 311 were accepted by my Gate of Death. I then asked her what happened to the 400 who did not make it. She said the Gate of Death judged them and sent them back to the Eternal one above us, who either ascended or descended them. I asked her if there were cases of those who the Gate of Death recommended descend actually ascend in this dimension. Devika tells me that many do, because the laws and spirits were different in these men's life. I explain that evil is not permitted in my Throne's dimension, with severe punishments issued to those who commit evil crimes. The Throne also feels that all should be treated equal and that all receive food. When you take hunger out of the equation you take away, "A hungry man has no laws." Devika confesses that her dimension has not given the people the same that your throne gives them.

Therefore; that is one reason why Lake of Peace and Lake of Love will not accept anyone who has not be passed by me or the Gate of Death. Devika told me to reach up my hand and pull down a leg. This time, my luck ran out as I pulled down a black leg. As this thing began to appear, Devika spoke in my mind telling me to say nothing. We would see their evil deeds and at the end either raise our hand for ascend or down for descend. The first scene we saw was this man cutting into a tent, to steal their food; nevertheless, he found three children in this tent sleeping. He kills all three while they were sleeping, the youngest still a baby. I ask Devika why the baby would be left unintended. She claims that all mothers did this while doing tribal chores and that someone always kept on eye on the front of the tent. I then said to her that must be why he cut a hole in the back of the tent. The next thing we see is him sneaking up on three women who were bathing in the river. He hides in a tree and begins shooting arrows at them. One by one, he kills all three, and then joyfully walks back to his tent in a nearby tribe. Both tribes belong to the same Indian nation. We also notice grain and fish in his tent. Next, he finds children playing beside a pond. Here, he once again kills all four of them. Consequently; the next day he kills two women, then scalps them to make it appear like white settlers did this. His scheme did not work because the white settlers used their thunder sticks to kill and not arrows. This angered him greatly. I motion for us to pause and point my hand down. Devika also immediately points her hand down.

Moreover; She tells me that presently, I must tell him his punishment, because the voice of my judgment will accompany him to the Prison of Evil. They will not admit him without it. I call him forward and tell him that I find him to be wicked and shall be sent to my Prison of Evil. I then look at Devika and ask her if we also receive the immoral ones who were with him. She tells me that they have pulled 1,232 evil ones who have worked with him and that both the Gate of Death, and the Gate of Blood are processing them and should be finished within about five minutes. I ask her if we can send this one away, and she nods yes as a group of warriors come and chain him, and then take him to the Prison of Evil. Devika tells me that we have thinned out this cloud of lost souls. She also tells me that my Wohpe has sent out around 1,000 maidens to pull out spirits. They are pulling from above where they can see the color of the hands. A couple of evil ones have tried to latch on to the white ones at which time these maidens struck them with some sort of built-in laser immediately freeing the white hand, that was then pulled to freedom. Devika tells me that these maidens are telepathic and can read souls. I tell her that this is true and that the maidens are the strongest, and most combat ready women in the Universe. I tell her that both Emperors Queens were maidens, and now the rule easily among the most powerful Empires in that Universe. Devika asks me the names of the two Queens. I tell her Orenda and Woape. Devika reveals that they are the ones who are constantly asking her how I am doing, and that in order to get them to stop for a while, she has allowed them to watch this activity.

Naturally, I ask her if they are watching now, and she said yes, therefore, I waved at them and smiled. Devika tells me they are waving back. Then Devika asks me if I want to see them. She knows a way to sneak me out of this dimension, although we can only stay for two hours and then must return. Once out of this dimension, the queens will have their fastest Tunnels to bring us to the planet we will meet at. I ask her how the queens can leave the throne. She answers with fleets of combat warriors in combat Tunnels. I must remember that they now rule and are expected to travel throughout their Empire. We meet on the planet they selected as a large combat tunnel warship appears. Devika tells me that is the ship we must board. As we board it, the warriors point to the door that says Queens, which they open as we walk in. They then close the door, and my two Queens appear. I quickly realize that this is a royal chamber. Realize it or not, Devika and my clothes disappear, and completely cleaned and reappear beside my door. Devika walks over and hugs my queens telling them how happy she is finally to see them. She also wishes Earth had some sort of similar custom. My Queen, standing with Devika in the middle, ask me how I like this gift they gave me. I told them that Devika was wonderful.

Afterwards; they then tell me if I think she is good out of bed, wait until I visit her at night. I ask Orenda and Woape if they would not be jealous. They explain that jealousy does not exist around the throne and that if I am in a situation where they could not satisfy my needs, then they must find someone who can. I ask Devika, who naturally, has a perfect body, if she agrees with this. She explains that she told me when we first met that she was mine. Any ways, from what the Queens told her; she would be in for a wonderful experience. I look at my Queens who both say, "So True." Therefore; I tell my Queens to join me and to tell how their day went. They said it began early when some rogue groups accused them of killing me. It was not until the Throne's special investigators reviewed our censored chamber videos and declared this was a Dimensional Transitional Event. I looked at my Queens and asked what was a Dimensional Transitional Event? They said they had no idea; it just sounded so true, which, in reality, it was. The public bought this as Wohpe verified it. I could feel the tunnel moving. The Queens told me they would take us back my entry point and that my ship was attached to this tunnel. This would give us more time together. I just hope that my return will not be as bad as my arrival. Devika told me it would be smooth. I ask her if she could also read my mind. She said yes and that it was mandated by my Queens for my security, and if I was in need of some sex. My Queens nodded their heads in agreement. The warriors would not allow the Queens to enter my Tunnel ship; therefore, we bid our farewells, exchanged kisses and hugs, as Devika got me back to my hospital.

Additionally; my sister had returned for evening visiting hours and thus asked how the rest of my day went. Devika had released her after my first lifting. I told her we went back to my Empire to visit my Queens. She said it was so strange to take a nap and not see anyone from the throne. She also added that my wife would visit me tomorrow, so be prepared. She wished me luck for the next day. Naturally, I could not sleep; I hate waking up in a hospital; it usually means something was wrong when you went to sleep. As I drifted into my dreams, Devika informed me that we had some more work to do and zipped me up to the clouds. I reached in and get a white hand. He had three sons, all of which were killed in tribal wars. Next, he told me that is wife, and he lived very quiet lives thereafter. Devika tells me that his wife was available. I ask him if he would like to see his wife. He joyfully shouts yes, and they are reunited. We now go to pull down his friends and family. We only get 74. I send this man and his wife to the Lake of Piece and his friends to the Gate of Death. I tell Devika that this last story was so sad. I drift up to the clouds and pull out another hand, ouch, which is black. As the warriors bind him, we return to our judgment cloud, As I study his face, I discover he is not Indian, but instead European. I ask him that nationality, is he? He claims to be a Viking. I can see some anger in Devika's eyes.

Moreover; I ask her if we have jurisdiction in this case, since he is not an Indian. She initiates some inquires and returns with a yes. And that since they are not Indian, we can speak with them. Just say no names. I ask this Viking how he died. He explains that we, and his small group of six men were burned alive at a steak. I can look over and see the men burning. In addition; I ask him why they were burning them? They claim because they were white. Devika stands up and calls him a liar, as she now shows videos of them hunting Indians and killing them for sport, actually competing to see who killed the most. I then said to the Viking in front of me, and ask him how many kills did he have? He said he had 83. I asked him if he was the winner. He said no and pointed to one of his friends who were watching, and said that man had 96. I thought to myself that this was not right. It was not their land, nor were they planning on settling there. Accordingly; I look at Devika and point my hand down, as does she. I tell our warriors that we may need some additional warriors, which immediately 500 appear. I tell the warriors to bind this man and the six who are watching and take them to the Prison of Evil. Devika now pulls down an additional 32 Vikings, claiming these were most likely all who were aboard their ship, and that in the early years, they tended to sail in single ships or extremely small fleets. I asked Devika if we had enough warriors to transport them. I then waved for the warriors to bind them and take them to the Prison of Evil.

Questionably; I asked her if we had any more for tonight. She said no and invited me to her lodgings. She actually lived in the clouds, and once inside her room appeared to be a normal room. She thanked me for helping them clean out the clouds of the lost spirits, and that we should be able to finish within five weeks. It was so important to separate the good from the bad. I agreed, and then asked her to tell me about her life. She tells me she was born in an Indian tribe; the name has been erased from her mind for security reasons. When she was 13, her tribe was attacked and the warriors killed. The women and children were marched back to the enemy's village and sold as slaves. She was sold to a family that had four children, and the mother was sick most of the time. She verified that they always treated her as one of their families. When she turned 18, the tribe freed her. She did not know where to go or what to do. She was in reality starving to death when a woman appeared and took her up in the clouds. She does not even know if she is actually dead, and that her body may be up here somewhere. She adds that the body they gave her feels and functions as a real human body. She takes my hand and rubs it on her legs.

They feel real. She then rubs it on her head. It feels real. She then rubs them on her breasts, and they feel extremely real. We then kiss, knowing that something had to be done with all this positive energy that is flowing through our bodies. She wants to seduce me; my queens want her to seduce me, so what do I do? She is a materialized being, and we are in the clouds. Therefore, I just need some more time to think about this.

Accordingly; I then fell asleep only to awaken in my hospital room in the morning, just in time for breakfast. Once I have finished eating, Devika appears and tells me she is putting me to sleep. We need to go, and away we go into the clouds. Today our courtroom is enhanced, and actually looks impressive. Devika and I sat in the front. We have plenty of space for the warriors, and a cage to put the black spirits in. Today we have a large rubber funnel that extends over to and into the clouds. Devika tells me I no longer must go and pull out a spirit. This device will pull them in for us. Accordingly; I ask Devika about the 10,000 maidens. She informs me that they have arrived and are working along with their 50,000 combat warriors. Next, I ask her what happens to the spirits they collect. Devika tells me the white spirits go to the Gate of Life and the Gate of Love. The black ones go to the Gate of Hate and the Gate of Pain. They have kept the Gate of Death open for us. Devika reveals to me that we have a special guest before we start to judge today, and that is Chief Isham. He will be the primary chief at Kosh Kosh Kung. I ask Devika if I should get and put on my crown. She said that would not be necessary, since he has visited Wohpe and the throne. Wohpe told him that you were his king. The Chief arrives, stands in front of me and starts to bow. I stop him while standing up and tell him we can suspend all the normal royal courtesies, but only with him. Once I get to know others, I may also suspend courtesies for them. Chief Isham begins by thanking me for cleaning up the lost spirits. He has tried for almost 400 years to get it cleaned, and he can notice a big difference already, especially with those female maidens reaching down and pulling up evil spirits.

In addition; he asks me if it is safe for those girls to do such dangerous work. I explain to him that these maidens are fierce combat ready warriors and that not even I would challenge one of them. I also add that my two Queens were previous maidens. And the final line is that I have five male warriors for each one of my precious maidens. The Chief confessed to not knowing this and was rather curious why there were so many in and around the Throne. I explain to him that if we are fighting, we want to draw the enemy out into the open and then destroy them. Maidens are highly effective in drawing out the enemy, who many times viewed them as weak and easy prey. I begin to laugh when I say, "man, do they get a surprise." I ask the Chief if he enjoyed the food at the Throne. He answers that it was clearly the best. Next, he tells me that he inspected Coon Hollow last week and could not believe the great achievements made so far. He tells me that he would have no objections to beginning our summit whenever I wished. I thank him but ask for a delay until we can clean up these lost spirits, because a day for me is not the same as a day for the righteous to be tormented by evil. Chief Isham now confesses that he has never met a more caring white king in all his life. As he says this, Devika reaches over and kisses my cheek, saying, "Absolutely the best." Chief Isham reveals to me that he has known Devika for over 300 years, and if she likes me, then his belief in me is founded in logic. I did not really understand his last sentence, thus told him thank you and hoped that our summits would be a great success.

Therefore; I told him that if he wanted to review what we were doing here and at my gates, I would have a command warrior tunnel take him back to the throne with 1,000 warriors to protect him. He accepted my offer, as I called for my warriors and a command warrior tunnel to escort the Chief to my throne and my gates. This special tunnel immediately appeared and gently pulled the chief aboard, loaded up with warriors and flashed back through the dimension wall behind the throne. I asked Devika how they were crossing the barrier so easily. She said she would find an answer and give it to me, she then said for me to hold on, because Orenda was going to answer it. Orenda tells me, oh mighty King, Wohpe makes special provisional holes in the barrier; they are temporary and only tunnels may pass through, in that they are sometimes unstable. I now said, oh Queen of great beauty, how are the maidens and warriors passing through? Orenda explains that the gates handle this. Then I ask her how are things, in which she replies they are miserable without me. I tell her to keep my love in her heart and to be strong, like I know she is. With this, she bows and vanishes. I tell Devika that I am ready for our first spirit. She motions for our special tunnel to activate, and it starts to make strange noises as the tubing appears to be stretched to it limits, as if to make a hard pushing sound and two black spirits appear. They are chained together by their feet. I tell my warriors to remove the chains then to get something that will clean their uniforms. Devika, of course, snaps her fingers and both black spirits are in sparkling clean uniforms, with even some sewing to ensure they do not fall apart.

Accordingly; I look at her and shake my head, asking if the snapping fingers something you girls are born with? She laughs and says, "no." I tell them to rise and face me, when I notice they have on civil war uniforms; one is northern; the other is southern. I ask them if it is not odd for a northern soldier to be with a southern soldier. They explain that they were chained together by some evil spirits. I inform them that they have black spirits and are considered wicked. They explain that the only ones they killed in the war was each other. They were hiding in Koon Hollow waiting for the war to end; however, it just kept going on and on. I look at Devika and ask why these men have black spirits. She examines their Book of Life, and both are well within the acceptable parameters. I asked them what they ate in Coon Hollow, and they told me crawdads and minnows from the creeks and fruit from the fruit trees that we scattered around both hills. I knew this to be true and asked Devika how soon we could give them their white spirits. Once again, she snaps her fingers and both now have white spirits. I tell both that I wish they would become friends, in which would make the future so much better in the place I am sending them. They shake hands and off, I send them to the Lake of Peace. After I sent them off, I remembered that I forgot to ask them where they died in Coon Hollow. Devika shows me Coon Hollow on a giant monitor in front of us. She tells me that both died in the creek beside my grandfather's grain storage building. She then highlights the area and drops a gold coin to where they each died. Devika tells me that only I can see these gold coins.

Therefore; I tell her that her support is outstanding, and that I could not be here or stay here without her. She blushes as she walks over and gives me a kiss on my check. I ask her if she notices I am getting a lot of white raced people. She said that was because I am closer to them than my Indian counterparts are. Devika further states that they would have sent my latest two both to the Prison of Evil. I ask her if we can make this last case part of their training, after all we must all work hard to find the truth. I ask her how many more do I have? She tells me a couple of weeks work, and we will be done. Furthermore, she adds that the maidens are processing the white spirits. Then I say that I did not realize that so many white people died in Coon Hollow. Devika advises me not to forget Coon Run Road. I tell her that I got it, and it is time for our next visitor. I wave, and our tunnel begins a light wiggle and before us stood a black spirit. This one is extra-large. The monitors come on behind him. He is identified as British, and had 72 deaths attributed to him. Indians accounted for 27 of these deaths. Although I am not supposed to, I ask him why he killed so many White people. He claims they were harassing his Indian friends. The monitors declare this to be a lie. I then asked about the 27 Indians. He said they were attacking their fort. The monitors report this as a lie. I look at this man and declare he is a liar.

Afterwards; I then look at Devika who motions a down wave. I call for my warriors to bind him and take him to the Prison of Evil. He easily shakes off the first two warriors, as the backup warriors began to fire hitting him and knocking him down. Then the four of them bind him with three belts. They place chains on his feet and handcuffs. The warriors after that place him on a caged roller and roll him to the tunnel and then into the Prison of Evil. I asked for other British, in which 844 were delivered. Another 6,000 warriors appeared and began binding these as their crimes were being displayed on our monitor, which reported that all 844 were evil and should be sent to the Prison of Evil. The monitor was helping us on this one, sense the Gates were overwhelmed now with the amazing work from our maidens. Devika tells me we are making great progress currently. I tell her I forgot to get our Civil War friends and family. Devika calls them forth as another 64 appear. I thought this was a low number, considering this war divided our nation. Devika tells me that most of the fighting was in West Virginia. The monitor only convicts 61 of them in which we need to study three, which are women. Devika calls for some security warriors to bind the 61. They have a special soul container that they pack these spirits into. We call the three women before us and ask them to explain why they have been put into black spirits. Two of them claim they did this voluntarily to remain with their husbands. The monitors verify this as the truth.

Accordingly; we transfer these two women into white spirits and erase their memories of being married and send them to the Lake of Peace via one of my Royal Tunnels. We now speak to the third woman who tells me the spirits claimed they were going to kill her children. Once again, the monitors verify this as true; we transfer her into a white spirit and send her in one of my Royal Tunnels, which can make the round trip in three minutes. Therefore, I recommend to Devika that we take a small break and wait until at least on off my Royal Tunnels return. Devika tells me we have some French to speak with. I push our tunnel button, and a French mountain man appears. The monitor lists him as killing 43 Americans, 38 British, and 74 Indians. It is the Indians whom we can see the most heinous murders. We see these murders on our monitors, and both give our hands down. I call for the warriors to deliver this one to the Prison of Evil. We call for his friends, of which 17 appear. Lights begin to flash, and Gate of Harmony begins piping music in through our Tunnels. This is rather clever, but what is this, as I ask Devika. She pauses and waves for me to be quiet. She is listening to some message. She declares that we have cleaned the Lost Spirits, not only over Ohio but over the United States and put-up anti-spirit barriers to keep them out in the future. Devika asks me if we can use one of my Tunnels to verity that the layer of lost spirits is clean. She wants to use my Tunnel because it can detect any invisible spirit's. I tell the warrior to drive slowly and to put on our invisible spirit's detectors. We make multiple scans and verify it is empty. We also cleaned up big chunks out of the oceans.

Furthermore, Earth's dimension has cleaned up their spirit that leaves the body transition processes.

Additionally; there will no additional lost spirits. I feel good about our accomplishment here. Devika asks me if I have met my wife yet. I tell her that she keeps postponing our meeting, and since we have been so busy, I have not worried about it. Devika explains to me that everyone believed that I would never recover from my coma, furthermore, would be dead within two years. She could not afford the mounting medical expenses and was forced to divorce me. They scanned her soul, and she did the only thing that she could do, that would keep me in long-term care and a roof over her head. If we remarry, then they can come after her. They will be watching to make sure we do not contact her. I was extremely angry and thought about erasing the United States government. Devika claims that would place the citizens in danger of being made slaves to other nations, plus could make Coon Run Road unsafe. I ask Devika if we can rest at her home for a few hours, to give me a chance to pull myself together. As we enter her home, she asks me if there is anything special, she can share with me now that I know I am single. I told her yes, although I may not live up to what my Queens told her initially. Before we started, I asked her if she was the jealous type in that I would keep my Queens. She just asked that I not flaunted other relationships in front of others if we had an established public relationship, just for personal shame and embarrassment issues. I told her today was physical and not the establishment of a relationship. She agreed and performed the actions she promised my Queens she would. I felt so much better, even though I was not completely physically recovered, I did push it to the limits. Thank you so much Devika.

CHAPTER 10

The Tribes

Devika invited me once more to her chamber. It really was so much better than that hospital bed. She felt that my physical body needed time to rest, although this body I was in felt good, with one exception, the physical eyes could not see it. I was not all that excited about the physical world, especially since it now offered me an empty house. Devika told me that my wife and son worked hard to keep that house for when or if I woke up. I figure there will be time for that after I get my things in order. Devika said that tonight she was going to work hard to relax me and make me feel special.

Next; I told her not to work at it too hard, because that could lead to disappointment, considering my age. She prepared a meal for us through her food processor.

She told me this meal was designed to help make me more alert and have more strength in what she called my cloud body. Furthermore, she also told me that she was giving my physical body all the nutrients it needed to heal itself. Now, the important thing was for it to get the rest, so she put some extra (transparent) sleep medicine in my IV's. She further added that as long as my monitors were not beeping or continue to give good numbers, and I was asleep; the nurses would not bother me. It was the ones who did not sleep that disturbed them. Consequently; I do know that the physical therapy, which Devika ensures I do not miss, is tiring, but I feel it is important. I have no intention of fighting with the medical people here, in that I know they also have their lives and are nearby to ensure that I also have a chance at a life. They call me their miracle patient in that after two years in a coma, I came back. I had spent the last two years in a coma research center, in which they were always testing new things. Every day, they would hook my legs and arms up to the machine that would extend the limbs and then retract them. This was to provide the muscles some movement exercises. They also had machines that would send electrical pulses through my limbs, not at the same time as the extender machine, to assist in keeping my brain active in the movement of my limbs.

Accordingly; I heard my nurses talking that if that coma center did not have done these things for my muscles, I would have never walked again. Speaking about walking, I have taken up to three steps in a row so far, which the staff claims are excellent, and that they are not going to push it. Devika brings my head back into the clouds by inviting me to her table. I look at my plate and ask her if she is a nurse. She tells me she is feeding me what Orenda and Woape told her to prepare. I ask her if they had made the calorie adjustments, since the food on the Throne had no calories. Devika said that unfortunately, spiritual physical bodies in this dimension required calories; nevertheless, she would make sure that I only gained muscle weight. She said that we would be spending time in a gymnasium, almost a few rooms down, which the dimension had made available just for us to use. She said we would lift weights, play sports such as basketball, tennis, and batting cages, plus so many other things. Additionally; a lot of stringent sex, all that I wanted anytime that I wanted it. I just hate to bust this gorgeous angel's bubble; however, I am 67 years old, and the baseball batting cage actually appeals to me better than the chamber rigid exercises she has planned.

Notwithstanding; I would probably never forgive myself if I did not accept some of her hospitality. Our meal is a nice thick steak, cut into the small squares that I like, mashed potatoes and gravy, plus one half of the plate with vegetables. Yep, no doubt about it, my Queens had a big part in these selections. At first, I thought it strange that they fussed so much over my health, until I realized that I will die possibly millennia before them. I wonder, which is worse, watching someone die or be the one who is dying. Devika is also serving us some alcohol-free extremely healthy wine. I ask her how she knows this is healthy. She points to the number 91 on the bottle and tells me the higher the number, the healthier it is. Any number above 80 is considered great. I ask her how she usually spends her free time. First, she tells me that she does not get much free time, although with me, her superiors have awarded her a lot of free time, which she plans on spending this with me. Second, she says that she spends a lot of time at the gymnasiums. She says that it is always enjoyable to put on tight exercise clothes and exercise in front of the warriors. She further qualifies this in that all the girls do this, in order to make puppets out of the big, strong warriors. I tell her that this is something that goes on everywhere and throughout time, and most likely will continue until the end of time. Out of curiosity, do you have an educational system up here? She pointed at her monitor and said they always had thousands of courses available. After we study through the monitor, we go to the designated center and take the exam. I ask her if they have a degree system here. Devika informs me that the degree systems were developed in the heavens and sent to mankind via dreams.

Following up; I ask her if she has any degrees. She snaps her fingers and one of her walls opens, and I see a wall full of degrees. She tells me that she now only tracks her highest ones. Additionally; she tells me that she holds six PhD's. I walk over to her wall and then gaze at her wonderful degrees. Accordingly, I ask her how old she is. Devika tells me that she is 7,555 years old. In fact, she is going to share with me the history of the Indian tribes later today, and much of it; she remembers seeing first hand. Next, I ask her if she has ever been married. She tells me that they are not given to marriage and that actually are not given genitals. Devika tells me she was given female genitals at the very tough request of my Queens. I just could not get over the ages of my girls, and how strong and young they appear. She now recommends that we watch their training film on the Indian history in North America. The video will appear in two halves; the left is the true history, and the right is what the humans claim to know. I tell her I do not want to see the half that is based on human history. The first to arrive in North America in the modern era were the Paleo-Indians. They began arriving over 100,000 years ago and continued for over 90,000 years. They initially entered by rafts and later crossed a land bridge that began to appear between Asia and North America. This land bridge appeared gradually, and by 100,000, the bridge had depths that ranged from 10 feet to 100 feet. The Small rafts could make these crossings, and could be carried between the smaller land bridges. The greatest migrations came through the Aleutian Islands, which made the raft use very popular. These tribes tended to follow the big-game animals, being careful not to scare them in returning to Asia. Seafood was the primary source of protein for the initial few thousand years.

As the initial ones settled in, they would fight against the new immigrants. The big game needed more time to increase their herds. Conditions improved in Europe, Asia and Africa, causing a mass reduction in the migrations to the Americas. As the ice ages began to freeze the northern areas of North America, many migrated back to Asia or toward Central America. The human groups were minuscule and scattered and represented nothing more than to support the claim that there was human life in the Americas. The small groups began to depend upon farming, and could produce enough to sustain them. Ohio began to host some large herds of elk and deer. Ohio began to stabilize their Indian populations as it moved toward the 12th century. The Shawnee, Wyandotte, and Delaware began to pass through Ohio having a nomad lifestyle and avoided building long term villages. The Shawnee soon saw their numbers dwindle toward extermination. Battles over hunting grounds and everything you could think about continued to weaken the tribes, as subsequently diseases once again spread throughout the state. In 1650, the first Europeans arrived and began settling in what the new to be colonies, later labeled as their Northwest Territory. In the meanwhile, the French and Indian wars sent more to their graves, after which the British began taking their shots. Soon, wagons of white men began to pour into Ohio.

The Cherokees were the primary Indian force in the southern parts of Ohio, even though the Eerie fell along the northern lake above Ohio. The Indians had a temporary relief in that the white men began fighting among themselves in their war for Independence. Even though they killed many among themselves, so many more crossed the Atlantic Ocean and flooded across the mountains into the Ohio Valley. Their Armies began to focus on the Indians and started to drive them across the Mississippi and eventually into their graves, stealing their lands and killing the large herds that they hunted. I could see tears begin to flow from Devika's eyes as she claims that even those who saw this could not believe it. She looked at me and said that yesterday many of those tears were freed as lives would once more proceed, unfortunately, only in the world of the spirits. I confessed to being rather confused with this history. Devika tells me not to worry about the history, in that it is what is now that counts. She also warns that what goes around comes around. Devika claims that the white man will soon lose his lands as other greedy men will take it from them and leave their bodies to rot on the ground and homes to burn. Devika claims that man will continue to kill man until the end of time. Devika flooded my mind with so many images of killing and pain. Devika explains that it is important to have felt this hurt prior to talking with the chiefs at Kosh Kosh Kung. Accordingly, I asked her what tribes did these chiefs represent. Subsequently, she explains that Chief Isham dissolved all the tribes and formed only one, which has no name. He declared that in order for the Indians to survive, they would have to survive as one tribe or one people with one law. Devika said that she wanted us to go to bed now, and a little later go to the Gymnasium.

Subsequently; I asked her how our adventures last night functioned for her first time. She tells me it was every bit as wonderful as Queen Orenda and Queen Woape had told her it would be. I asked her if when I left would they take that back off her body. She said maybe, unless the Queens and I petitioned on her behalf. I promised her that we would, even if we had to ask Wohpe. As we lay in our bed, I could see the painful images of all the massacres, until Devika slapped me and told me to stop causing myself pain and to accept my reward. I think she is like a kid who just discovered candy. She soon began to slow, and then looked at me and said, "let's hit the gym." When we arrived, she showed me the list of exercises we would do before we ran. She told me it would take 55 minutes, in which it did to the minute. The kid, or should I say ancient aged grandma, is well organized. Devika asked me if her age bothered me. I told her I considered it a miracle and a gift from the spirits. Consequently; she tells me that when I meet with my Eternal one, someday I will also reach and pass her age. I guess when she puts it like that, then it makes sense and appears to be natural. Devika looks at me and tells me she senses something is wrong. I tell her it is the aftershock of learning that I am divorced. Moreover; I completely understand and would have done the same thing. When something is deceased, it is supposed to stay lifeless. That is the law of the physical realm. She tells me that she has lost some great friends in battles against the evil ones. It always hurts, especially when you ask why.

Subsequently, I ask her that if a good spirit dies, what happens to it. She explains that it is recreated. Therefore; I tell her they do not die, but live. She argues that when it dies, it does not come back like it was. That is gone. I could not think of a valid argument against this, yet again, I do not hold six PhDs. Devika tells me it is time to get me back to the hospital. She will be by later to give me additional sleep medicine at that time. Tonight, she will speak with Chief Isham and make our arrangements for Kosh Kosh Kung. I ask her what can I expect to gain from this meeting. Devika says not much now, considering all the obstacles have been removed. However, he may try to get something extra. I ask her, if so, should I give him something extra? She said absolutely not. If you do, he will make life on Coon Run Road miserable. Devika returns me to my hospital bed, or back into my dreams, as I start to wiggle in this bed. I lay here for a little while when a lab tech comes in to draw some blood. I have to try and put things together. Furthermore, I have too many places going on, yet at least two of my objectives can be crossed off. The lost spirits are found, and the blood-stained soil has been cleaned. I will have to stay strong and run the course. Devika now sends me a vision of her speaking with Chief Isham. They first discuss where to meet. Devika suggests the open field below Coon Hollow. This is where the seed of the problem was born. Since it is spiritual, no one in the flesh can view it or disturb us. Devika asks the chief why we are having his meeting. The chief said he wanted to open lines of communication, so that when problems arose, we could all have a face to discuss it. It is the unknown that causes fear, and then killing. Devika agreed and assured the chief that my face was a face the Indians needed to have an avenue to speak with. We could not do as we did in the old days and expect a different tomorrow. The Chief agreed. The Chief said we will walk this new road for a new tomorrow. Wohpe begins building the spiritual meeting place.

CHAPTER 11

Kosh Kosh Kung

Where is Devika? I am walking to do my morning Physical Training here in the hospital. She is usually with me. It is easier to push tired muscles when you have an almost 7,000-year-old woman to push me. I must confess,

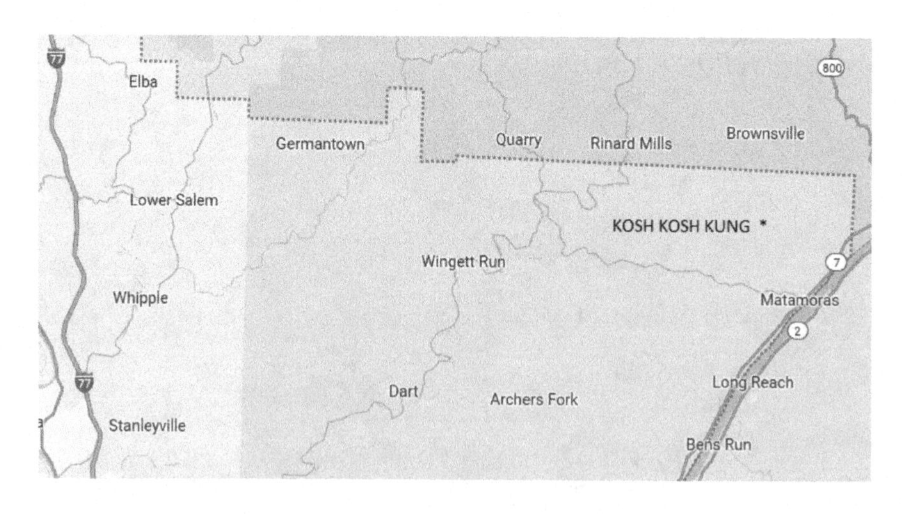

my body is feeling a little bit better. I wonder how many steps I can do today? For now, I will wait for my hospital breakfast. I still cannot figure out why everyone complains about their food? It is much better than what I make at home, and easier, they bring it to my room. I have not heard from my Queens in the past few days.

Moreover, I guess I will ask Devika if she can hook us up. Oh, there she is, good morning Devika. She also tells me good morning and that we have a busy day ahead of us. When I finish my breakfast, she will give me some additional sleep medicine, but just a little because she wants to use my physical body for a short appearance before the chiefs. I guess to verify I am still alive. She explains that the original Kosh Kosh Kung is no more, due to age and time. Wohpe has built a new, extremely gorgeous summit center for this meeting. It will occur today at my grandfather's farm, across the road in the old corn field in view of Coon Hollow. It cannot be seen in the physical world. Today toward the end of the meeting, it will be moved to the original Kosh Kosh Kung site, so when the chief exit, they will see the original site. Devika tells me that you will go by the title, "King James." Your sister, whose physical body will be asleep, will also attend. Devika now let me see the inside, which had statues of me, and monitors showing my coronation and two Queens. I asked her about my physical body and if it can handle this. She will make that determination at the time I am to appear, and if I do not look capable, she will leave me in the hospital.

Subsequently; Devika tells me that she will make sure my body handles the introduction, and then will transfer me back to my spiritual body, which was aborted. She will send my sister and I back earlier so we can walk around the farm for a few minutes. Devika also says, "By the way, the meeting will begin with a speech from you." I look at her, as my heart is now beating faster, and I can feel some perspiration soaking my clothes, and try to mumble some words. She comes over, gives me a kiss on my cheek, then tells me not to worry, she will give me the words to say. I start to return to normal, and ask her if she can dry my clothes. She will also appear as a doctor today and tell the nurses not to come into the room until lunchtime. If a nurse enters the room, she will rush my sister back. By then, my physical body will be back in the room. Devika tells me to hold on, because the show is starting to begin. I ask her if she will kiss me in front of my sister, this way no one will be bugging me about my wife, and it will look like I am moving on. Devika tells me that both of my Queens will appear today and kiss me as well. Devika explains that she will be the moderator, since all the Chiefs know her. My sister enters the room and says hi to me. I ask her if she knows what will happen today. Devika, who is now with the both of us, explains to me that she has briefed my sister.

After this; Devika disappears, as some nurses are entering my room. They congratulate me on my physical therapy today and for eating my breakfast. While they are getting my meds ready, and updating my charts, Devika walks in, having a different older body, wearing a doctor's white robe and having a doctor's identification, introduces herself to the nurses, my sister, and I. Her face flashes for my sister and I so we can identify her as Devika. She explains to the nurses that I am not to be disturbed today until no earlier than three in the afternoon. His sister will be here to insure this. She looks at my chart and physical therapy list and tells the nurses that the following changes need to be made. She increases some repetitions and adds two exercises. She then says her office will talk to Dr. XX about these med changes. She looks at me and asks if I have any questions. I look at her and say not now, although I was hoping you would decrease my physical therapy Dr. XX. She answers, "That would be over my dead body, James." We both laugh as she leaves. The nurses' comment on how nice my doctor is, in which I tell them she has been my doctor ten years now. After they have left, we fall into a sleep as my sister and I appear at our summit building. I ask my sister if she is getting use to this by now? She says that it is coming around slowly. We both look at this giant building, with the standard white marble outside and ten columns in the front. It is a little over 100 feet tall and has a nice large round Roman style dome on the top.

As we enter, we witness a long hallway with pictures of me shaking people's hands and my two Queens with me. Another set of pictures shows Devika and I am rescuing the lost spirits. As I look at some of the pictures, I ask Devika when was the last time she spoke with Orenda and Woape. Devika tells us that Emperor Queen Orenda and Emperor Queen Woape will appear today, soon before I give my speech to meet with the chiefs and my sister. Devika says to my sister that the Emperor Queens want to give her a hug and kiss and thank her for caring for their King. There are two large statues of me, one on each side of the stage, and a large table in the middle of the white marble floor. Devika tells us we have ten minutes to walk around outside now. When we go outside, the first question my sister asks me is why I call my queens by their first name only and Devika calls them by their title and name? I explain that only I may call them by their first name, because I was the one who gave them their crowns. I also tell her that all three of them are over 6,000 years old each. My sister asks how this is possible. I explain that they live in the spiritual realm and as Devika explained it to me, someday when we are in heaven, we too we have ages that will increase throughout eternity. She tells me that now she understands this; having always heard about it but never have seen it. We walk up to the road and see how all the junk and buildings had been removed. It was mowed, as we could see all the way up Coon Hollow. I ask her if she knows about the 13 houses. She said she did not. I told her I would have to battle them next. Devika told us it was time to enter the center and meet the Queens. We entered, and my two Queens appeared, they went up to my sister, exchanged hugs and asked her to please take good care of me.

I whispered in my sister's ears that they have planned all my non-hospital meals for Devika. We both laughed. Then I saw my two Queens appear before me, both had tears in their eyes. I asked them why they were crying, in which they told me it was because they miss me so much. I asked them how the kingdom was going. Woape told me she had to do her first execution yesterday from a man who tried to start a rebellion. They complained how some warriors were harassing them that they will not serve maidens. I then told today to send back a copy of my robe and crown to Devika and I would make a video that would warn warriors who will not serve their Queens that they will be discharged and could be sent to the Prison of Evil. They both told me that they missed me so much. I told them to be strong, and then in my mind told them I had discovered recently that I was no longer married, and that I might change my future plans. Telepathically, I asked them to inform Wohpe that my wife had divorced me, believing that I would not survive my coma. Each of my Queens now gave me a big kiss and declared their eternal love for me. My sister looked at me and told me how, that even though she saw it in her dreams, she did not know if it was indeed true. I then asked her that because she can now feel it, if she believes it to be so? She asks me how this is possible. I explain to her that I do not know, and that I did not choose this, and that it comes with a price. Devika comes up to me and tells me that she now has my robe and crown in her quarters and we will make the video tonight while I am sleeping if not earlier if we finish in time.

Devika tells us it is time to take our seats around the table and that Chief Ishan will soon be here. She motions for the Queens and I to go into a special waiting room and that the Spirit of Harmony will introduce us. Devika looks at my Queens and tells them, "That which you do, do quickly." Devika tells my sister to stay with her. She asks Devika, "What must they do quickly." Devika explains that the Queens miss their husband very much and that their love is deeper than the deepest ocean and higher than the highest mountain. Chief Ishan enters as Devika introduces my sister to him. Devika explains that she is sitting in since she will be helping to revenge the 13 houses and helped in secret with the freeing of the lost spirits. The Chief tells her she has done a great service as he shakes her hand. Devika also tells the Chief that she has Cherokee ancestry. Devika now tells the Queens, telepathically, that the Chief is coming in. She knocks on the door as Orenda tells them to enter. Devika opens the door and introduces the Chief. Orenda asks him to come in and have a seat. Devika now must excuse herself as other Chiefs are arriving. Soon all nine of the additional Chiefs have arrived, as Devika introduces them to my sister. With Devika, who is well known among the Indian spiritual realm introducing my sister, none question her right to be there. Soon thereafter; the Spirit of Harmony plays the Royal welcome for the king, then plays the Royal welcome for the Queens. The door opens as Chief Isham enters and takes his seat. Once more, the Spirit of Harmony plays the Queen's Royal welcome as a warrior escorts each one to their seat and remains behind them. Subsequently, the Spirit of Harmony plays the King's Royal welcome as I enter with four warriors. When I take my seat, I excuse the warriors who will remain by the doors. Devika tells me to begin my speech, which she has put in my mind:

I would like to thank the chiefs for arriving here today, as I hope we can lay the seeds for eternal peace and forgiveness for the evils of the past. Recently I deployed almost 70,000 warriors, Devika and myself as we freed the lost spirits trapped in your clouds, sending the good ones to my Lake of Peace *and the evil ones to my* Prison of Evil. *Chief Isham, has verified these places. The Evil ones included Indian, Viking, British, French, and American. Only the good Indians were sent to my Lake of Peace, any good white spirits, who had died while defending Indians, were sent to this dimension's eternal rest for the good. My throne will punish those who have wronged the Indian nations and people. I have seen the terrible crimes committed against our people and the land that was stolen. Soon, my sister and I will fight the 13 houses of Evil which were located on this land. They will spend their eternities in my Prison of Evil. Today, we will hear from each of you concerning any concerns you may have and issues you need to be solved. Our focus is on the spiritual realm, with little we can do in the physical realm. My biggest concern is Wohpe's dedication to all that no one goes hungry. If you have people who need food, tell Chief Isham, who will tell Devika, who will tell me or my Queen, and Wohpe will feed them. Remember, no one goes hungry. I have also spoken to your Eternal one, who has fixed it, so there will be no more lost spirits. Mistakes were made in the past, as today we begin to prepare a future where those mistakes will never be made again. It is a spirit of forgiveness that will make this possible. I truly hope that for those who forgive, that their descendants reap the great rewards. It is when we act as one that we will climb the highest mountains, yet when we act as one, our enemies can defeat with ease. I hope we leave here today with one mind and that we share victory through peace. Thank you for dedication to victory.*

Devika congratulated me on a wonderful speech. I was thinking she had better like it since she wrote it. She now introduced Chief Isham who spoke as follows:

Thank you, King James and your wonderful Queens, Emperor Indian Queen Orenda and Emperor Indian Queen Woape. I really appreciate the time you spent with me during my recent visit to your throne. I also wish to thank Devika for the wonderful support she provided me the last time I visited our heavens. Furthermore, I believe that the mistakes of the past need not be the mistakes of the future. To settle disputes with violence and killing only leads to more violence and killing. Our tribe has one name now, and the name shows the power of being united and working as one. Compromise does not always mean getting what you want, it means that our group gets what it wants. That is always better than giving our enemies what they want. We must keep our focus on a future for our children. I have seen the wonders of our host's throne and the magnificent gates that adorn its walls, the gates that can make yesterday today and today tomorrow. The Lake of Peace where our ancestors can have greater joys than when they lived here on Earth, *a land without hunger, without pain, without greed, and without wars and deaths. Our tomorrow has begun today.*

With this, Devika asked the other chiefs if they had any questions or comments. They did not really have much to say, except thanks and that their people would now have great hope. They all voted yes, and the hate between the Indians and Coon Hollow came to an end. With this, the Queens had the warriors bring a meal in for all to enjoy. Afterward, they departed. The Queens took their King back into their special chamber for a quick goodbye, as they had to rush back to the throne. Devika invited my sister and I back to her quarters. My sister was so shocked to know that such a place could exist. Devika escorted my sister through the clouds and above her city in the clouds. When they returned, we created the video for my Queens and transmitted it back to the throne. Even though today turned out very favorable, it could have turned out disastrous. I believe they were just so tired of living in fear and wanted some sort of hope of a better tomorrow. No one wants their children to live in a world full of hate and killings. Hate makes the hater a slave that can never be free to love. Devika delivers my sister and I back to my hospital room just minutes before the nurses entered to give me my meds and update my charts. My sister must rush back to her home.

CHAPTER 12

Dreizehn Häuser Black

As I prepare for another day of physical therapy in this hospital, fearful of the increase that the doctor prescribed yesterday, something just doesn't feel right. I tried to put my finger on what it could be. It is something I know, but what, and another good question is. Why am I alone in this room? Seldom; can I remember being all alone, but then again, I cannot remember ever being with someone else? What is going on with my brain, if indeed I still have a brain? I'm trying to remember what happened the last few days, yet those memories are evaporating. I can now feel a standing rush of pain beginning to overwhelm me. Furthermore, I tried to think of what my name is; even that evades me. Likewise, I look at the clock, and realize that breakfast has not been delivered; however, I'm positive that is usually delivered by now. Are not there supposed to be nurses coming in and out, making all the noise that they can? I look at my clock and see that it is 10 AM, yet there is no sun up yet.

That begs to question; why it is still dark? Why is it so black in here? Why do you have all these questions with no answers? I am so used to having someone help me, yet when I cry for help now, I received no answer nor a response. Could just a few hours of sleep produce such a catastrophe? Help! Help! Is there any reason for all the silence? To say that I'm confused would be the understatement of the century. To question if I'm being punished for something would also be a question for the century. To wonder why my bed is spinning would equally important be a valid question, yet why is it spinning, and why can't I see my room spinning? I can now feel myself spinning quicker and faster. I think to myself that I'm moving across the ceiling of this room. Nevertheless; as I prepare to crash into my ceiling, the ceiling opens and into the dark sky I find myself shooting like a bullet to somewhere I have no idea to where. Then, as quick as this began, I feel myself crashing to the ground. I am weak and tired, confused, dizzy, and every other abnormal thing that I went can think of. As I prepare to stand up and walk; I make it just two steps before tripping on a rock. And yes; that rock hurts and cuts into my leg.

Fortunately; my watch had a light that will glow in the dark and tells me that it is now 10:20 AM. All this excitement for only 20 minutes? I wonder whether I will make it until 11 AM? I am, for some strange reason, able to hear the nurses screening in my hospital room, "He's gone." I do not know why I am hearing this, because I know that not in the hospital, or do I know? Furthermore, I guess a better question is; why am I gone? Likewise, I need to find some answers; nevertheless, if I cannot see nor can I walk, how will I be able to find some answers? If only; I could escape this darkness! I can never remember being in a place of total darkness. My body is so tired as I feel the sudden urge to sleep, and maybe sleep forever if that were possible. While I am sleeping, I hear a voice of someone speaking. The voice sounds familiar and identifies herself as Devika. I asked her if I know her? She assures me that I do know her and that someday I will once again know her. For now, she hands me a set of eyes that she puts into my skull. I can feel this squashing as flesh is being rearranged and reconnected. Slowly, the damn light because clearer and clearer until I can see the surrounding land. I asked her, and I can Coon Hollow? She verifies that I am. She reveals to me that trouble has taken me as a prisoner. Furthermore, she promises to fight as hard as she can for my rescue. Likewise, she hands me a nice long Golden sword and sticks in my mouth a pill. Not only that, but she tells me that this will give me enough knowledge to begin my journey toward my rescue. I will have to fight harder now than ever before. She does not know when she can see me again, if she can indeed see me once again. I can feel her wrapping a bandage around my cut leg and feel a needle sewing up my cut leg. Actually; now that I think about it; she sewed up my cut before applying the bandage.

For some reason; I'm having difficulty in processing the sequence of events as they occur. As she bids farewell; she tells me that the battle is mine to fight and win, or lose. If I fight hard and strong a victory will be mine, although these are my victory and battle to fight alone. Subsequently; I can feel her presence depart from me. Consequently; I can feel another presence approach me. This entity is black and feels evil. My only defense thus far can be that this force does not know I can see. Even though I cannot completely see it, I can see where it is not. As the footsteps slowly approach me to where I can feel it is within my swords range, I began swinging and swinging hard in total chaos. Although it feels like I am swinging at air, each swing appears to fill in the air slightly, until my last few swings make solid contact. I continue to cut this thing into as many small pieces that I can. Having no knowledge of what is going on here, I can only hope that whatever I am swinging at his some of the trouble that I am to face, and not a badly needed ally whom I would need. I can feel that this was among the trouble that the previous voice warned me about. Therefore; I get up and begin to move around on the ground surrounding me. I noticed that there are a lot of black holes. Without my current eyes, I would never have been able to make it past the black holes. I reach down on the ground beside me and pick up some stones and drop them into these holes to try to determine how deep they are. I cannot hear any stone ever hitting the bottom of these holes. These holes must go deep inside the Earth. I could never remember seeing any holes in the grounds here at Coon Hollow.

The only exception, being the caves on the hill to the south of Coon Run Road. Suddenly and surprisingly; I hear a noise coming from one of the black holes. Up to the hole comes another black thing. I feel inside of me the need to fight; therefore, after swinging hard multiple times, and finally I am able to cut this thing in halves. Just to be safe, I also swing and behead it. I scoot these weightless body parts to the side, not wanting them to fall back down into this hole, and potentially warning any of the dangers coming my way. This process continues throughout the entire day, as I believe I am able to kill about 200 of them. Be that as it may; thereby they are not slowing down, and I have another dilemma facing me, and that it is now getting dark. I look around and see some boards laying on the ground, which must have been left from my grandfather's old buildings. I start to place these boards on these holes. For some strange reason; I find a cigarette lighter in my pocket. I collect some of the dead dry weeds around me and start a fire, and put some boards on it simply to get the wood to start burning. I then began to drop the boards into these holes. Fortunately; as the boards fall deeper into the hole, they began to burn faster until reaching the bottom, where I can hear some agonizing screams. I frantically continue this on all the remaining holes that I can see, dropping the burning wood into these holes and hearing frantic screaming.

To my amazement; I can see some light coming up from the other holes that I have yet to drop burning wood into. I can only conclude that these holes all going to an opening at the base. Either way the screaming, to my delight, intensifies. I now, while crawling on the ground with a burning piece of wood to act as my light, to make sure I do not step into a hole that is not showing light from below. I do find three more holes without any light flowing from the bottom, in which I drop a piece of burning wood into them, hearing streams in all of them. Furthermore, I now crawled back to where my fire is, and verified that I have enough wood to burn for the remainder of the night until morning comes. Fortunately; for me, this is the first week of July, and our nights are not quite as long as it were during the other months of the year. It is now 10 PM, and I believe the sun will be up around 5 AM; therefore, somehow, I must hope that this fire keeps them away from me until the morning daylight. I was awakened three times during the night by these black beasts, in which each time I stabbed them with my burning wood, which immediately sent them on fire. I will never know if any others came up while I was asleep. Likewise, I can merely hope that the fire attracted them to their demise. Early in the morning as daylight approached, I collected more wood, raked some of my ashes to reignite the red coals and placed more wood on them. I then began my search for additional black holes, and by noon identified another 40. Each one I dropped in a piece of my burning wood, as I could once more delightfully hear those screeching screams of agony.

I continued to search until around 5 PM when I determined all the black holes have been neutralized. Not wanting to take any chances, I continued to search for black holes but also for anything else that might be strange. Considering that it has been such a long time since I've actually scoured these grounds, I really would not know for sure what was normal and what wasn't. I thought about going up to Uncle John's old house and speak with the new owner, whom I met the earlier this year and see about getting a ride back to the hospital. And then again, whatever brought me out here from the hospital, then most likely would bring me back here again. Therefore; I think I'll restart my fire and camp out one night and hopefully something or someone will happen tomorrow. As I woke up the same time as the sun came up, I notice that there are some black cement blocks lined up in a row, actually they are lined up in a square about 50 feet on each side. I can't think this is good, especially with me inside it. Once again, I don't know what to do. One side tells me to let it go, whatever is being done, while the other side tells me to destroy it as fast as I can, before it gets out of hand. I know from the black holes that were black something right, so precisely to prevent myself from getting behind because each row does represent almost 200 blocks, I start knocking them down. I think what good is knocking them down, something, which will almost put them back up, so I decide to smash them on top of each other. This worked out pretty well as I am barely able to keep up. Whatever is making these blocks, is starting to make them faster now. Subsequently; I learned a new trick, instead of mashing them from above. I will mash them from the side. Along about the afternoon, I began to start to become exhausted. However, the black cement blocks are not slowing down.

Be that as it may, I force myself to continue, even though I have not eaten for this being the second day. I just have to think of it is burning off advance calories. I feel it's starting to get a little chilly in the air now, so I take and quickly break another round of weeds and start another fire burning the left-over wood that I have. Strangely; as my fire began to burn, the blocks slowdown in their arrival rate. Could this be the second time that fire has saved me? As my fire is raging, and I have collected plenty of wood for another night of fire, and moreover, not one black cement block is left unturned. In fact; everyone who is still here is mashed, because I've had my fill with black today. I'm trying to think what this could amount to, a 50 $ft.^2$ solid black brick building, its height I will never know. I am sitting here on the ground beside my fire, as a plate of the food appears beside me. Without hesitation, I start eating it as quickly as possible. It looks like the savings in my calorie bank just got spent. The time now is about five in the afternoon, and I say time to get up and try to walk around, as I can feel my muscles from so many black blocks today beginning to tighten. I then look about; I see the small Coon Hollow Creek began to flow with black water. Once again, I know this cannot be good. How can I think of a way to stop this water, then I remember once as a kid when I was playing here, I built a nice damn of wood, rocks, and whatever other junk I could find? It worked for how long; I could not remember.

Accordingly; I immediately began to throw the black cement chunks into this water. I have enough rocks here to build probably 20 dams. I kept throwing in every bit of broken cement block that I could get my hands on, and additionally work on reinforcing the front of my dam. Then I reinforced it with mud, actually dirt that I was digging up with some of my leftovers, or still remaining wood. When I threw this dirt on it, the water slowly turned into mud. Within an hour, my dam built. Now the question was how soon before the water started going over my dam? I had one more idea, maybe I can carve out some tunnels toward the black holes. The water could probably pour into there for days, if not for months. Consequently; my sword turned out to be an excellent canal maker. And soon; I had canals going to many of the black holes. Although technically; they really need to go to only one hole. So far, I've stopped the black holes; black cement blocked walls, and now the black Coon Hollow Creek. I keep trying to figure out, what is the deal with all this black? While I was thinking, I was also trying to scrape up some more firewood. The wood was getting tougher and harder to find. Fortunately; I started to take branches from the other side of the road where that lumber company had been, before they declared this place to be haunted. Now there is an original thought, that this place is haunted. Hell yes; it is definitely haunted. And lucky me I could not get out of here. Now, the only positive thing I have noticed is that after each encounter with something that's black, I seem to be getting better. Moreover; what better was, I had no idea.

As the darkness was beginning to appear, a dim white light began to shine. At first; I tried to focus on where Coon Run Road was in order to make sure that this light was not as a headlight to an approaching vehicle. It wasn't, in that it was coming from the direction where my grandparent's house used to be. The light started getting larger and closer. Considering that it is a white light, I figured it might be safe. The white light stopped in front of me and opened. Out of the door came a very now familiar and beautiful face. Considering what I have been through the last few days, that face could belong to a guerrilla, and I would say that it was beautiful. Although, being serious, this is a beautiful face. Then suddenly; I remember her and call out to her, "Devika, how are you this evening?" She smiles and says she has both pleasant news and bad news. I tell her to start over the good news, I had enough bad news for a lifetime. She says the good news is that she is here to help me; the bad news is she has no power in this area; something is sucking all the power away. She told me that for two days now she's tried to reach me, and that only this afternoon was she starting to make headway. I told her that last night I had a maybe 200 black holes with black things coming out of them, and by accident discovered that fire would kill them. Today I something tried to build a 50 ft.[2] wall around me with black cement blocks. Once again, fire slowed them down, giving me a chance to mash them up into small rocks. Then just within the last hour, Coon Hollow Creek water turned black. I could build a dam, using the broken black cement blocks and the sword that you gave me, to carve out some canals so that I can pour the water into those black holes.

I asked her if she knew what the deal was with all his black? Devika currently tells me that there's still more black to come in that we must defeat the Black Gate before she, and I can once more work together with her power. Furthermore; she tells me that she has been studying this gate for weeks at the moment, yet not been able to unlock its mystery, except that it can be defeated and turned off. Together; she and I must determine how to turn it off. I asked her where we can find this gate at. She tells me it only appears in the morning, close to where our fire is burning now. I asked her if she thinks I should move the fire? She tells me that it does not matter because the gate is not afraid of fire. She goes to her white light, opens the door, and pulls out a blanket and comes toward me. Furthermore, she says that we could have a very busy day tomorrow, in that gates usually are not solved in one day. That night we slept under the stars, as the clouds were gone. This meant for me that there would not have any rain this evening. When we woke up in the morning, Devika was once more opening the door to her white light and brought out some food for us. She also had a rope in which she tied to my hand and the other end to her hand. I asked her why she was doing this? She explains that when the gate appears, we must jump in with each other, so we can stay together. If you do not stay attached to each other, we could forever lose each other. Notwithstanding; I asked her why we must jump over the gate? She explains that this gate can only be defeated from within. Her white light began to flash, which warns her that the gate is approaching. Ironically, this gate is appearing where the wall was being built yesterday.

The gate appears; we made the jump, and the gate disappears. Devika believes the reason that it disappeared was because it's building was not built. We were both laying on the ground in the middle of a field. I feel the ground beginning to tremble; therefore, I warn Devika that we must run and hide. She wants to know why, as I informed her that I would tell her as soon as we were all in danger. We still had the rope tied to our hands. I told her to trust me, she would soon discover the reason. Accordingly; a few seconds later, some dinosaurs come rushing past us. She asked me how I knew what they were, and I told her that I watched a lot of history Channel shows as a child. I told her that we must be at least 65 million years in the past and wondered how we are getting out of here. She says we must find the black box and open it. When we opened the box, the gate will reappear. She claims now, all we had to do was look for a black box. I asked her where do we start looking? She said for us to put our swords together, and that they would point us in the right direction. We put our swords together, and started walking and walking until we approached a mountain. Subsequently; it was really a bunch of steep hills. Renewed, we maneuvered our way through the first set of hills, and then we went to go up the second set of hills, when I noticed a very large Tiger sitting on our black box. I said to Devika that it was time to use our swords. When we untied our hands, and she stored the rope into the backpack that she was wearing. As I approached the Tiger head on, Devika came in from its side. This Tiger was fierce and tried to swat us. I got a good stab in initially, could pull my sword out and cut his palm as he was swatting at me.

Meanwhile; Devika was getting multiple stabs in, when she then begins to gut this creature, cutting a line from his chest down to the bottom of his belly. This of course created gushes of blood as this creature died. Accordingly; I told Devika that we had better grab the box and run. We ran up the hill for maybe 100 feet and stopped. Devika wanted to know why we ran this time? I told her because of predators who can smell blood and with it will be coming big appetites. She agreed that this was a good reason and wondered if we were secure here. I told her that the blood was downwind from us, so we should be protected, we took our swords and opened the black box. Inside it was a button for us to push. Devika believes it is smart if we both pushed it simultaneously, since we both came through together. We did as she wanted as she once again tied up our hands, confessing to me that she did not know how soon the gate would appear. Either way; since we pushed the button simultaneously, the gate could not leave without both of us. Accordingly; the gate did not come until the next morning, leaving us scared to death of all the strange sounds that echoed through the forest throughout the entire night. I could talk Devika into climbing up a tree with me. At least, this would give us a little protection against any predators who could not climb. I guess with that giant Tiger only being one hundred feet away, most of the predators feasted on that for this night. When the morning came, we climbed back down to the ground, make sure we were tied together perfect, and simultaneously push the button, as a gate appeared. Devika recommended that we pause for just as a minute, to allow the gate to bring us closer to our desire timeframe. Then before I knew it, she jumped into the gate, and once again we landed in a field. I could recognize the hills that were not far from where we landed, and suggested to Devika that we were in the same place, yet another timeframe. I cannot see anything that could give me a clue as to where we were in time.

Devika reminds me that it does not matter what time we are, unless we are in our time, and the only way to get there was to find a black box once more. Therefore; we put our swords together, and this time begin walking across this field. I was trying to keep an eye out for any dinosaur tracks. Fortunately; there were no tracks on this ground. We kept walking until we approached a small River. I recommended that we try to find a shallow crossing, which was in about three miles, where we found a crossing with large rocks in it. I suspected that this was where the animals crossed. We crossed here, backtrack back up to where our swords provided us once again a solid direction to follow. This time, we were not so lucky to find a black box on the same day. Therefore; we bundled up on the first no branch of a tree and prepared to sleep. Suddenly, I noticed something strange in the field on the other side of the river, and those were several small fireplaces. I told Devika that we were apparently in one of the ages of the Homo Sapiens, which branch I had no idea, but that they had learned to master fire. It would be better if we try to avoid them if all possible, since they might not know how to take us, as a friend or enemy. I reached inside my pocket, and pulled out my lighter, showing it to Devika. I told her that this was I get out of jail-free card. She told me that she had no idea what I was talking about.

Consequently; I told her that I hoped that she would never need to know. The next morning, we continued our search for the black box. This time it was on a rock in the middle of yet another River. Devika told me not to worry, that she was an outstanding swimmer and jumped in that water like a frog, reached the rock standing up on it securing the black box and dove back into the water, swimming quickly to our shoreline. I helped her out of water as we opened up our second black box. It was now around lunchtime, so Devika figured that this box could not summon the gate until the next morning. We, therefore, continued walking throughout the day. Devika wanted to get away from these rivers, and that they could prove to be a nemesis on our future searches. Much to our delight; we ran into some fruit trees and selected some of the fruit that had fallen on the ground. Devika told me that this would give us some much-needed energy. I was actually quite surprised that my legs were holding out as good as they were, and asked Devika if she knew why? She told me this was because these events were before my dimensional jump. I told her that a man was lucky when currently not only to have a smart woman but a very beautiful one. Devika hopes that this would be enough to help get us back to our home. I asked her why she jumped with me? She said it was because she loved me. I could not think of any time previously that I had heard a woman say that she loved me. Although I'm sure that if I thought long enough, I could come across many examples where they said just the opposite. Be that as it may; we had some buttons to push and time to travel. We position ourselves and together simultaneously push the button, as a gate appeared.

Once more, waited for just a little while, but different amount of time as previously, and jumped. This time we landed on the top of a five-story building. Devika recommended that we match our swords in order to determine which side of the building to come down. Once we made that determination, we broke down a door on the roof and started going down some steps, hoping to reach the ground before being discovered. We were lucky, in that the direction that our swords were sending us on was toward some woods. While on the first floor, I noticed a trash can and went to scrounge through it hoping to find maybe a newspaper or a piece of mail that had been date stamped. I did find some junk mail that was date stamped July 3, 1939. I told Devika that this was not a good time in man's history. Sure enough, I scrounge through the trashcan; I noticed some mail with German addresses. I told Devika that this was during the Nazis, and that we had better get out of here as fast as possible. Unfortunately; we happen to run into a Nazi soldier seducing his girlfriend. I immediately stabbed the both of them with one thrust of my sword. I retrieve the machine gun beside him and his ammo belt. Fortunately; this belt had three grenades attached to it. Our swords finally landed as next to our black box. I really recommended to Devika that we not try to wait until the next morning but try to get out of here now. We pushed buttons, and nothing. I could soon hear some dogs barking. I told Devika that I hoped these were not Army dogs. One of the dogs began to approach us, as it was Devika tossing her knife striking the dog in his throat as he was beginning to approach and attack us. By hitting him in the throat, she cut his vocal cords, and thus he could not make any more noise. I quickly retrieved her knife for her and drug the dog beside some bushes nearby. Still no gate. I then told Devika that we would try something else. I pulled the hammer from one of the three German grenades and tossed it down the hill.

Apparently; this bought us some time, as the Germans continued their search away from us. Then finally, and not a moment too soon, the gate appeared and with our hands tied, and with a two-minute delay, we leaped in. This time the gate dropped us where we began in Coon Hollow. Devika tells me now, we must fight and destroy this gate. I asked her if she thinks maybe these two German grenades could help us. I noticed that the gate was remaining and asked Devika if she understood why. Then he told me because we had conquered is time movement; therefore, it was no longer a time portal for evil. To test what would happen if something was thrown into it, I tossed in a rock. When a rock hit the open part inside the gate, the rock was frozen situated properly. That was all I needed to know, in that if I tossed in a grenade, it will be held situated properly until it exploded. I toss in my first grenade, as it was locked in place it exploded, shattering the rim of this gate. Consequently; the gate was still semi-functional. Therefore; I tossed in my second grenade, and it immediately exploded and completely destroyed this black gate for good.

at this moment in time; I asked Devika what had we just accomplished. She said two things: The first since I can stay with her in her white light at this moment in time and be safe at night. The second thing: I can now do battle against the 13 houses, as they no longer had the evil protection, they previously had. She recommended we go to her white light, clean up, eat, and rest because tomorrow the war would begin. I do not really know what to expect when I climbed into this little white light. I was quite surprised when inside it was a very large two-story living area, which was identical to my house in Washington state. Naturally; knowing my way around this structure, I immediately prepared to take a shower. After taking my shower, Devika entered, collected my dirty clothing and asked me how we cleaned our clothing. I got her clothing as well, and showed her how to use our washing machine. She after that asked me; did not the clothing come out wet after being soaked in this water. I afterwards showed her my dryer and told her that this would dry our clothing. I also told her that I had some extra clothing upstairs that she can wear until her clothing was finished drying. Now she asked me how she could clean her body as well. I told her that I had two showers upstairs, and that I would show her both and let her decide which one she wanted to use. She preferred to use the one in our master bedroom. I turned the water on and told her to stick her hand in and tell me if it was too hot or furthermore cold, and I would adjust it to exactly the way she needed it.

Next; I then showed her our shampoo and soap and gave her examples on how to use them. She actually found this to be quite stimulating. I, therefore, asked her if she'd ever taken a shower with water before? Devika explained to me that she had to take on a physical body in order to join me in this war. She further clarifies that this is all new to her, especially the pain that she's feeling in her stomach. I told her that this meant she was getting hungry; I would go downstairs and make us something to eat. Consequently; she asked me if it was a man's job to do the cooking, or was it the woman's job? I told her whoever had the time to do this. I also told her that with my recent divorce, I would be doing a lot of cooking for myself. Out of curiosity; I asked her how she got this large house and my backyard and front yard into this little white light. She claimed that it was some process of molecular regeneration. That was not the obstacle, the obstacle was that this white light could not leave Coon Hollow, until we won the war against the 13 houses. She told me not to worry, but she developed a strategic plan in which we could slowly knock these houses out one at a time. We also knock them out from the back forward, so that the front houses would not become alerted. I asked her if they just could not talk to each other? She said not now since we had destroyed their four major black power sources. She confessed that she never thought it could be done without the use of magic. To her amazement, we came out victorious today. Accordingly; tomorrow and the days after would each be days of fresh new battles that had to be won.

CHAPTER 13

Dreizehn Häuser

The next morning came and Devika, and I prepared for our first day of battle. Devika showed me the 13 keys that she got from the gate before it exploded. These keys would allow us to enter the gate that each of these houses used to commit their crimes. Our mission was to view some of these crimes, mentally transferring them to our records log. We would need these recordings during the final battle against the whole remaining, if any, scourge that by these monsters would sink into the mouth of hell. Once we finish collecting our evidence, we were to kill this heinous murderer, if in the flesh with our swords, if in the spirit, with the salt that Devika would bring in her backpack. Once the murderer has been killed, we entered the gate, yet while going through it, we would release some salt, which would destroy the insides of the gate. Once outside, we can borrow some hammers and destroy the outside. We would get to take that evidential recording to her white light for safe storage, before proceeding to the next one. Devika told me of one additional requirement, and that was if they were detected by any member of the family, we had to execute them. If we did not, that family member would someday execute us. Naturally, in order to avoid detection, the 13 houses did most of the killing in the past, which of course created additional dimension forks that had no effect on our dimension. Sometimes, the killer would jump to a different year, and their commit more crimes. Devika said not to worry, because she could track them down by analyzing their gate, because if they went through it, they were planning to come back and had to leave some coding in the gate. Devika said that when we were watching them, we had to be quiet, and if we were killing them; we had to be fast. Neglecting to do so could result in our death. She now handed me a recording device that she attached to my eyes. Everything that I saw was recorded and when we returned a backup copy was transmitted to a receiver inside her white light. Each time we went to the gate, the gate would readjust our clothing to match those of the time that we were in. Devika said it was time to begin.

Therefore, we went to the house of Zane Gray. Devika used her master key to unlock the door. Inside we went to find an empty house. These unpainted shacks were small with tin roofs. In the center of the floor was a black gate with a portal. As we prepared to enter the gate, Devika told me to stand beside her before entering, because we had to make sure that no one was watching. Once the coast is clear, we would jump through the gate quickly, and find a place to hide in whatever house or place we were. When we arrived, Devika immediately pointed towards the door and ran outside. Once outside she began to climb a tree and naturally, I had no idea what we were doing while I followed her up the tree. When up in the tree she pulled out a little white light opened the door as initially began to expand we entered inside and while closing the door, it contracted, which had no effect on us. I told her we had two choices, one choice we set on my front porch and see what was going on, which were to reduce it to my backpack on my back table and see what was going on. At this time, something opened up one of my sheds and pulled out two sets of binoculars. We could use these to determine who was in the house. Once Zane was out, we could follow him in his little white light to determine what he was up to. She recommended that we follow him a couple of times just to get the hang of his routines. She further told me that the keys knew when he was going to murder and also of all the murders he committed thus far. Furthermore, she was in the process of transferring these videos from the key to her transceiver that was here in my house. Likewise, she told me that Zane had a history of causing trouble in exacting revenge. Once, he got mad in school, and burned down the school buses' garage.

He got three years in a reform school for this. I noticed that there was some snow in this area and that all the vehicles had Alaskan license plates. I told Devika that if she got cold, I had some coats in the house, in fact, my ex-wife had left a few that she no longer wanted. They also told me that Zane was excellent with weapons and was considered to be an expert hunter in this area. She asked me if I like hunting? I told her I did not like hunting. I definitely had never butchered an animal, although there's nothing wrong with it; I just did not have the stomach for it. She said our subject was married and had two children. To be on the safe side, to put them in her Family Member Container, which is no bigger than a coffee thermos. I can smell donuts and other forms of bread being baked. What that does to cool still Alaskan air is remarkable, making me starving. Devika recommended that I eat some cereal, so that way, my stomach would not be growling when we were attempting to capture Zane. Devika came up with an excellent idea, since our subject worked in a bakery, and I was hungry, we go to the bakery and pick up some pastries. This would give her a chance to run some scans on him, which could help with her videos and the location of these dead bodies, since most likely where he buried them and their locations would be in his head. They had a different way of killing, that also satisfied his intense love of hunting. He to enjoy the services of prostitutes, however, did not like the quickie part of this process, instead wanting to have some additional time. Subsequently; he used his creativity to, after the sex, to take a nature ride with him.

Sometimes, he had to spike their drink, with a nice sleeping aid. Once he got them into the deep wilderness, he released them. Afterward; he went to his home, and after that considering most of these releases were on a Friday, returned on Saturday with his hunting rifle, and then began the process of tracking her down and killing her. The thrill of killing evolved beyond hunting animals to that of hunting people. He continued this process no less than 23 times, until on the 23rd time, some other hunters discovered what he was doing, and used their cell phones to call 911. The police could triangulate their location from their cell phone and quickly came to the area in question, only to arrive in time to hear a gunshot. The police and the reporting hunters rushed to the site to catch the same and capture him. There was of course an exchange of gunfire. One of the hunters hit him in his arm, which was enough to allow the police to handcuff him, and be taken to the jail. Additionally; the town assembled a large search party with dogs in order to locate these missing women. Unfortunately; due to the low number of actual residents, this search took a few months. What helped them, was as the police had missing person's reports on these girls, and could retrieve some of their personal items. This helped greatly in the search.

We also helped with the search and were credited with five discoveries. This was possible by us knowing where to lineup in the morning and how-to guide the dogs, sometimes sideways. Having to cross creeks and avoid higher hills, most times, justified our deviations. Zane was sentenced to 461 years plus life. Now the trick was to find a way to contact him and murder him. Devika recommended that we come in on her little white light, enter his cell at night, and then stab him at least 23 times. This would lead the police to suspect one of the victims' family. We were fortunate enough that no one on the search crews witnessed decaying bodies. All the bodies were of course dug up, and reburied in the town's cemetery. I thought this to be ironic, and that these girls were sex workers, and as such were snubbed by the non-customer residents. Any ways; Devika could accumulate our video data, that is something two things that remained, one was the execution and the capture of the family members placing them in the Family Member Container. That evening we entered the prison in her tiny white light that is color adjusted to a warm white and thus resemble a lightning bug. I told her to make sure that we did not get close to any people because some people kill any insect that they see. Devika told me not to worry, because there was no human being even with a gun that could contact her little light because it can move actually faster than the speed of light and, if I need to be, through walls.

When we got inside his cell, I grabbed two knives and immediately rushed out to his bed. My first knife got his throat, the second one I stabbed him through his ear. The other 21 stabs were spread out over his body. Devika, upon verifying that the 23 stabs, recorded his death. She now told me, let's go pick up his family. I asked her what happened to his family, considering that serial killers usually don't broadcast their activities to their families. She told me that they would be sent to a spiritual court who would examine their innocence or guilt, and then they would be dealt with appropriately. This court was located in Florida. This was so that the family would not associate anyone in Alaska being involved with this kidnapping and transfer. We returned to his home, and Devika released some sleeping gas into the room. She then allowed her Family Member Container to suck them in, naturally, using their molecular regeneration technology. After securing the family in the white light, we had the gate return us to Coon Hollow, as her white light strategically released salt throughout this process. We had to get both sides, and that can only occur during the transfer, yet with salt in this transfer process, it would destroy both sides simultaneously. Devika now submitted our materials to the Council that was monitoring our progress.

She congratulates me, one down and 12 to go. This is not the first time I'd ever been involved with the project requiring 13 separate encounters, but could only hope it would be the last time. Devika used her master key and unlocked the second real house. She was afraid that with taking 13 keys everywhere, she could lose one. This house belongs to Harry Dearth. Once we are inside, we examine the summary of this killer. It is rather scary; it is that he killed more than 33 teenage boys near Chicago before 1978. He buried most of these bodies underneath his house. Curiously; I asked Devika she could do this, because my belief had been that teenage boys are extremely strong, especially the football players. He used many different techniques that employed trying to con these boys into his vehicle. He carried his Sheriff's badge, and that he owned some local businesses that would hire teenagers, thus promising them jobs. As men, we get weaker with age. She tells me that he would trick these guys into putting on handcuffs, telling them this was some sort of magic trick. Once they had the handcuffs on, that was it. He would rape and torture them and then kill them prior to burying them underneath his house. He used to try many tricks and deceptive methods in order to get his young boys to have sex with him. Furthermore, he had a sodomy conviction which was for 10 years in prison, of which he was paroled for the vast majority of this time. That taste of prison convinced him that he was not going to go back. Previously, he would have sex or attempt sex with these boys who always told someone, which was presenting a series of challenges for Harry. This was when he decided to meet and kill them after having sex with them. One method that he used a lot was to put a rope around their neck and tighten it with a hammer, thereby choking them. The overwhelming majority of his victims were killed between 3 AM and 6 AM. Devika tells me that there was enough decay from the bodies they stored underneath his house to satisfy the proof or evidence requirement from our counsel. Now all we had to do was go to his prison, execute him, and come back to key out of this house. Therefore; we jumped into her warm white light and zipped to the prison that was holding Harry. I wanted to do some extra special for the sick master; therefore, first, I slashed his throat, and then cut off his family tool. He died immediately, as Devika collected the proof of his execution. We returned to his house in Chicago and, with the key turning on the gates, preparing our salt to be deployed during our transfer through the gate to Coon Hollow. Once we arrived and shot salt over this gate's end, and through some salt through this portal, watching both ends dissolve almost simultaneously. Moreover; as the portals vanish, so do the buildings that are surrounding them.

Devika, congratulated me on our second victory, unfortunately reminding me that 11 remained. She submitted our requirements to the Council, and recommended that we try for the third one, which was Jacob Koon. Jacob was the oldest resident of the 13 houses. Devika got out of her key and told me we were heading for California. I told her California was a lot better than the Alaska we had been in recently. As we gazed through the portal, we could determine that Jacob was left in there. In fact, he already has been arrested for the murder of 25 orchard workers. We, therefore, began to search the orchard in Devika's warm white light for their scans to detect body parts. We had arrived late in this process, as most of the bodies had been dug up and reburied. There was no requirement that we get all the bodies, just so we get evidence of multiple murders. Jacob enjoyed stabbing and slashing his victims. Devika returned really excited and that she got enough evidence to justify 20 of the murders, which far exceeded the requirement by the Council. I told her; it was time tonight to sneak into his cell and stab and slash him with my sword. Devika told me, as long as we never entered between 3 AM and 4 AM. That was when evil liked to roam, looking for fresh prey. I told her usually in prisons they put them to bed around 10 PM, so he should be well asleep by midnight. We arrived at midnight and once more I slashed my victim's throat. I also stabbed him a couple of times, once again trying to make it look like a friend of one of his victims was exacting revenge. Devika acquired the proof of death, as we both quickly jump back into her light, and went back to Jacob's California work shack.

Fortunately, the gate was not moved since the previous day. We accumulated our evidence as Devika submitted it to the Council for their review. After preparing our salt for release we jumped into the gate and upon arrival at the Coon Hollow gate of Jacob's house, we dumped some more salt, dissolving this third gate and house.

Three down and 10 to go. I asked Devika if she thought our luck would continue, as she replied as long as we keep working. We can't take any chances on them forming allies. So now we took the key and opened up Moses Barnhart's Coon Hollow house. Once we entered, it was to portal from an appropriate time to exit. Moses was staying with his mother and sister at the time, so this gave us some breathing room in order to accumulated evidence of the 23 bodies of the victims he killed. Among his targets, all-male, with two in their 40s. Their ages ranged from 17 to 46. He would wake them prior to killing them. He had to be a bit more creative in his attempts to lure, attracting alcoholics and drug users among others. Devika, quickly accumulated the body parts that we needed for the evidence. To do this, we had to visit several of the local parishes. Her scanners would lock in on the body cells, to record information on her device for the Council. We returned to the prison that they were holding him based upon an eight-life term's conviction. Moses reported to the infirmary complaining about a sore back. The doctor verified it is, and specified, that he should remain in his cell for a couple of days and gave him some sleeping medication to help with the pain. We arrived there when he was already asleep. For this kill, we used a small skinny knife, and that Devika felt it more represented weapons available inside the prison, feeling that my sword could alert them of outside interference. She just said that would cause more trouble in the long term, although tonight we were safe. I cut his throat and stabbed him in his heart. The reason I cut their throats is to inhibit their ability to scream or make noise. Plus, it creates a lot of blood. Devika collected the evidence of the execution, combined it with our evidence of the murders and submitted it to the Council. We did the salt trick on our return to Coon Hollow and watched his shack and black gates vanish.

We now had four down and nine to go. It was currently time to look for Larry Young's Coon Hollow house. Devika opened the door with the key as we stare through the portal in order to determine the appropriate time to jump. He lived alone and was apparently outrunning some errands. We entered through the gate, went out his window and began searching for the 30 bodies he killed and were disposed of here in Florida. He committed murders and other states as well, with an estimated total of 88 beginning in the late 60s and continuing until the police caught him. Unlike all of our other killers; Larry killed young women and girls ranging in ages 16 to 25. It took us the remainder of the day to accumulate enough evidence for 23 of these murders. Devika once again assures me that this is plenty. This time for the execution, Devika sets off the prison's escape alarm, which that put everyone in lock down. Once we had Larry in the cell, Devika put on her transparent suit and walked over, giving him a high drug shot mixed with some other deadly chemicals. Even though there was a slight wrestling match, Devika easily gained total control, as he soon died. She collected the execution evidence, combined it with the murders evidence is submitted to our Council as number five was on the books with eight more remaining. We did our salt through the gates trick as one more house vanished from Coon Hollow. I look at Devika with a now confused expression on my face. She asked me what was wrong? I told her that it was scary to think that so much death had its roots in the evil gates from this small hollow. It just did not make sense to me as having trouble grasping it, but be that as it may, I still have eight more houses to liquidate.

The next house belongs to Tom Bouters. The question for Devika and that was what if this beast is already dead and has been dead since 1928? She said it was okay as long as we provided evidence that he was indeed executed. I said then we have to go to Winnipeg, Canada on January 13, 1928. I also told her that he killed people throughout many states and even Canada. Furthermore, I told her the West Coast, Seattle and Portland, San Francisco and so on. She wanted to see what was giving me this information so she could program it into her scanner. I transmitted the data to her, and she put it into her scanner. Now she said it was time to go to Winnipeg as she punched on January 13, 1928. She said it will be better to use her white light and then return using the gates to get the execution evidence. When we arrived in Winnipeg, we could see Tom standing on the gallows was a rope around his neck. Devika immediately started scanning to verify that it was him, and her machine verified. It was now a simple wait until he hangs and recorded his death. Fortunately; they were ready to hang him and did so rather quickly. We had on film him standing on the gallows that he was talking to someone as they put the black hood over his face. And then they hung him, as his body, hung from the extended rope. We had the evidence of his death, so now Devika said we will return to Coon Hollow and cancel out his gates as we get some evidence of some murders. This time we remained in her white light, racing through the gate after she had unlocked it with her key. Tom had no less than 22 murders, ranging from an eight-month-old boy to mid-60s. Except for the boy, all his victims were female, ranging from 13 through mid-60s. He would rape these many times financially successful women, and have sex with their dead bodies. Although he didn't do this to all the women, he did it too many of them. It was his last two murders in a small town in Canada where he was caught. That town does not exist to this day. To be on the safe side, Devika collected evidence of all 22 murders. We did our gate thing with the salt dissolving both sides and removing Tom's house from Coon Hollow. Devika accumulated and assembled all the evidence we needed for this house and submitted it to the Council, who approved it, as they have on all the evidence we have thus far submitted. We now have six houses down and seven remaining. Devika asked me if I was able to continue; I told her absolutely, the sooner I get this weight off my chest the better I will feel.

Our next house belongs to Darrell Walters. Devika motions me to follow her as she heads toward the gate. I tell her that Darrell was executed on February 23, 1996, the first few minutes of that day at Quentin State Prison. She next looks at me, says well let's head for Quentin State Prison as she punches in the time. I told her that he was executed by lethal injection, so we should get a good video of him alive, injected, dying, and deceased considering the prison usually has a medical authority to pronounce time of death. We arrived; Devika accumulated her visual evidence, and a few cells that matters and can ever collect off of Darrell's dead body. As we were returning to Coon Hollow to Darrell's house to use his black gate and collect some executed bodies. He had 21 murders that were known, and they ranged from ages 12 to 19. They were all boys whom he did the standard pick them up through deception that if they didn't agree to bind them, next rape them, and finally kill them while at times tossing their bodies out into the road. He would purposely try to toss them in areas away from where he killed his victim so that way with the police would go on a wild goose chase. I gave Devika his victim list and where they were killed at as she plugged it into her scanners, and the evidence began to pour in. After running around on the first couple of houses we destroyed, she now uses the position data and lecture scanners who read the body cells. She explains that the Council matches the DNA to verify the executed body, and with the bodies having been dead for a long time, there is no reason to get shook up on the details. Once again, she assembled our evidence and transmitted it to our Council, who instantaneously approves it. Now all we have to do is salt the gates as we return to Coon Hollow. The gates and Darrell's house vanish. We now have seven houses destroyed, with six remaining.

The next house we will attempt to negotiate belongs to Timothy Hamilton. Devika arrives, and I give her the initial briefing. Timothy is still in prison for life at California's Mule Creek State Prison. He will be in there until he dies, which today we will speed up this process. He would discard the bodies alongside the roads, yet unlike the other synergistic serial killers; he would shoot them in the head with his gun, and thereby not tortured them before their death. Another reason he had to use a gun was his size, he was smaller and would have been unable to overpower many of his victims. His 35 victims ranged from 18 to 21. He would also have sex with their dead bodies. I transmitted the victim list with their known locations of death and burial information to Devika, so she could transmit it to her white light. For this one, she wanted to accumulate the victims' evidence, since our killer was not going anywhere. First things first, they had to find a place in California to station ourselves. She took out her key and unlocked Timothy's back gate. We can use her white light with its long-range scanners to collect as much physical evidence of these crimes that we could. Although we did not get all 35, we did get 21 and Devika said that was more than enough, as a Council had already approved our victim remains. Devika also told me something interesting, and that was the blood of these victims would cry out from the ground wanting their revenge, and each execution we do today frees them from being in limbo. This little tidbit made me feel better. Now we were taking a trip to Mule Creek. Devika currently had assembled what she called her poison missiles that she could shoot them into the body of the person we were trying to execute. This would allow us to essentially go and execute and leave. And that's exactly what we did, as her scanners accumulated video and biological data related to this execution. I believe that it is when his victims began to cheer in the limbo world that the Council had actually received verification of this execution. Devika assembles her packet and transmits it to the Council, who approved it almost instantaneously. We return to our arrival point go inside the black gate, with our salt dribbling, and exit the black gate in Coon Hollow. Both gates and Timothy's house vanish. We have eight victories, with five more battles to fight. Devika tells me to prepare for our next battle.

Our next house belongs to Thomas Harris. I informed Devika that Thomas had been executed by electric chair on January 24, 1989, in Florida's state prison. She pushed the data in her Time Machine, and instantaneously we were there. She sat up her sensor equipment as we watched them strapping Thomas to that chair and electrocute him, causing his smelly death. Furthermore, she collected the execution evidence, and asked me if I had the victim's list. I transmitted it to her, as she looked puzzled, commenting that these were a lot of dead people. I explained that Thomas confessed to 36 murders, yet others say there were as many as 100. Only the blood in the ground could verify that. He would rape these women before killing them, and attempting to store their bodies in a place ready for him to return and have additional sex, until the bodies were too decomposed to perform the function. Her scanners started transmitting the victim's DNA, for a total of 72 confirmed, by blood in the ground and victims. Devika assembles this package and submits it to the Council for their review. They instantaneously accept this. We return to Thomas's black gate and using our salt, it through to the Coon Hollow black gate, escaping just as the gates and his house vanish. We now have nine victories in four more battles to fight. This time I looked at Devika and asked her if she wanted to continue, as she said absolutely.

Our next house belongs to Tom Scott. Devika and I enter his Coon Hollow house, and she uses her key to unlock his gate. I tell her that he died of AIDS in 1994. Therefore, we jumped right in and land in the Midwest, where I give her the victim list that I compiled. She gives this information to her sensors, who began their nationwide scan. Being in no hurry, because we could not go anywhere until the sensors bring back the victim DNA sources, Devika recommends that we take a nap and with a little rest, we may continue throughout the night if possible. I am tired, so I go upstairs and jump into my bed, as Devika snuggles in on the opposite side of this king-size bed, and we immediately fall fast asleep. What seemed to be like just a few seconds, the sensors were sounding off in our room. Devika got up and collected their victim evidence, and the evidence they got from Tom's body. She wrapped this up, and with her fingers crossed submitted it to the Council who approved it. I told her, and this is just for her information now, that Tom killed 21 teen boys ranging from ages 16 to a straggler at 29. Devika currently claims that there are 21 new boys celebrating tonight. We proceed to the black gate on Tom's end, and afterward have been through we began dropping our salt. Both black gates and Tom's Coon Hollow house vanish.

We now have defeated 10 Coon Hollow houses, with only three remaining. Accordingly; I inform Devika that the next house belongs to James Powell. Devika now inserts her key to this house's black gate as we zip off to the West Coast. I provide her the victim data and her sensors began receiving the victim DNA data that are Council is in need of. I asked her if she had another little poison missiles, which she replies that she has plenty of them. Furthermore, I tell her it is time to head to the Oregon State Penitentiary. Likewise, I explained to her that this killer was suspected of killing at least 44 people, most of them women. It is also believed to be have committed at least 60 unsolved rapes. As a little white-light flashes into James's cell, Devika releases two of her deadly missiles. I asked her why she released two, and she said that she wanted to make sure he was dead. We appear to be working together as a team very effectively. I do not believe I could've done this with our little white light, nor little missiles, nor her sensors. We now have verification that James is dead and is receiving the victim DNA as proof of execution. Devika assembles this evidence and provides it to the Council, who accepts it. With this, she takes out her key and sticks it into James's black gate, as we slowly began to start to release the salt jump into and through to Coon Hollow James's house black gate. Both gates and house vanish. We now have just two more battles to fight. We are going to message on this one as we immediately begin our preparations.

I explained to Devika that the next house belonged to the Glen Campbell. They asked for her key into the Glen's Coon Hollow house black gate. As we prepared to begin searching for bodies, I gave Devika the list of the victims. I also told her that Glen had been shot by the FBI during a gunfight. I also told her that he had between 18 and 35 confirmed kills, and that he killed young and old, male and female. Once more, her sensors returned with all the evidence, both victim and killer, whom we needed. Devika, assembled this information and presented it to our Council. The Council for the 12th straight time approved our evidence. We stand beside each other in front of Campbell's black gate, so to salt dropping while holding hands, this time jump through in our famous stream of salt. Once through, we watch both black gates, and Campbell's house vanish. I look at Devika and tell her that we are now on our last house, with 12 victories under our belts.

This final house belongs to Lewis Palmer. Devika walks over, sticks her key into Lewis Palmer's black gate, as we leap through together. I immediately give Devika the victim list, and tell her that we must go to South Woods State Prison in Bridgeton New Jersey where he is still alive. We leap into her little warm white light and almost instantaneously arrived in Bridgeton New Jersey. She explains that once she neutralizes Lewis, then we have access to the gates. She gives her sensors the information I gave her plus the information they have on Lewis and released it. Even I am feeling a bit uneasy, being this close to a touchdown. Then I see a smile appear on Devika's face as the wonder sensor lights began flashing. She looks at me and reveals that Lewis Palmer is now deceased, and that she has 17 victim body parts to submit as DNA evidence. She assembles her package and submits it to the Council. Within just a few seconds, they approve it and congratulate us on the victory of this war. I explained to Devika that I would feel better celebrating this in Coon Hollow as soon as Palmer's house is destroyed. We stand beside each other and with our little stream of salt jump through Palmer's black gate and the right in his Coon Hollow black gate. As we stand beside each other, we watched the last two black gates and the last of the 13 houses vanish. There are no more 13 houses. I asked Devika what had we just accomplished? She said the main thing was that I was now free to go after the Coon Run Road Ghost, and I could also fix the dimension crack above Coon Hollow. I asked her how does someone fix a dimension crack? She told me that she would get the answer and be with me as we once again go forth into the unknown and do the impossible. She also told me that I was now free to depart from Coon Hollow and asked if I wanted to spend the night in her warm white light. That warm white light is the closest thing that I have to my Washington home. I, therefore, told her that I would love to. Once again, we leap into her warm white light. Once in my house, we remember that we forgot to eat this day, and thus raid my refrigerator.

CHAPTER 14

Fizard Sealed

I could actually see the sun come up from outside my window. In reality; I was looking out my window from inside Devika's little warm white light. I remember as a kid, when the sun come up from grandma's upstairs window I would sit at the top of the steps because it was so easy to look out of. Of course; before the sun comes up, there will be roosters making their racket. My view from here is it really is only about maybe 25 feet from where grandma's old upstairs window was, before they tore down the house. Now here is a good point, why were they in such a big hurry to tear the house down? They tore it down about 10 years ago, and for 10 years have done nothing with this land. I sometimes cannot figure out the government. Devika is getting up now and wants to know what is for breakfast.

I brought up some of my sausage links and tossed in some toast with Philadelphia cream cheese spread on it, and finally a glass of chocolate milk, with two sunny side up eggs.

Yes, chocolate milk. I still like it. I think that is because of the third-grade teacher that forbid it in her classroom, so we had to buy regular milk for our afternoon snack. Always has to be somebody to take away what is rightfully yours. Anyway; it is time for me to cook Devika some breakfast. First off; it has been only fair, since the only reason she's in a physical body, was to help me. I was blind, trapped in total darkness with my feet hurting so badly I could not even walk. She eventually gave me some new eyes and helped me with my feet, although the feet came back rather naturally. Consequently; that is a story within itself, she is here in a physical body just to help me. Accordingly; any chance I get to spoil her, I will without question. I asked Devika if she has heard anything for my Queens? She says she's heard nothing from the other dimension. I said the reason I'm asking is that it is Wohpe who was always worried about this crack between the dimensions.

Next; I asked Devika if her superiors have mentioned anything about this crack? She said; "Someday will have to fix it." I then asked her why we are so worried about it, then? She tells me that it is above Coon Hollow and if it is breaking, why do we need to fix it? I asked her if she knew how to fix it. She told me that nothing changed from yesterday; except she found the name of the ancient one who could tell us how and his name is Emerick, and he lives in the hills beside a town called Loki. I asked if she knew where

Loki was. She said no but as you pointed to the ceiling, my light does. Devika then asked me why I was acting so strange today? The only thing that I could tell her was, from my recent activities; I must be tired. She then recommended that we lay around and relax for a day. She wanted to taste some more of the delicious food I make. That's when you can tell that she has spent way too long in a spiritual body and too few days in a physical body. Being curious; I asked her if she has ever been in a physical body previously? She told me this was her first time. I asked if she liked it, which she replied no. I told her that I understood exactly what she meant, and that I was at the upper end of the years needed to suffer here in Earth before being set free or, in other words, dying. She told me that I had better not expect to be leaving my body too soon, because she was going to take good care of me. I told her also make this pic on and tease Devika day. She flexed her arms, looking me with a grin and said, why don't we play hit James's day. After hearing this; I said that I recommended we rest today rather than playing games. She smiled and said that was a good idea. Then she clarified, that she would never hit me.

Subsequently; I told her this must mean that I have a chance of being alive tomorrow when I wake up. Devika looks at me and tells me that sometimes I say the strangest things. I told her I thought that is because my brain doesn't want to work anymore. She laughed and said that my brain was working very well, in fact has saved her life so far way too many times. Currently; I am trying to think in my mind when I have ever saved her life, but then again, I might as well keep my mouth shut and take the credit. Consequently;

Devika, why do you want to have a physical body? She tells me, "To spend some time with you and try to keep you alive, if this is even possible. "I told her that I truly did enjoy this time with her. Then I asked her, again had she, heard anything from my Queens, as she looks at me and says that they have heard nothing from that dimension. Now I wondered if they were having some kind of trouble. I asked her if she could contact them to make sure they were okay. She reminds me about the following, that while in this physical body she has no powers except occasionally what her light can give her, who most times are simply it performing the things that I had requested. Since she had finished her breakfast, I asked her if she was ready for our morning nap? She looks at me and tells me you have never taken a morning before, so why am I am calling it our morning nap? I told her since this was the first one, we would make it a tradition for us. She then tells me that she would be demoted in her job if she tried to take a nap every day. I asked her how much longer she can stay with me? She said their big boss told her for as long that it took to fix my situation and me. Thus; I then told her that a nap would help me temporarily.

Accordingly; I picked her up to carry her upstairs for a nap. This was the first time she had ever held or picked her up. She appeared to enjoy it. That was good because I just had a bad feeling about this in that crack in the sky above us. When we awoke, I felt that something could maybe see me. I needed to get the ball rolling on this crack in the sky deal. I asked Devika if the light can make contact to my Queens. She said that was a possibility, therefore let's go check if it can. The light was able to make contact, although someone else picked up my Queen's communication device. I asked who this was. She told me that she was one of the servants that previously worked in this world's chamber. I then asked her if she knew where the Queens were. She says she has no idea, that they escaped when the new masters took over the throne. I then asked her if she knew where Wohpe was. She told me that the new masters destroyed his stones and him when they took over this previous throne. How is that possible? She says, then no one knows, however we have new masters now. I asked if she knew who I was. She said you were our previous King and that if the new masters ever caught me, they would behead me. She also warned me that the Masters claimed they would search every universe to find me. This is when I said to Devika that ceiling this crack was very important now. She agreed, commenting how unbelievable such a great throne could fall. I told her that all it needed was to have one stone removed, it lost all its power and without that power it was easy pickings for anyone who wanted to destroy it. She asked me if I was worried about my previous Queens? I told her that they were maidens before, and knew how to survive in very difficult situations, I hope. I then looked at her and said, I guess you have me all to yourself now. She laughed, then said, what made me think that I wanted her all to myself? I told her I would answer that question some other time.

For now, before we go to look for the crack in the sky repair guy, let's take a walk around this farm. She agreed and seems to be following the almost invisible now old cow paths that I used to walk on. I was surprised, that some of this area had been bush hogged, and that a line of the brush had been cut down. That is good because once these wild bushes and trees take off, the land would be almost impossible to navigate. We walked around the hill that sat behind my grandma's house, then follow the actually repaired fence line down to Coon Hollow Creek. Now; I told her we could travel up the fun hill. Accordingly; up the hill we walked to what must be the property line, because this is where the fence formed a T. We, therefore, headed back down the hill, this time in a diagonal fashion considering I did not want to follow the fence line down to Coon Run Road. I can see evidence that a logging company had done some work up in this area. They cleaned up their leftover tree parts quite well. At least we had somewhat passable routes that we could follow down to Coon Hollow Creek. When we reached the Creek, I asked her if she remembered where we were. She said we were at the place where there used to be the 13 houses. I told her very good.

Then; I asked if she wanted to meet Bob, the man who helped my sister and me when we were out here previously. She said why not because until I agree to it, I would just keep pestering her about it. I said that was very true, because when a man has a very beautiful woman beside him, he wants to show her off. She looked at me said, "Oh boy, you are so funny. "Hence; I held her hand as we walked up Coon Run Road to visit Bob. Once there, I knocked on the door, yet no one answered. I told her that they must have gone into town for something. As a result; we walk back to her little white light to visit some sky repair guy. Devika prepared her white light to take us to a man she called Emerick, who lived just outside Loki. Upon arrival, we knocked on the door, and he answered, allowing us to enter. Once inside; he asked us why we were visiting him. Then Devika explained that we had to repair a crack in the sky that was just over Coon Hollow. Nevertheless; they were warned by the scientist that if the crack expanded, it could destroy both our dimension and the dimension beside us. He looked at us and said that this was very serious, however the expendable supplies that he had he could not afford to let them go. Devika explained that she might be able to get the money, if you give me an estimate? He asked her if it was possible for him to see this crack? She told him sure, as she waved, her little white light came and this time expanded large enough that we could easily walk through the door.

Emerick claimed that never seen something like this previously. Devika explained it was only used primarily for planet saving missions. We allowed him to set in the copilot's seat. Devika showed him how to adjust the camera and the equipment to obtain information that he needed. She also told me that if he got stuck or confused, to let her know, and she would fix it for him. She started where we believe this crack began and continued to its end. Witnessing this; I told Devika that this crack was expanding. She made three passes to ensure that Emerick got the information that he needed. After the third pass, she told her machine to provide the summary report. Devika asked Emerick what information he needed? He told her how wide your crack was, what was the material that the cracks were made of. She told her machine that as it printed out another summary report detailing this information. Emerick was so surprised, revealing that usually it took him weeks to compute this information. He looked at this report and gave Devika an estimate of how much the supplies would cost, saying that he would provide 10 men for the first two days to help install the connecting cables, then after that it was up to her and me to finish his out. With this information; I asked Emerick what kind of work that would be? He explained, that the cabling will completely connect be crack, yet however before connecting it we would put some sealer in there. After this, we would put some mesh over the top of the crack, followed by additional sealer, and some of his white cloud mud. This would reinforce where the crack was making it stronger than it was previously, and with the steel cabling they had installed to connect it in this crack was never again coming open.

Accordingly; Devika informed her bosses that we would need an additional three white lights to help deliver all this material to the sky. The purpose of these white lights was to make sure we did not put too much pressure on the sides of the crack. They understood this completely and sent her five white lights, so that way each of the two men crews could have a white light right there beside them. We agreed that that was a very good idea, it would find white lights available, she paid Emerick. He agreed to help us load our five white lights telling us exactly what to put into each one and the order that we would load the supplies, the first part for each white light was 20 rolls of his metal reinforced cabling. He had showed us how to line them up so that way they can be easily rolled to the installation station. It was very important that two people were with the role when they are rolling. When they reach their installation station, there they are flat on the ground. This way the cable can easily be fed from the top down and there was no danger of rolling it into the crack, which if hit someone on the ground would instantaneously kill them. Next, we distribute the mesh on to each white light. The final thing was to distribute his magic white cloud mud and some tools to help apply it. After about three hours, we completed our loading. Emerick said it was good that we did this today, so that way when his men show up in the morning, we can proceed right to the worksite. He also invited us to stay at his house tonight, and that he had an upstairs that would be completely for us. Therefore; and the morning, we would make some breakfast and head up to the clouds. This part of the question for me as I asked Emerick what to do with our lunches while in the clouds.

Moreover; he said that his men always brought their own food and that we would be wise to prepare some food for us. Devika told me to follow her into the white light; she took me to another room that I never knew existed, basically because I had no reason to be looking around. She opened up three refrigerators and asked me what I will want for lunch tomorrow. I was very impressed with the collection of food that she had available. I so want to do it and asked her what she liked. She told me not to worry, because it was a learning experience for her and that if she ate something she did not like she would definitely remember it the next time she saw it. I told her maybe she could stand beside me, and I could feed her small samples of the sandwiches that I was preparing. She asked me why I was making sandwiches, which I told her that this was the most popular lunch time work food. She thanked me for teaching her this. She now had all six of the flight lights to retract small enough so that she could put them into the little holders on her waist belt. Emerick came rushing back into the house all frantic about 10 minutes after our retraction. He was terrified, believing that the white lights had left us. Devika, explained to him that the white lights were in a very secure location. This calmed the him down immediately. I whispered it could be because here is why she didn't tell him where they were. She told me telepathically that she still did not trust him for sure and that he had no reason to know where her vehicles were with her paid supplies on them. I gave her a kiss and thanked her for being so wise. Emerick asked us if we were married, in whom I replied I'm still waiting for her to say yes. She asked me back telepathically, saying the answer would be yes, every day and every night for eternity. I whispered in her ear they would have start making some wedding arrangements very soon. I also asked her if she was allowed to get married. She whispered in my ear she could, but she would have to give up her spiritual body.

At this time; Emerick asked us if we wanted to join him for supper. I asked him if he had enough extra food, in which he answered he had enough to feed an Army. Emerick explained to us that his wife got sick the previous winter and died. He had two sons and one daughter, who all were married and moved away from the mountains. I felt so sorry for him, knowing how painful and lonely an empty house can be. Emerick also told us that since this is leveled wisely and moves so easily and that he could travel up there, and he would go up there with this and supervise the operation for no additional charge. This way we would know without a doubt everything was done by the books and that our dimensions should be able to handle this. He asked us if we knew of any other cracks. Devika said that currently there were no other known cracks, however that did not mean that there were not any additional cracks. I finished eating and went upstairs to retire for the evening. Devika was not going to let me retire, especially on the night of my proposal. I went with the flow because when the candy store is open it is the only time you can eat the candy. We got to our room, I asked her if it was okay if I asked it out loud? She said if you must silly boy. I told her that I must because this question was always answered with a big kiss has tight hug. I don't know if such a custom exists but I could easily guess that neither did she. Therefore; I asked her if she would marry me? She quickly said yes and made sure that she obeyed that custom with a 20-minute hug and kiss. Boys, I don't know if this old man can keep up with these young whippersnappers.

Then again, who am I calling young, in that she is well over 6,000 years old? That brought another good question to my mind, and this was what if she gave up her spiritual body and took on a physical body which would age and eventually die. She said she would almost die, meaning that once her physical body died, her spirit would reunite with her current spirit body and resume her heavenly duties. Devika also told me that this was very common for many of the females who were serving in the heavens now. I asked her what about the males, and she said many did as well, it's just that she never paid much attention to them. Well, I told her it was time for us to snuggle up and get some rest. Just after this, I asked her if she was telling the truth about not knowing about any other cracks? She verified that they had no idea about this, and that they continue to appear, and many disappear without any human or spirit ever knowing about them. She said the main reason that we had to seal my crack was because it was apparent that evil spirits were aware of it and using it. Subsequently; it would only be a matter of time before they established another 13 houses, and black holes in all those other little nasty surprises, some of which we may not even know about yet.

Once this crack was sealed, the ones that we did not know anything about would be of no threat, considering their power source had been disconnected. I said, I guess let's see if we can get this bad boy rolling tomorrow. She told me that sometimes my words did I make sense to her. I asked her what words and at any time if I said something that confused her, she needed to tell me. What do they mean by bad boy? I told her that I meant this job or project. She then laughed and said sometimes human speaking is strange. I agreed with her and recommended that we get some sleep. The next morning, Emerick woke us up and already had a really nice breakfast prepared for my new wife to be and I. Devika went outside and expanded her white lights. She wanted to do this before the workers arrived, in case one of them got an idea, may be to steal it. I can't blame her for being fussy over these wonderful, powerful and so convenient spacecrafts. When they arrived, she put out that no one touch any controls, because she had all the controls synced into her panel. If someone accidentally pushed a button, it could result in their deaths. She therefore recommended that everyone sat in the chairs and washed their monitors or go to the game room and play some ping-pong pool or anything and just have some fun. She estimated that our landing site was about 400 miles above the earth in a straight shot up. This long trip could take as much as five seconds. In other words, as the doors closed, they would be opening up real soon and remain seated until you hear the all-clear button and hear her voice telling them to disembark. Everyone jumped into their respective white lights, and just as she told them, they were immediately at their direct worksite.

When she told everyone to disembark, everyone came out amazed and happy. Emerick said that that was the best ride, and fastest, smooth space ride he ever had. Devika showed everyone some oxygen tanks that were with the mask that came with them and recommended that everyone take one. Because oxygen deprivation has a nasty way of sneaking up on you. And you don't want to be dizzy around such a big crack in front of us. We all did exactly what she said, because we knew she knew what she was talking about. The workers now prepared to unload all the materials, in which Devika asked them not to do this, because of security reasons. If pirates or other bad people were to come here and see our supplies, that were in convenient piles, they would load them up and steal them; however, if we only had out what we were using and with the remainder in our ships, which were transparent and invisible, they would leave. She told everyone to look at the ships, snapped her fingers and they disappeared. Then she snapped her fingers again, and they reappeared. She told these men that you do not want to be out in the open when these pirates arrive because everyone would send you down to the surface ground. She had radars and alarms set to give us plenty of time to hide before these pirates arrived. Furthermore, she then looked at Emerick and asked him if he had ever worked on a crack in the sky. He told her this the first time; the previous installers would assemble the panels and take them up to the crack and install them over the open crack. I asked him if they used the cables that we had. He said unfortunately not and that is why so many of these cracks expanded beyond the large panels that they installed and fell to the ground, killing so many people. He said last year he refused to sell any crack filling supplies unless they showed him, first, that they had installed the cables.

Accordingly; I told him we might as well start installing these cables if he would show us how. We also got around him as he began pulling out five sets of tools. This first set actually came in two parts, both identical. It looked like a five headed single-line drill bit. He told us that first we had to drill the five holds, and after that they had to be at least a foot from the crack; as even two feet the from the crack was good, if we did not want to stand close to the crack. He said after we had drilled these holes, we would return these drills to our respective spaceships; and then roll out one role of the metal cabling to this side of our crack a few feet from the holes that we drilled. Furthermore, he showed us how they put the cable around the object, in which he turned it on and some lights began to flash. Likewise, he turned it back and the lights stopped flashing. At this time, he handed each one of his 10 employees a small, round badge to attach to their shirts. He told them that the cable came back it would head for that badge and make my contact with them, so please do not be standing by the crack by at least four or 5 feet back. Once they had the cable in their hand, all they had to do was come over and insert it into their next available drilled hole. They will continue this process, sending it back and forth until they have filled every hole. Once they filled every hole, they would simply call for him, and he would cut the remaining cable and prepare the end for its final attachment, in which after the final tightening this part of the cable would tie itself around any part of the cable that it could.

He further told us we do not adjust the tightening; this is done by the cable. Each time we get a new role, we roll the empty role back into our respective spaceships. He said this was a very simple process and is so essential in saving the lives of people who would someday travel underneath this crack, so for them give it our best. Take the time and work smartly, because we had a lot of roles to spin out today, since when we start today, we have to continue it, so that the crack does not rip out the cables that we had already installed. Therefore; take your time. It is the complete installation of these cables along the crack that provides maximum connecting power. Quality, not quantity, will save lives today and tomorrow. They continued this process throughout the day, with each crew having to install 20 roles of these metal rolls. When we were finished, Emerick motioned for the cables to begin tightening. We can feel our ground moving slowly toward the crack. Each tightens, it was leaving about one and a half inches open. He explained that this was for when the sun would overheat the ground, forcing it to expand. It was now extremely late in the evening, he therefore reminded his men to meet at the same place we did today for the next two days we would seal these holes, lay down the mesh, apply his white mud and then see what happens. It was not hard work. It just required careful attention to detail. Tomorrow, just like today, would only take up the supplies that we needed for the area we were working on. I also assured him that Devika and myself would be wearing weapons for their security tomorrow. Everyone goes up and will come down, hopefully in our wonderful ships. So now is time to head for home.

We loaded up and landed at Emerick. He once again requested that we stayed in his house with this evening in fact until we finished this job. Devika believed that this was a fair request and agreed on behalf of both of us. Emerick told us that there was a nice creek to bathe in below his house. Devika told him that the showers in the ships worked perfectly, and that he was welcomed to use one of them. The ships also had waterless clothing cleaners, so you take a shower with the clothing on the come out dry with clean clothes also. So Emerick jumped into the ship that he'd ridden on throughout the day. We all three met a few minutes later with clean clothes on and clean bodies. Emerick commented that he felt this was impossible. Devika explained to Emerick that we were using top-secret technologies and that he was not to tell anyone about it. We had also explained this to each of his men throughout the day. As we lay down that night, Devika told me that she had applied some powder around the side of the crack. She also added that no spirits were coming through that crack tonight. She just couldn't believe how much detail and comprehensive progress we have made today, and that for all generic purposes the remainder of this work was for cosmetics and of course future protection against the crack expanding for someone attempting to sabotage it. Furthermore, she also said she sent pictures of the work that was going today to her superiors, who were so amazed and felt very confident in the high quality of wrongful crack entry prevention in the future.

She said that they had been forbidden to engage in the crack sealing in the future due to the unfortunate deaths of so many people. She said that the crack sealing was forbidden for any complete panel assembly on the ground and then transferred to a crack site for installation. That was how she got around this, by saying that the material was scattered to the crack for installation on the crack itself. Since it back being used today showing all the drilling and cable being installed in these drilled holes then tightened in place. I felt good, having survived a day in the opening decided crack in the sky. Just a thought of this makes me cringe. Devika wanted to remind me that this would protect Coon Hollow and Coon Run Road. She also wanted to make sure that I remembered that this would make it almost impossible for me to revisit the other dimensions, while at the same time would make it almost impossible for them to visit here, considering that I may now have the entire force seeking for my head. I told her that you usually cannot have your cake and eat it too. Then I put my arms around her and said, "Why would I need anything from that dimension when I have everything that I need in my arms now. "With this we called it a night. I asked Devika if she really thought that marriage was worth all that she was throwing away. She reminded me that she was not throwing anything away but only taking maybe 30- or 40-year break from it, and all the sex would make up for that because she could have sex legally, something she wanted to do for her entire life. I mean, if she is so convinced that this is what she wants I should be thankful that I happened to be here when she wanted someone the most. She reminds me that the same can be said about so many other people, in that they had made great sacrifices only to have a world that did not know or care about the sacrifices that they had made.

While the next day came and we began our meshing. Devika and I decided to join the crew on this activity, and that it did not look that hard nor labor some and that the faster we had done the faster we can get back on the ground where I felt a lot more at ease. In the middle of the afternoon, Devika's alarms began to sound. I told everyone to lay down your tools and head inside the ship they came up in. Devika grabbed what looked like a light antitank weapon and put it on her shoulder with her legs secured, waited for the ship to stick its nose up on this cloud. The second it did she shot it, blowing it into thousands of small pieces. With this shot, her alarm went off, signaling it was safe to return to work. I asked her why she shot it, it was, she told me that her stick has told her that this enemy had to be eliminated. I asked her if she thought it got any messages off to the remainder of its group. She told me that all six of her ships scrambled all communications in this area and that her weapon completely shattered everything on that ship. Therefore; I asked her, does this mean we are safe now? She said, of course, called all the men to resume their work. I noticed that now the work pace was picking up. Emerick believed that the first coat of sealer was drying up now and that we can start putting some meshing on it tomorrow.

The only problem he said was that it was too late in the day to start the meshing, even though the meshing would go quick tomorrow because we all had cut enough pieces to complete our job. Tomorrow we would lay our cut pieces on top of the ceiling that dried today and then apply her final any coach of sealant and his magic white mud. Once we knew that the meshing was not going to move, we could mark this as a finished job. When we returned to Emerick's house that night, Devika told him we had to return to our home because she had some important business meetings she had to attend. When arrived at my house, I invited her in for a cup of coffee. She told me that as soon as she drank that coffee, she had to meet with her superiors. Somehow, they had discovered her intention to marry me. I asked her if this meant she was any kind of trouble? She told me absolutely not. They just wanted to know if I was okay and what our intentions were so that way, they could make the proper personnel adjustments to ensure that her position remained filled. I told her that I was married to her, and I was not going to have her replacement watching over me. She said that they would never allow that anyway, that replacement will be reassigned to other cases. I began thinking in my mind that there was no way to back out of this now, even though there is not an ounce of blood in the that did not want to completely see this thing through. I just couldn't live with myself if I knew had I shamed her from all her friends and people that she has worked with for thousands of years. Furthermore, I'm sure that everything will work out for us. Because worst-case scenario, or float around her little white light and hope that we were not destroyed by some flyswatter.

I prepared our supper, leaving one full plate in our refrigerator for her to eat when she came home. I also prepared our sandwiches for tomorrow's work. Furthermore, I didn't mind this. The only thing I mind is being here all alone in this house. Our final day of work arrived as we headed for our site. Our crew was feeling much more at ease now and completed this job by lunchtime. This track was metal tightened, double sealed, meshed, and muddied, so it no longer represented a portal in any form or manner into another dimension. I had two missions now: number one destroys the Coon Run Road Ghost; number two get married to Devika.

CHAPTER 15

Coon Run Road Ghost

I can see that the sun has risen, that the sunrays are making my face warm. Nevertheless; I appeared to be alone in this king-size bed. I roll around just to make sure, yet there is no doubt about now, for some reason, I am all alone. I should not be alone. I wonder where is Devika? After all this is in her white light in that I cannot think of anywhere else, she should be at this early in the morning. Therefore; I decide to get up, since there is no way, I can get back to sleep now. Consequently; I strolled downstairs to the kitchen and made me some coffee. I wait there for about one hour before Devika returns. When she returns, I asked if she wanted some coffee. She agrees to drink one cup, which I made for her. As we drink our coffee, she's unusually quiet. This prompts me to ask her if everything is, in order? She tells me that it is not all right. Notwithstanding; that is all she says.

Consequently; I asked her what is wrong? She explains that her superiors are calling her back and want to assign her to a new mission. I'm curious now, so as to why would they want to assign her to a new mission since first will not have finished this mission, and second, we want to establish an official relationship. She confesses that she never told them about our relationship, because if she did, they would have reassigned her. She does not understand how they discovered our relationship. Somehow, someone had been spying on us. But then I explained that when we were in public we behaved; we only did couple things when in this white light. She now suspected that some sensor or monitor in this white light had transmitted that information. Now she told me that they had restored her spiritual body to the original condition prior to this assignment, and that we could no longer engage in couple's intimate activities. I told her that that did not really matter to me because I was too old for that stupid stuff anyways. Moreover; they had agreed to allow her to help me find and destroy the Coon Run Road Ghost.

She warned, though, that they would be watching us. I thought that was good, in that if we got into any kind of trouble, they could help rescue us. Accordingly; I thought if they were watching us, we might as well get to work. Moreover; I asked Devika if she knew how we can find this Coon Run Road Ghost? She said that the only thing she knew to do was to program in information we had concerning this ghost, and then wait to see what her processors had determined. At the end of the first day, we had no luck, as Devika's supervisors questioned her about the status of our search. I decided to get involved with this conversation, and told them that if they had to stick their nose in our business, they could at least help us locate this ghost. With this, Devika's monitors began to blink and light up, and her large printer, which was hidden in one of her walls, appeared and began printing on a large sheet a map. I took this map over to our table and with Devika beside me, started to discuss its contents with her. It appeared to have a long winding river that ran across the called the Narfi River. This River ran between two extremely steep hills, which are called the Mountain of Flavius. The actual Valley in which the river ran through was called the Evander Valley. I asked Devika if she understood what this map meant, or for that matter what was this a map of? She had no idea, so I therefore asked her supervisors, what was this a map of? They explained that this is where the Coon Run Road Ghost resided at. The one thing that bugs me is I asked something a question, and that thing only answers that exact question. Is this a map of the entire Valley sandwiched in between a mountain and the river, with the sides naturally covered in forest?

Therefore; how the hell would I know where to look for this ghost. But I decided to play their little game and; therefore, asked them where on this map does this ghost reside at? I mean, if my mission is to eliminate this ghost, then it would make sense if I could at least find it. This is when the voice told me it did not know where the ghost was at this time, and we would have to simply wait. I call this so-called Devika supervisor, "the voice." I have yet to see this thing, only to hear it when he speaks. Furthermore, I then asked this voice if our presence here could be detected by this ghost? The voice said we cannot be detected by this ghost. Subsequently; now would just be a waiting game. I recommended that when the ghost does appear, that we study it before planning on how to execute it. The voice agreed, as now all we could do was wait. I then asked what was our attack plan, namely when the ghost appears what do we do? The voice now says, first we will spray it was a special ghost tracking spray. This way, when he goes disappears, we will be able to discover it once more. Next; we will shoot it with some of our spirit destruction missiles. I asked him how effective were these missiles. They claimed that they had about a 25% destruction rate. I then asked where we would fire these missiles from? The voice said they did not understand the question. I said that if we shot a missile from this ship, and it did not destroy the ghost would have a reference point for the counterattack. I recommended that we have three or four ships spread in somewhat of a circle; this way when that ship fired a missile it could relocate, and set up its defensive measures. While the ghost was messing with determining where the first missiles fired from, the second ship could fire a missile, take its countermeasures, while the third ship could fire a missile, take its countermeasures, while the fourth ship fired its missile and took its countermeasures. If the ghost was still not severely damaged, then the first ship to fire a missile, and we continue this circle until the ghost was executed.

Afterward; I asked where we actually were? This is when the voice told me, somewhere among the land of the dead. Okay, how did we get here, and how do we leave when finished? The voice then told me not to fear, but the light that I was in could move back and forth. Following this; I asked the light if there was anything else I needed to know? Except for some strange noises, this place was relatively quiet. About an hour later we could hear some strange noises as if something was clamoring into these rock walls. And there it was trying to look into our front window. I noticed that a red light on my dashboard was blinking. To be honest, this is something that I would consider as being something else that I needed to know. His voice was able to volunteer some information when I asked what this blinking light was all about? The voice told me that this was to tell me that the ghost was nearby. Since it was right in front of me, I cannot fire at it from another one of our ships, for fear that the ghost could move in our laser beam and damage my ship. The voice told me to be patient and wait for this ghost to move. About five minutes later, the ghost did move as my ships began to lock onto it and in sequence began to fire.

This ghost was seriously damaged, and making some strange, eerie painful sounds. The voice ordered the ships to continue firing. However; the ghost was able to limp away and drop into a black hole beside it that just became visible. The voice recommended that remained here and drop charges into this hole. We could be entering into an ambush if we attempted to follow the ghost in. We had a tracking powder so we knew where the ghost was going. Actually; as I had no idea what we were or where anything was down here, the only thing we might know is where the ghost was hiding. The voice now discovered that the ghost was hiding in a large chamber, with enough space for our lights to enter and once again circle it. Once in place, again our ships began firing in circular motion, scoring multiple hits. These hits were not enough, as the ghost was able to ascend straight up toward the surface. This forced us to find another route out, to avoid a potential ambush. A few minutes later, our sensors were able to locate this ghost. It appeared to be motionless, as our ship sensors were reporting that it was no longer alive. Devika recommended that her and I exit our ship and ensure that it was indeed dead. I tried to explain to her that by definition ghosts were dead, this will put our lives in danger to receive valueless information. We could just as easily safely continue to fire from within our ships. After a few minutes, the voice recommended that we exit this ship and attempt to put the ghost into a container that could be removed from the Earth. Now this made sense to me, so Devika and I took a container and exited the ship. Devika made it to the ghost a few steps ahead of me and attempted to place the ghost in her container. When she touched the ghost, I saw sparks flying everywhere as her arm vanished in the air now filled with a burned flesh smell.

At this point the voice put in front of me a large container with the unique grabbing device in which I was able to secure the ghost and place it inside this container. The voice along with some small robotic devices placed the container inside one of the lights. Once inside, that light exploded. The ship, container, and ghost and vanished. Devika motioned, with her one good arm, for me to follow her into another light. Once inside, we activated the monitors, to see if they were detecting the location of the ghost. Unfortunately; the ghost was still in existence and had once again descended into the Earth. I noticed that one of our lights vanished and then about one later we reappeared as two lights. One of these lights began shooting a thick laser beam into the Earth, approaching the proximity of where the ghost was. We could see where the hole was materializing extremely close to where the ghost was. Next, the lights began to drop a lot of missiles down this freshly dug tunnel, exploding around where the ghost was alleged to be. Two additional tunnels were created with this laser beam, as missiles were released almost nonstop for the next 10 minutes. Each exploding missile was taking something from this ghost. After about 20 minutes later, all of our ships verified that the ghost was indeed no more. With this, our lights sealed the tunnels that they had created. The ghost of Coon Run Road was no more, with Devika paying the price with one of her arms.

At this time, I could feel some ropes tying up my feet and arms and can see the same happening to Devika. I asked her why we were being tied up? She told me we had to appear before her superiors. Soon we were once more in her clouds, except this time we were not released into our chambers, but instead placed inside jail cells. Unfortunately; our cells were not visible to each other. I then asked something why we were here. The voice once more began talking, telling me that the spirits were reviewing the recordings made by our spirits on charges of an illegal human spiritual relationship. I was so confused that I simply fell into my cell. The next day, I appeared before some lights, in which they declared me to be innocent. I then asked them what would happen to Devika? They told me that she had deliberately deceived them and me and broke many of their sacred laws. As such, her existence was to be terminated. This made me feel really sad inside because actually I truly did have some intense feelings for her. I started to think why she did what she did, unless it was to have what my Queen's had. This is just me guessing, because I had no idea why, except that love can sometimes make people do some very strange things. I can never forget what a great warrior she and how we fought side-by-side to acquire the 13 stones and terminate the 13 houses. Personally; I think her superiors actually were a bunch of jerks who had overreacted; however, that would be something, someday I would have to discuss when I entered the spiritual realm.

Her spiritual supervisors once again appeared before me and told me that their mission on Coon Run Road, Coon Hollow, and the Coon Run Road Ghost, had finished successfully with a complete victory. It was now time for me to cease my contact with the spiritual world of this dimension and return to my physical realm. When they clarified the spirit realm of this dimension, I asked them if that was inclusive of our sister dimensions? They told me that this was being decided currently. Prior to my transfer, they informed me that all knowledge of my sister concerning my spiritual activities had been erased and that there would be no dissolving of the split in the dimensional lines. They had to erase these memories from her mind to prevent an evil force that had destroyed my previous throne from entering into this world and destroying them as well. This was strictly for her protection. I could now feel myself being sucked back into my body, which had been transferred back from the hospital to the coma center. My muscles felt so weak, as I could easily acknowledge my end was near. I felt the pain returning. And it absolutely experienced how debauched this felt. I truly thought I was past this, but then again, I must be on a revolving circle that just seems to be spinning in a circle. I do not even know if I can muster up the energy to fight these battles, once more. Furthermore, I can merely hope that the previous battles had their victories somewhere in time. Was this my reward from so much hard work to free Coon Hollow?

CHAPTER 16

The Ending

The sole thing that I remember is that I could not remember. I felt as though I accomplished all my objectives and was preparing to return to my home out somewhere; however, even that location is escaping my mind at the current time. For some reason, I feel as if I did not belong in this body that will not move. This is something that is going to get old real fast and that is having to lay in bed all day without the ability to move. My solitary source of information is from listening to the nurses talk. They were claiming how disappointed they were in my return, considering I was making such great progress. They were saying that I was out of the regular hospital and existing at home without the need of any medical attention. In other words, for some strange reason, I had awakened. I don't really know what they meant by that phrase except that I was doing well.

My confusion lays in the fact that I do not remember how I made it back into this so-called coma center. I do know that I am tired and just want to go to sleep, question being what would happen to me, if I would want to sleep. There may not be any good valid reason why I should resist, considering one minute I was recovered and the next minute I relapsed months back into a prior unhealthy nonfunctional condition. There is one constant, and that is the increasing pain that I am feeling throughout my body. And let me tell you, I do not like pain. To me, it is a punishment for trying to survive. Each breath is also becoming more problematic and strenuous. This being; there is a pain associated with this difficulty. Nevertheless; the harder I fight not to breathe the harder my body fights to get that fresh air into my lungs. One of many things I detest about this current condition is not knowing where I was or where I should be or where I want to be. I'm having difficulty in formulating a solid thought. I do know that the more I think about this stuff, the less time I have to concentrate on this pain.

At this time; a doctor and two nurses enter into my room. The nurses tell the doctor they noticed no change in my condition, that my blood pressure is dangerously too low and my blood oxygen levels are disappointing to say the least. The doctor believes my body is preparing to shut down, and based upon my current relapse it may be advisable to go ahead and let it shut down. Even I find myself agreeing with this analysis, and if I'm not going to get better than maybe I had better move on, just as the rest of humanity has done the previous thousands of years. After all, it is appointed unto all men to die. A terrifying thing about this, is that those who are dead appeared to be at peace. Who am I not to know that they too are screaming inside their bodies? Either way; whatever the doctor says, will be my destiny in that I had no way to communicate a desire otherwise. Why is my memory so empty? I've had to do something in my life; but what was it? Were there other people in my life? It is hard to imagine that someone could have lived an entire lifetime as a hermit. I realize that I have been in this medical facility for three days now with no visitors. That has to tell me something. And what it is telling me is not good nor is it completely bad. It's just like everything else in its current condition and that is a big fat nothing. The nurses gave me a couple shots and replaced the bags that are feeding me intravenously. I would assume that one of those is food considering I'm not eaten for three days nor am I hungry so somehow the food is entering my body and these tubes are the only things that are going in my body. I also noticed that I am wearing an adult diaper. Strange that we would wear a diaper coming into this world and wear a diaper leaving it. At least this time around I do not have to change these diapers because they don't look or smell good at all. I am noticing that for the first time in a few days it feels like my pain level is dropping; which leads me to believe that one of the shots or maybe both of my shots are for pain management.

Subsequently; I really had no idea what these shots were for; however, the pain is going down but also so is my blood pressure, blood oxygen, and my heart rhythm is starting to become flatter. Now there is a tall slim totally black faceless thing sitting in a chair beside me. It looks at me and introduces itself as death. I consider death as a chance to get out of this nonfunctional body; however, I do not want to jump out of the frying pan and into the fire. In an attempt to communicate with this thing, I ask it why it is here? It tells me that my appointed time has not arrived. One of the janitors comes into my room, with a few boxes of cleaning supplies and begins to restock the shelves in this room. I noticed a shipping label on one of these boxes and an address in the state of Washington. When I saw this address, I remembered that I lived in the state of Washington. I finally got some little piece of information about my body or life only with death staring me in my eyes. Once the janitor left my room, a nurse came in to record some numbers from my monitors. While she was recording these numbers, another nurse enters and starts talking. They are in agreement that my time is quickly approaching. I have always had disappointment in the current medical profession; yet at the same time feel fortunate enough not to have to had relied on the medical profession in my preceding centuries. It appears to me that they are simply waiting for me to die, rather than trying to think of ways to improve my current condition, if it can be improved. I just don't know enough to make any sort of determination.

At this time; three little white lights enter into my room. At the sight of these white lights, death gets up and vanishes through the wall. The white lights reformed into Angels. They form a triangle around my bed saying nothing. I; therefore, asked him why they are here? They tell me to have no fear for they are not here to hurt me. Therefore; once again I asked him why they are here? They told me to be patient for they were waiting for the light to guide me into eternity. Everything that I could ever remember about a white light and going into eternity was good, which basically means that I might as well relax and be patient as they told me to do. I think it may have been the excitement of being able to talk to something that led me to question if they knew anything about my life? Unfortunately; they told me that they did not know, except to tell me that good things usually happened to those whom they came for. I asked them what they meant by the word usually? They told me that meant to the best of their knowledge and that they had no knowledge of any unfavorable events happening to those who they guided into the white light. Now the white light became so bright that I could not see anything in my room. These angels took my arms and guided me into this light. At this time, I can vaguely hear the monitor alarms in my room began to sound as if to signify that I had died. I can see my bed being moved down the hallway and my body being stored in a room in the basement. This begins to fade out as I am now concentrating on being inside this bright white light that is spinning somewhere. I guess my story is over, if only I could remember what this story was. I guess it does not really matter now, does it?

The judge

I survive one more day in my serene daytime world, spending the entire day with my family. Consequently, I realize that having them another day is revealing rivers of miracles. It amazes me how humanity can create great technological things; nevertheless, still has vastly limited knowledge about the functioning of the human body. My exhaustion plummets with me going into a deep sleep. I feel a smooth wave of tranquility flow through my nighttime soul. Just as I begin to take a deep breath, enjoying the harmony of this new place, I notice something that changes my serenity. I am sitting in a courtroom, with George sitting beside me.

Many of the people sitting in this courtroom were fellow neighbors who were nothing more than acquaintances; nevertheless, so far, they haven't been hostile. When I take my daily walk, several waves, others sit on their porch and stare through me. I consider ignoring better than aggressively challenging. The judge and defendant's seats are empty. The prosecuting attorney and his aides are prepared. Next, the judge comes into the courtroom as the bailiff calls for everyone to rise. Everyone rises, then the judge seats. After everyone sits down, as an attorney with Ben beside him came walking into the courtroom. The judge jumped up, as did everyone in the courtroom, except for George and me. A man beside me begins screaming for us to stand up now. Two men behind us lift us up on our feet. We elect not to struggle or intensify the situation. We hold our peace as those around us divert their attention back to the courtroom. I ask George what sort of courtroom is this.

I have never seen the defense have so much power as this. Ben stands up, turns around looking at me and declares that I should be the one sitting in his seat. The judge tells Ben to relax, because they will find a way to put me in that defendant's seat. This quickly puts a lump in my throat. I ask George why we came today. He explains the sheriff asked us to be here to back up his deputy's testimony. The defense calls Ben to the stand. I never heard of a case where the individual charged ran the courtroom. This was scary indeed. Rumor had it that Ben had more anger against the sheriff than he had against me, since the sheriff showed him, his cat and then gave it to the animal shelter, which ended putting it down forever. Ben vowed never-ending revenge when he heard this. Fortunately, my neighbors told him that his cat purred around my legs. Ben knew that George, and I would provide a little catnip and treats occasionally. We did that, for the most part, to lure him back into his yard, as we never gave him the treats, unless we were in his yard. I did not want to motivate him to camp out in my yard. I constantly wondered why I was not fond of that cat, yet suspect most likely; it was because of my intense dislike for Ben.

I have been around cats long enough to mask my genuine intentions because if they believe you do not like them; they will hover around you. Somehow, that cat could read our true minds; nevertheless, he would not forgo his catnip and treats. I suspect that cats, like people, think differently when their bellies are empty. I return my focus to the matter at hand. The judge reads the charge and each time he mentions Bens' name everyone cheered. Ben had control of this courtroom, much to the bewilderment of George and me. He did not do anything special around the community, except drive into town after work, shunning all who came around him. This forces me to ask George what we did to make these people so angry. George replies that all we had to do was breath and appear to mourn over the loss of our families. We still held contempt because no one in town, except for a few of my wives' closest friends, showed any remorse or concern for our bereavement. I was shocked when the girl scouts and 4h clubs came soliciting at our door. We felt as if they believed we had a disease or through secret evils deserved our fate. George and I both kept a full suitcase in our trunks as part of our contingency fast evacuation plan.

We each also kept a crossbow and two containers of arrows that came with it. We live too close to a state border and therefore, cannot keep firearms in our vehicles and travel over state boarders. I often wonder why we stay in this town, even though a part of me claims this is to hold onto my previous family life memories. This makes some sort of sense; however, that would be at the subconscious level, which should predominate now. Somehow, this is not as great for a concern currently, as I can see Ben looking over at us. It is only a matter of time before he unleashes on me. He is most likely exploring his options to decide when best to attack. Considering, I am not as lost in this episode as I usually am, realizing I just jumped from an earlier part. Nonetheless, I have yet to determine the true underlying cause of this friction. George believes it stems from his old European heritage and racism against the Asians. Ironically, his German ancestors caused the same, if not more, grief as the Japanese, as my wife was. This is hard for many westerners to realize the variations in the Asians resemble the variations in the Europeans. A Frenchman is as much British as a Filipino is Japanese, just as a snowball has as well a chance in Hell as I do in this courtroom on this day. The sole chance I have today is that I am not on trial. I appreciate George's advice that I keep my cool, which I must agree.

A victory in a battle today would have little effect on the outcome in the battle ahead of us. Any ways, I want to get a feel for what Ben has planned. I wonder how psychotic he is going to get in each stage of this waste of life. We recognize the sheriff is merely the first hurdle on the road we must negotiate. A strange-looking man came running through our courtroom. He was yelling at people and quickly gained control of all who were here. He appeared to be concerned that the court had not built a special cage for George and me. The judge explains that police officers are guarding the doors and that he has muscle men sitting around us. Nevertheless, the man begins to yell at the judge, as Ben stands up and tells him to wait outside this courtroom. The man at once obeys Ben, as everyone, including the judge, applauded him. I hear the men behind me tell his friend that this is yet, but another example of the high moral character of Ben. The applauding continues, as many begin standing while they are clapping on Ben's behalf. George and I also stand before Hercules, who is sitting behind, puts us on our feet.

We pretend to clap and merely lip serviced our cheers. Even though infinitesimal, we wanted to make sure not to be contributors to our own fates. Ben finally stands up and motions for everyone to be quiet. The audience and judge obey his most-recent command. I wonder how I was stuck living beside this lunatic; nonetheless, I find it harder to place the sole blame on him. The people who surround him are feeding him. I wonder what I would do if I had a mob of people begging to obey my every command. The judge finally calls this court in session as Ben takes the defendant's chair, and two police officers come back to me when the lead one bends over and whispers in my ear to follow him. I get up on my feet and walk behind him, as the second police officer guarded me from behind me. They escort me to a dirty chair positioned center of the courtroom in the wide open. The police officers report, aloud, to the judge the agitator is seated in the guilty man's chair. The courtroom naturally applauds, creating within me a desire for a future event in my town where I can torture each one of them. This is not as any courtroom should be, forcing me to accept this mad house as my temporary existence. The trouble with the provisional part is that this temporary is now. Once it becomes as before, I will be relieved, or at the minimum work harder to keep it in our history.

Considering that, I must stand tall and defeat this now; my testing moments presently manifested their desire to engage. The judge ordered his quest for justice to begin. I wondered what fantasy world he lived in, because this room had everything but justice. Ben looked at me and asked why I constantly tortured his cat. Accordingly, I told him that my sole contact with that cat was to provide stress relief and treats to offset the horrifying neglect he unleashed to that poor creature. George stands up and seconds my statement. The judge tells George this is a court trial and not a procedural hearing. Ben stands up and tells the court, this is the proof of how George and I live lies and are solely interested in defaming him. The prosecution asks that I not be permitted to lie in court. My attorney tells the judge that Ben is the lone one to lie in this court so far. Ben asks the prosecution that if the judge does not allow me to speak, how can he prove to the jury about the extent of the lies and attempts to deceive the jury.

The judge orders the attorneys to sustain and let Ben continue proving his innocence. I turned to the judge and asked why I was here, as there is no evidence throughout the world that could ever prove Ben innocent. The judge asks me to tell the court what happened that day. Accordingly, I begin by telling the court that Ben had other crazy spells and this time combined his threats with actual gunfire. Ben asks me why the sheriff did not take any pictures of my shattered windows. I told the Judge Ben's company agreed with the sheriff if they replaced the windows, he would let Ben slide on that part of the charge, with a promise that if he ever did it once more, these charges would be added. The company sealed an agreement with the sheriff, including signed statements with photos of the damage and physical evidence of the broken windows. Ben asks me what happened to this evidence. I told Ben that I did not monitor the internal administration of the sheriff's office; however, I am sure if they would cooperate with even a corrupt court.

At this time, Ben officially accuses me of lying about these shots. I ask Ben if he shot two of my windows. He stands up proud and tall and denies any of my windows were shot that day.

I felt so relieved that he denied any of my windows were shot and thus claimed no windows had been damaged. At this, I walk to the jury and ask them to open some dated emails on my phone. Ben, who was foolishly convinced I had no evidence, allowed me to show this to the jury. Fortunately, for us, our neighbor from across the street took pictures of Ben shooting my house and emailed them to George and myself. Considering this, George opened his copy of the email, and we viewed these pictures and downloaded them to his spare laptop, he kept in his attic, we elected not to open my email. The jury opened this email and looked over the pictures. The judge then asked to see the email. The jury member forwarded this email to his fellow members and next gave my phone to the judge, who looked at it, pushed a button, and afterwards asked where the pictures were. I asked the judge how he knew there were pictures on my phone. He stuttered and explained he heard the jury talk about seeing pictures. Thereafter, one jury member tells the jury, this is the judge's lucky day, because he will email him another copy.

The prosecution became angry that evidence has been exposed to the jury that is not favorable to Ben. George asks the judge how such a guilty man can find justice. The judge tells George he will find the answer for that question when I stand trial. I shake my head in disbelief, yet must accept at least the injustice that is in the open here and not hidden like a secret as in most other courts. I am appalled each day when I see the injustices and corruption in the judicial system in my daytime world. The foolishness of a few greedy police officers can doom the life of an innocent man. This is a prime reason I am exercising much patience during this process currently; in that I truly want to find the legitimacy behind Ben's perception. I know when two people look at the same thing; each may have a different view of what they see. It appears that so many in my community share Ben's view, which is a mystery to me. Accordingly; I turn and ask Ben why he has treated my former family and me so unjustly. Ben claims that he had tried extremely hard to accept the wicked ways of George and me, nevertheless, must accept the views of the others who live in our town that I am too malicious to reform. I decide to withdraw my offensive and play it conservatively until I get out of this challenge.

I hold many views against the power of the American government as they have stripped away too many of our rights. Understanding the realm of this issue is beyond my adventures in unconscious. I am finding the openness of the prejudice to be refreshing. I consider it a sense of security in the judge has yet to be hostile. Nevertheless, this was about to change. Ben tells the judge he is done with me, that since I continue to lie, it might be better to let me think about my evil ways before my confession. The judge told me to take my seat and for the bailiff to call in the sheriff. The sheriff comes in with TV crews from two area stations, plus dozens of reporters. The judge told the reporters to get out of his courtroom, or he would declare them in contempt and sentence them to long prison terms. The sheriff tells the judge not today. Notwithstanding, he walks up to the judge and hands him an official order from the State's Adjutant General. The sheriff looked at Ben and told him to sit in his seat beside his attorney. The sheriff then looked at Ben's attorney and asked him if he would tell the court what happened that night. The sheriff explained the event as it happened.

Ben continued to disrupt the proceeding by objecting. Finally, the sheriff looked at Ben and told him he would get his chance to talk, and if he interrupted him one more time, he would arrest him for obstructing a police officer. Ben asks the judge if the sheriff can do this. The judge told him he did not know; nevertheless, he recommended that Ben sat down and stopped interrupting the sheriff. The sheriff told the judge and news reporters that I had no business being here and that George, and I should be released. Afterwards, the sheriff released his frustration on Ben. The sheriff told Ben that it was only a matter of time before they get him across the county lines and then send him to a federal prison. Ben smiled at the sheriff and told him to keep on dreaming. The sheriff hands Ben a judgment that his construction company be dissolved and that anyone still associated with it in two days be sent to prison. He also hands Ben a subpoena to appear in a federal court located in our state capital in two weeks. The judge asks the sheriff why the federal government is interfering with local jurisdictions. The sheriff explains that some homes in West Virginia, with many in Ohio are complaining about receiving threats if they did not purchase this unwanted construction.

Ben's lawyer explains to him that by going over state borders, the federal government could take jurisdiction. Ben asks him about the subpoena. His lawyer explains they will talk about that later. The sheriff takes George and me with him as he leaves the court. The judge demands he leaves us there. The sheriff tells the judge that he no longer needed us as a witness, and since they are not on trial here, he will give us a ride home. The sheriff makes us a strange offer. He recommends we get out of our hometown for a few months for our own safety. He tells me that his neighbor died last year and that his estate needed someone to stay there and make some small repairs, supplies at the estate's responsibility. George and I thought this might be a good idea. The farm is five miles off the highway and tucked off the country road with merely a small path back to it. The sheriff asks us to give him a list of things that need to be secured in our homes before they yellow tag them as crime scenes.

He also asks for a list of clothing and volunteers to bring any perishables, such as leftovers in the refrigerator and fruits. We made our lists as he sent his deputies to secure them for us. We got word later that week that by some great mystery, Ben was found not guilty of the charges. Most commentators attributed this to the pronounced lack of justice in our county. Unfortunately, for Ben the state highway patrol with some federal marshals took him to our state capital, where he was convicted for tax fraud and sent to prison. He sold his house to pay for legal counsel. We vanished during this social event, thereby keeping ourselves disassociated. The judge was also convicted and sent to prison. George and I worked our way back into our homes. Life was different now in our hometown, as most neighbors simply avoided us in their shame. George and I readjusted rather harshly. We could solely feel pain and death around us. It did not help those two men who were shot in my front yard. Consequently, it is almost as if I can sense them being in my yard. Each night I could hear them scream, as they continually call out my name to save them. This tortures me in that how could I save men who would kill me on sight. George and I were victims, yet things worked out fine for us in the view that we were on the road to recovery.

I wish consequently, that this road was not so long, and it would not be over so many events. Ben sent me a letter apologizing. My minister, or should I say the minister of one small church in our town recommended that I keep a low profile and ignore the letter. If Ben writes an additional letter, we will deal with that when it happens, if it actually happens once more. Somehow, the sanctuary farms the sheriff provided offered enough distractions to divert my normal concentration on my self-pity, as George would label my behavior. I had not realized it has endured this long. I am not the first to have faced this type of life event, yet I am truly sad that I hope to be among the lasts. Subsequently, I realize that healing is a process that takes time and effort. Suddenly, I was going to, for the second time; during my life learn how to walk. Accordingly, I looked at George and asked him if he was glad to be back in town. He looked at me as if I had lost my mind declaring the farm, we were temporarily safeguarding was at least 100 times better than our small lots in this town. He so much enjoyed feeding animals and playing on the tractors. I knew other events lay ahead of me, and my time here, was ending. I lay down; hoping tonight would be the first night.

Psychotic Phantasmagoria Divulgence

Vision 30 Insect Invasion and War

Vision 13 The Baby Factory

VISION 30

Insect Invasion and War

This was the third day that we had rain. And I am so happy because we just went through the no-rain season. The last three months have been dry, with my sprinklers almost working nonstop to keep my front yard somewhat green. My yard was doing wonderful as in order to show off my green, which I fertilize with Max green from Scott, I raised my mower to number four. The trouble was that the grass was wanting to lie down, which killed the grass it was laying on. Accordingly; I decided to lower my mower back down to three. This created a bunch of bald spots which turn a nice yard into a hideous giant pile of bold spots. I was wanting to take one small area where there were a lot of these spots and expand our flower bed.

Annika pleaded with me not to do so. I was just standing in this light rain, allowing the water to soak into my clothing. Then the rain stopped and the sun came out bright causing me to blink my eyes, and there was Twister. The rain returned as did the darkness because I was out quite early. Twister opened her door, and in I went. Accordingly; Annika came stumbling in, wearing her robe and appearing somewhat sleepy. Twister apologize for the disturbance as she went transparent, so that no neighbor could see us. Twister explained that this mission was going to be much more difficult than the previous ones, yet the survival of humanity rested on it. Twister assured me that every Twister like unit, to be honest I don't know what you call it other than wonderful, magnificent, many times unbelievable, had been assigned to this case, as also over 100 science labs. I looked over at Annika and said good morning the humanity saving girl. She took a sip of her coffee, then said her good morning to me. I looked around the area where I was sitting and sure enough there was a cup of coffee. I also took a sip.

Twister placed on a video which she had made although appearing as a human, and of course an extremely beautiful human female. I have to listen and look at this gorgeous female, while sitting beside my gorgeous wife. I was thinking, was my luck, was changing? The video began showing three boys playing baseball with a gang of other boys. The three boys, even though intermingled with the baseball team, had bright yellow uniforms. Naturally, the bright yellow uniforms were only appearing like that for Annika and myself. They were in a small town called Stanford, in Kentucky. Unfortunately, for the three boys the baseball park was on the opposite side of town in the First Southern Veterans Park. However; they would move back and forth across town using their bikes. They lived on Redwood Drive, beside Arn Mowing and Landscaping. Ironically; all three boys fathers worked for Arn. Their mothers were fortunate to find work in a nearby store called Ump-Attire. They were not from rich families, yet in Kentucky some steady flow of cash, enough to cover the rent and the limited groceries that they purchased were enough to survive. A farmer a few miles out of town gave them a very large lot for growing vegetables, with a condition that he got one-third of the final harvest, and got to select the one third. They also were able to give the boys some money for McDonald's, which was on their way back home.

This was not considered a luxury; they just prevented the mothers from having to rush home and prepare meals for the boys. Instead; they would prepare dinner around 7 PM for their entire families. The boys always arrived home from baseball around 4 PM. This gave them three hours to do their homework in a leisurely playful manner. Because if they waited until their fathers got home, they would have their noses deep in those books accomplishing every little detail of the homework. The three boys were named Billy age 13, Randy age 13, and Timmy age 14. They currently were studying chemistry. The teacher gave them an experiment to work on for their homework. They were to mix three chemicals, actually two chemicals with water. The ingredients were sodium chloride and NaCI, with water. The purpose was to watch the water dissolved and breakdown the NaCI. They had a microscope in which they were supposed to view these chemical reactions as they occurred. While selecting the ingredients, they knew that the NaCI was salt, nevertheless, they could not figure out what the sodium chloride was. Unfortunately; none of the three boys were paying attention today in class. Somehow, their encyclopedia was saying this was salt. Now they looked at each other and wondered how they could mix salt with salt and water. I was just plain stupidity until Randy came up with a solution. He said his mother had some Clorox which had to contain sodium chloride. He suggested that they also used some vinegar to offset the Clorox.

Therefore; they mixed the vinegar, chloride, salt and watched throughout the weekend to see what happened. Something did happen, and that was that it filled the house with smoke and it was smelly smoke. Notwithstanding; the smoke wilted some of his mother's flowers. Randy could not think right now. That's when Billie and Timmy took control of the situation and opened the windows, so the smoke could leave the house, or essentially air out the house. Little did they know that the smoke from the house had soaked into the flower bed in front of the house. In this bed were some insect eggs, and for the purposes of this mission we will tell you the three of them were: first one was the Tsetse fly, the second was the kissing bug while the third one of interest to us was the assassin Caterpillar. The smoke settled into the dirt and when their mother watered her flowers each evening for a remainder of the summer, the smoke broke down into something else, these new elements mixed with some elements of the fertilizer that his mother gave her flowers. Their molecules and atoms re-bonded creating a new element that was able to dissolve itself through these insect eggs walls. While in there they continued their re-bonding, which resulted in something new and evolutionary. While most of the eggs died six of them survived, namely two Tsetse Fly, two Kissing Bug, and two Assassin Caterpillar's. And supposedly with the help from the evil ones they were male and female, which meant the possibility of being able to reproduce.

Once these chemicals kicked in the new insects quickly worked free from their eggs and proceeded to escape in the nearby woods. Kentucky offered them the woods to develop. They began to grow and grow and never slow down growing until they were six feet tall, with the Assassin Caterpillar being 10 feet long. Their growth created big appetites, and the creation of these new insects also modified their eating habits. They now discovered that vegetation was not working, although it would if it was combined with flesh. The animals were too quick to catch. Therefore; they migrated over to Junction City. Here they proceeded to School Street, where they discovered the Junction City Elementary School. Therefore; they picked the strategic areas for the attack on any kid that was standing alone. Once in such a target was established, they would have their other members join them. Their attacks must be brutal and quick. Their digestive systems also evolved to where blood could substitute for flesh. They were able to drain the blood from one small girl during the recess. Accordingly; the girl did not return to her classroom after recess. The other students claimed that she did not play with anyone. This gave these insects time to get back into the woods. During the next recess, some students, while playing discovered this deceased girl.

The coroner noted the insect bites and the lack of blood. It was this common notation that allowed the researchers to discover the bodies which had died from these insect bites. Therefore; the corner filled out his report in the town and moved on as normal. Notwithstanding, two weeks later the insects found another victim while hiking. This was perfect because it gave them the chance to feed on both the blood and also feast on the flesh of the young adult's body. The insects found that they had to eat at least once every three days. Accordingly; they proceeded back to the elementary school and selected another child and drained her blood. They continued to wait for another hiker to come to this trail. Another hiker did, and they got him. They were big enough that they could initiate a straight on attack. With the six of them having designated points to target they were able to quickly kill hiker. When they went back to the elementary school, they discovered that there were changes. With the death of the second child, the elementary school suspended operations until some state insect officials could make a determination. The state officials immediately had all the school and the area surrounding, both inside and outside, completely fumigated.

When the insects returned the chemicals from the fumigation lightly affected them, enough to provide them a solid deterrent. Notwithstanding; the two hikers had been discovered from their family members who returned to conduct extensive search. This was enough to request additional assistance from the state. Also, all hikers were advised to stop hiking. The buddy rule kicked in, and this was where no single person was allowed to be in public. You had to be with another human being. Accordingly; the trails were fumigated. The insects migrated to the north, with a child's killing an average of two per town. Not all of these towns took these deaths seriously; consequently, they all did mark in their notation, the loss of blood. The insects began to multiply, and when insects multiply, they multiply extensively. This was when they split off into the three separate directions. They continued to randomly feast as they spread throughout the neighboring states. Sadly; within one year they killed over 1,000 people. A few ambitious government employees began to notice a serious problem, yet could not identify what was doing this because the bites that were big enough now to be confused with animal bites, yet the extensive and strange footprints indicated insects. The insect portion was put on the back burner, considering insects do not get that big. It was not until two years and the death of 10,000 people, that the government began to take this seriously. The trouble was no one knew what to do and how do you fight an invisible enemy, one that had never been seen by any person?

That ended on a June day in 2028, when a hunter spotted one of these insects through the scope on his rifle. He was able to use his phone and zoom in capturing a low-quality grainy video. Luckily; the police were able to enhance the quality, however the police were able to enhance this enough to get a visible picture. The death toll in this state alone had already reached 30,000 people. The numbers of these insects were increasing so much that they were forced to start hunting in the open. As the police went to release this photo, the governor of the state asked them not release it yet, to give them some time to set up some emergency facilities to treat the mass hysteria they predicted that would occur. The governor asked for two weeks to do this. Naturally the police had no choice but to comply. Consequently; hunters in other states began to release photos of these giant insects. Naturally, some hysteria occurred but not to the degree the government originally thought this would take. The public knew that they had a serious enemy existing among them and therefore began to take many precautions to slow these creatures down. Reports began to surface as a few of these insects were killed. Information about the dead insects was released as the media flooded their publications with these details and additional higher-quality photos. The trouble was that these reports were only released in the state where these insects had been killed. Notwithstanding; the deaths were now manifesting themselves nationwide, with one federal estimate that now over 300,000 Americans had died.

This was when the president issued a nationwide warning and update declaring a state of emergency. Twister informs us that this warning went out yesterday, and that they now estimated that over one million of these insects currently existed in the United States. I personally have never liked insects. I particularly hated the fleas and mosquitoes. This is why I permit spiders to create their web's outside of my house. They, in essence, help me catch some of these two insects plus a few other species. The flipside to this is when I see the reason my vegetables had so many holes in them and even my flowers. Especially my dahlias, where they were eating these completely enough to kill the plant. When I got my insecticide out, the label claimed to kill over 100 types. Then I sprayed it; it killed nothing. I have used foggers before, with limited success. My best victory was what I did when living in the barracks in South Korea. I used this poison that claimed the insect would take back to their nesting area and spread some kind of disease or something to wipe them out.

A couple of months later by accident I found that nest, was in my container for my 360 floppies. There must have been at least a 100 of them dead. I asked Annika about her experiences with insects. She claims that until today, she never saw an insect. That was because the generation before her ate them all. Therefore; they were completely nonexistent when she was born. I immediately ran for Twister's restroom and began to vomit. My stomach was extremely upset. I do remember getting a friend of mine to eat some worms. I ended up paying approximately $1.50 as he ate eight worms. I always thought he was a strange person; however, he did not get sick. The reports that are coming in now were dismal at best. These darn things were now busting into stores and homes, leaving nothing alive when they left. We could not make any solution currently because they all were being trained now in all states. Somehow, they got into some tourist ships that went to Alaska. With the limited cold currently, in Alaska due to summer months the insects were not reproducing at the rate they were in Hawaii and the lower 48. The United Nations had now placed the United States in quarantine and would allow no aircraft to enter nor with permit any aircraft from the United States to land on foreign soil.

Fortunately; due to the enormous size of these monsters, they were not able to work their way into the aircraft. However, scientists in other countries were not willing to take that chance and thus were attempting to develop insecticides. The Marines discovered that flamethrowers were more effective than spraying insecticides. They were having some success from these flamethrowers and actually were able to kill many of them. Naturally, the states were employing their limited supply of flamethrowers. The president personally called the manufactures of these flamethrowers and asked them to work on 24 shifts and mass-produce as many as they could. Fortunately; a few of the manufactures actually converted some their other production lines to producing these flamethrowers. Consequently, they finally ended up in trouble in that some parts of the flamethrowers were produced in China. Unfortunately; China refused to increase the production of these parts. Therefore; the president has some of his manufacturing scientists to reverse engineer this device. Subsequently; the deciding chip was similar to those used in other devices here in the US. Therefore; this deciding part was available within two days in factories, which manufactured the chips that we needed while working 24 hours a day this was now a national emergency because the United States was at war. The media hurdle was able to find a way to prevent them from breaking into thousands of other structures. This just was not going to happen because it was when you got into a structure; they were getting in.

Schools were now all closed and all National Guard and reserve military forces were activated. Nevertheless, the more that they killed these monsters, the more of them that began to reappear.

Intelligence reports revealed that they were covering mass areas, one report had a force of them over one mile wide. They also witnessed the giant Army of the Kissing Blood fighting against the Assassin Caterpillar. Consequently; this war was a place around St. Louis. Preliminary reports suggested that over one million insects had died in this initial confrontation. Sadly, this was a local issue that did not spread throughout their populations. The next emergency action involved barricading as many large facilities as possible for people to seek sanctuary. This was a deadly nation crippling emergency. Something had to happen now. Twister now notified Annika and me; she needed for us to figure out a way to save this continent. These insects were now beginning to expand into Mexico with limited expansion into Canada due to the colder climate. Annika looks to me in total confusion and said her mind was blank. This was something she never even knew existed and could not figure out what or how they were getting so big. Even farmers were now reporting the total destruction of their livestock. These insects now had learned how to attack moving prey. This sent off some apprehensions that there would be an immediate food shortage, as these creatures were even cleaning out large fields of corn, oats or whatever else stood in their way.

I was convinced that there was only one way to handle this crisis and that was for them to use some poison that would continue to spread to their nests. I told Twister that there were poisons available currently that could perform this function and for her to identify them and contact whoever had to be contacted for an immediate mass production. These poisons would be mixed with other substances that we knew these insects would be attracted to and distribute in any current and projected path that the masses were moving. I recommended that we airdropped these into some of the mass accumulation herds. As the idea now was to get as much of this stuff into as many of these insects as possible. It would take time for these poisons to infiltrate other insects that they came into contact with; nevertheless, it would happen. This had to happen, or mankind, truly in North America and eventually South America, would be extinct. All the wars, pandemics, and mass murderers when combined had a death toll that already felt far below the current tally. It just happened so fast with was such a deadly impact that our secret enemy became visible and almost invincible. The flamethrowers were able to divert some of these insects' movements, but as you burn one of these, they simply crawl right over it. These monsters had no sense of compassion for each other. Their existence was for one purpose and one purpose only and that was to eat.

This helped reinforce my belief that our poisons were the answer. The only way inside these now large beasts was through their eating. It took one day to get these poisons out among these insects. My only hope was that not only to kill them but spread whatever diseases it was designed to spread among these populations. Because if we had to hunt them down and find them, this would be so time-consuming, and even at that, all they had to do was for a pair, a male and female to survive, and within months we would be right back to where we were right now. The worst-case scenario was that these poisons may only weaken them, and if so, our bullets would be able to finish them off. Reports came in that these things with the poisons along with everything else around them was creating limited hesitation. Therefore; our dye had been cast. We know little about how insects' function, especially how much was instinctive or reflective. I really did not know how long it would take for these poisons to kill their host, considering they were not designed to kill them but to get into their systems to where they would spread it among other insects that they came in contact with. We immediately saw with the poisons was causing them to separate. When they separated, they headed off into different directions from the current year. Their behavior changed drastically, as they were now in full retreat mode.

This confused me because as a retreated they guaranteed themselves to become infected. Then again it could be because they were confronted with something they did not expect nor had an instinct to handle. I suspect also that this new poison took away their appetite, and with no appetite there was no need to hunt. The National Guard and the Federal Reserve's began to report they had no visible encounters. They would continue their patrols, however, they felt it was safe for the public once again to resume their normal activities. Subsequently; there's a massive job that had to be done quickly and that was to decide how to dispose of these dead giant insects. The original plan was to burn them with the flamethrowers; however, their bodies just made too much smell in the smoke. Initial air-quality tests suggested that the smoke was not good to breathe, as technically no smoke is good to breathe. The difference being that CDC felt that though the foreign substances in this airborne smoke people could eventually become hazardous to their health. Anyways; it was not good that anything from these insects anywhere enter a human. Subsequently; the military engineers came to the areas where there was a high quality of the dead insects and began to dig the large holes and bury them. The important thing was to bury them away from potential drinking water sources.

Even though; initially, it did not look like this would be a difficult job, it turned out to be extremely difficult because we're talking about millions of dead giant stinking insects. Meanwhile; preliminary initial reports indicated approximately 12 million human beings had been eaten or were taken by these incidents. This qualified as the greatest disaster caused by insects in the history of mankind. This raised another concern, and that was the bodies of these humans who were in these insects. Realizing that most insects digest with acid, these bodies would appear hideous at best. It was best to leave them buried inside these insects where their acids would continue to break them down. Approximately one month later the National Guard reported another shocking event. They had discovered one of the nests for these insects. Inside this nest were approximately over one million dead insects. An exact number will be impossible to calculate because these insects had molded into one solid mass. This provided evidence that the poison did return to the nest for final liquidation of their population. Another problem was beginning to surface, and that was people reporting to the hospitals and immediately dying within a few days with severe flulike symptoms. After examining their bodies through autopsies and extensive lab analysis, a consensus was reached, and that was this was a new type of the flu and unfortunately it was related to the insects. A drastic campaign began an attempt to find a vaccine. This was proving to be very difficult if not impossible.

Within one month; the hospitals were overwhelmed, and this was now a true deadly pandemic. The nation once again closed down as everyone remained secluded, as much as possible. Unfortunately; that did not stop the deaths. Even Twister and her network could not come up with a vaccine, that they could transfer through dreams, to humanity. The spiritual analysis concluded that this was a major attack created by the evil ones. The only hope was that this flu would die out on its own. Unfortunately; that would mean those who caught it would die. This disturbed Annika, as she became angry that everyone was giving up. I explained to Annika that sometimes is better to lose the battle, if you win the war. I told her that we would be saving more people by doing it this way. Twister gave us some good news; her network had developed the Insect Laser Egg Elimination and Detection Device. Furthermore; this device will be strictly spiritual and would not manifest itself physically among the world. These eggs were too small and spread out for any human to ever dream of detecting and destroying. Her device would begin scanning every inch of North and

South America. During the scans, if an egg was detected, it was immediately dissolved. They also included some chemicals that have traditionally been effective in slowing down flus.

They actually use this chemical against the Spanish flu in the early 20th century. This was a shot in the dark, but they had it and to put it out there and see if anything happens. You see this new flu strain floating in the air, and that this chemical was disturbing it. This new flu was called the bug flu. This day Twister formed another idea, she would go through their inventory of previous chemicals and they would pick different areas to release these chemicals and see if anything was happening. One chemical was able to attack the bug flu virus with a 75% kill rate. The remaining 25% were somewhat damaged. With that being said they began flooding the hospitals that had bug flu victims, and within days they could see about one half of the patients returning home. It was now time to flood the planet, while research continued for a 100% cure, 75% now was better than nothing. In the meanwhile; the mass campaign to bury the dead insects continued, as did another campaign to find the dead nests. Slowly nests began to appear in many strange places, such as under people's houses, with projections that this could take up to 10 years to uncover these nests. The blood flu took approximately 15 million additional lives, resulting in a total of 27 million dying because of the Insect Invasion and War. This just showed how fragile and combustible our environment really was. The chemicals are mixed forming new results that could also be mixed forming new results, and the process continue until something unpredictable and deadly emerges. As Annika strolled through the death reports she appeared to become extremely depressed.

Therefore; Twister came up with a brilliant idea and that being to immediately proceed to our honeymoon and what better place than in Rome? Annika had seen reports of ancient Rome; however, Rome did not exist during her time period. Twister apologized; however, we would have to keep this visit to a minimum for fear that the evil ones, angry over the failure of their insect invasion, would be searching for some new targets. With this being said I recommended, as did Annika, that we returned to our home. As we were returning, Annika asked me what the building was that we were in front of. I told her it was the Pantheon, and that we would someday explore it together. Upon returning to our home, we immediately put her tired bodies into her bed and drifted off to sleep. This is one of those days, or even weeks, where even though we lost a lot of people, humanity had been saved, at least for one more event. Good night!

VISION 13

The Baby Factory

I currently found myself in a strange structure resembling a factory with small white lights being captured in minute containers being monitored by larger formless lights. I rapidly found myself slipping out of the building, and viewing it from the outside. It appeared rather bland and made of red bricks revealing that it was an older building and appeared very rustic from the outside with plenty of windows, a tall tower which extended upward doubling the height of the building. I also witnessed what appeared to be a large furnace cone-shaped on the side with additional buildings extending as far as I can see. I can witness no entrance with only a yellow forklift parked along the side of the building. There is nothing to reveal what is going on in the inside with merely a simple sign, 'Have the Time

Pottery', on the outside. I establish that what was going on the inside of this building is well concealed. Actually, it appears rather scary and entered, nevertheless; I find myself drifting up to the inside. The inside is completely modern with devices, which are colorful and shiny. The pipes are silver and rust free. Simply put, it is beautiful yet strangely vacant. It appears to look very modern and lavish looking as if costing its owner, a ton of money. My primary concern is that this place is completely unoccupied, contrary to what looks to be a highly kept structure that would require a large crew to maintain. At this time, the inside becomes quite dark with white silhouettes resembling human form appearing at the vacant stations. I currently see little, minuscule balls of light dropping from the ceiling and landing on the stations, apparently to find homes in the small colored containers. The individuals or things that are working at the stations now begin to take a collar. They all have short, bushy red hair while wearing sleeveless blue shirts with white T-shirts extending from beyond the outer shirts and underneath completely covering their arms. It appeared that they all are conventional in just about every facet. I am currently focused on five of the stations, three of which have elongated tables with two shelves each that are on rolling wheels to roll underneath their station or be extended at their station master's determination. Three of these stations have little collared containers, two of which are red and the remaining one yellow. Each of the attendants appears beside and are concentrating on the task before them. I am completely confused as to what is happening in this place. To my surprise, this mystery was soon to begin to reveal itself to me through another white light shining inside me. I look at the colorless light and ask where I am and why I am here. I was completely comfortable talking with these white lights, since I previously talked to one while working in the cemetery and another while orbiting our planet. The previous two were very much helpful, leaving me to only hope that this one also would follow that trend. The light began speaking to me. The light emitted a warm beam into my body unconditionally relaxing me. For some unknown reason, my muscles were extremely tight, nevertheless, they were now completely relaxed. The spirit introduced herself as Laura, a name whom I never ran into that much in my life, remembering only one from my junior high school days. Strangely, that Laura and her family reported seeing UFOs. Both, she and her family immediately moved out of the mainstream and began to live excessively private lives thereafter. Laura informed me totally not to worry, but that she would guide me through each of the events that were planned for me during this almost supernatural experience. I had dealt with the supernatural so much recently that they most likely felt natural for me. Be that as it may, Laura told me that this was a soul unification center, and that I would witness new souls being united with their future flesh. While she was speaking, I began to scan this facility, realizing that it was much larger than I had originally believed. Additionally, there had to be over 1,000 such work areas that I just described. Laura began to scold me for not paying attention, of which I immediately apologized citing that this was so much more magnificent than I first realized. She emitted some warm energy signifying she found my explanation satisfactory. She further explained that this was one of many such stations, and, additionally, other stations existed in nearly galaxies in which the creator had also established beings much similar to those existing on Earth. I always wondered how this 'birthing process' happened with nothing related to what I was witnessing this night. I didn't know really for sure if it was night or day using only the abundant darkness surrounding me as a Q that this was the night. Deciding to take advantage of my friends and what appeared to be eager to help my assistant, I therefore, asked Laura if it was night or day. Her vague answer explained that it was the night which was the time of the day they unite most with their bodies. I asked her about the babies born during the day. She explained that this was not an issue because they would pre-plant these new souls the previous night. At this time, one of the station attendants took hold of their red box and slowly began to disappear. I asked Laura what was happening to this attendant, and she explained that the attendant had secured fresh souls, one per container, and was preparing to make his deliveries. Laura grips my hand, as we begin to approach this station attendant. He identified himself as James and promised me that I would soon witness what they all believed to be the most important part of our existence. As the total flash approached, we approached our first destination. James secured one of his containers and placed it on this pregnant woman's belly. Once secured it began to take on a reddish color exterior. After witnessing another flash, Laura informed me that the soul was now integrated with the flesh and that a new human being would soon emerge from his mother with a living soul and thus officially created in the image of its creator. This event was quick yet to be able to witness it was extremely rewarding. Laura and James then informed me that I will be provided a chance to witness this new being life in a quick summary as almost instantly a young man appeared in my vision after graduating from his high school. The next scene was not what I had expected; nevertheless, James and Laura informed me that it was the reality. This young man lay on a battlefield, guts exposed, and facing his death. I could also see a large number of Angels surrounding him. Laura explained that they were removing the soul from the painful mutilated flesh, thereby mitigating as much as the pain as possible. I could see a sense of peace overcome in his face. James told me that this man had just died a hero defending his country. I asked James if those that they were fighting received the same treatment. I acknowledged that they did, with all being treated equally until Judgment Day. I marveled at my first true glimpse of innocent until proven guilty, a concept that I had often wished existed in the United States in practice and not just some long-lost philosophy. I could merely think that this being was such a waste of a light. He never had the chance to marry or procreate. He would at no time witness a child of his getting married or the joy of experiencing the birth of a grandchild. As I was watching these events unfold before us, everything turned purple, and an alarm sounded. Laura told me we had to return to the so-called baby factory to witness something very heartbreaking. Upon arrival there we saw an abortion as the assembly lines stopped. I was witnessing this abortion. Laura explained this would require the reassignment of the pending soul. Subsequently, I saw a teenage girl get murdered over drugs as her unborn baby lingered in her womb. This baby quickly died along with his mother requiring another soul transfer. I could feel the sadness in both James and Laura. Afterwards, the lights or surrounding lights all turned white and returned to our deliveries. This time, we arrived in a small hut in Africa. This hat hut had no furniture, encompassing merely a woman experiencing pain, legs spread, with an elderly lady preparing to help deliver this fresh baby. After the standard color changes; I could almost immediately hear the cries of a newborn. Afterwards, I witnessed this young lady get married and graduate from her college. Laura after that told me it was time to move on, as that night I witnessed over 50 deliveries, with most of them maturing to an old age. James then informed me that he had been doing this for over two centuries at this point. I asked them if they knew who delivered me to my mother. To my shock; James confessed remembering my delivery. I could witness the first few moments of my life. We returned to the factory as other spirits came forward and introduced themselves to me. I was so fascinated by this comprehensive spiritual process. I felt as if I had finally experienced a positive visual experience. I petition that I could actually continue to witness this amazing process. Following this, Laura took me into the high spiritual realms; as I could see a spacious multitude of color flashes throughout our planet each representing a new life beginning. I asked Laura concerning why such a wide variety of colors and not just the white ones they revealed to me this night. She explained that each color represented different situations, and that it would take much more time than they had allotted be me to reveal all these situations. Accepting this answer, I thanked Laura for sharing these positive events with me, considering that these events were assuring the continuation of our species or the Homo sapiens. I was quite amazed that this was being accomplished through the actions of these angels and became curious as to the creation of the extra spirits. Laura was apparently reading my mind and thereby took me to another site well beyond Earth. I arrived at a bluish cloudy site which was soon filled with so many bright lights. The largest bright light began to take form revealing a bearded male in a white robe sitting in a brown chair. The chair sat upon a well decorated large almost transparent brown circle, extremely powerful looking yet beyond my ability to describe. Above he who sat upon this chair was an extremely large brown and white light with what appeared to be a tree in the center and the source of all this power. On each side were well designed circles of light, with one revealing a man hanging from a cross and the other containing a large white dove. Each circle of light was adorned by other divine looking objects, whose beauty and majesty being well beyond my ability to describe, except for what appeared to represent somewhat ancient symbols. James clarified that these symbols were from the Creators personal or heavenly language, of which they all spoke unless speaking with humans, at which time they would speak their language. This throne was also being circled by many additional smaller doves, which Laura explained represented the creator's massive love being released upon humanity. The large power source above this in what appeared to be a sovereignty, was producing many smaller bright lights that were forming into smaller spheroids and vanishing towards the baby factories. I truly wish I could have a better descriptive term rather than 'baby factory,' nevertheless, feel it is enough to get my point across. Laura explained that the smaller lights were being created from the Almighty and that he therefore was creating others in his image. This made me feel superior as I could verify that we were actually created in his image and better yet, individually, just as Adam was. I had previously I previously I previously presumed that this was a one-time process with the creation, of Adam and Eve. However; as I witnessed tonight, it was an ongoing process and that the Almighty was actually very much involved with humanity. Shortly thereafter, we returned to the baby factory, as Laura explained, that the Almighty did not like to be disturbed during what he felt was an extremely intimate spiritual process. I can appreciate this acknowledging how important, even though quite brief, it was to witness our active integration with our Creator. I was saddened by the thought that many of these new souls would unfortunately prove to be a disappointment, developing from this ongoing quest for the expansion of good and bombardment from the bad. I therefore asked Laura, if she ever had encounters with the fallen ones. She explained that they tried to always keep underneath the powerful Almighty's umbrella of protection. I informed her that this was a very wise course of action on their part. She then revealed to me hundreds of thousands of small black dots circling the earth. She explained that these were from the evil one and constantly seeking every available opportunity to corrupt and enslave the pure. Humanity, unfortunately, was the targets of these evil ones whose primary goal was to separate the good from the Almighty's umbrella. At this time, James, Laura, and what must have been over 1,000 of the angels began singing praises to the Almighty explaining that their work for this night had reached its conclusion. They all expressed great joy in serving their great and just master. Only the future would reveal the successes or failures of the newly created humans that would soon be within this endless battle. Laura then explained to me the importance of the Bible, alerting me to the fact it had all the tools that I needed to end victorious on the side of the good. She told me that if I did not have time to research this, I should cease what I was doing and make the time and that what she called the words of the Almighty, would be my sole source and path to eternal salvation and therefore be free of the torment unleashed by the evil ones. I should always strive to do so, as the rewards were too great to forgo. Make the time to arm myself was the proper tools needed in this battle was her strong and convincing argument. We then returned to the baby factory to watch some of the final deliveries of this night. I had to ask one additional question concerning reincarnation. Laura explained that there were situations warranting reincarnation as determined by the creator. The important issue was that all would receive a fair and equal chance to serve good and reject the evils ones. All who did not have enough entries in their book of life were provided an opportunity to establish these entries. I could not determine if this had answered by question; nevertheless, felt that it was indeed fair, and kept everyone on equal footing. I felt that I now could truly appreciate the importance of their work. As with my previous encounters, I suddenly became very tired and drifted back into sleep. Goodbye baby factory as I wished them the best of success in their work with humanity. Laura and the angels continued singing the praises to the Almighty, as I found myself compelled to join them being filled with such warmth and peace. I was actually struggling to continue in this warm experience, yet knew it was now time to await a new adventure, hoping that I would experience some more positive events such as I had this time.

Index

Symbols

A

B

C

D

E

F

G

H

J

K

L

M

N

O

P

R

S

T

U

V

W

Z

The other adventures from this author

Prikhodko, Dream of Nagykanizsai
Search for Wise Wolf
Seven Wives of Siklósi
Passion of the Progenitor
Mempire, Born in Blood
Penance on Earth
Patmos Paradigm
Lord of New Venus
Tianshire, Life in the Light
Rachmanism in Ereshkigal
Sisterhood, Blood of our Blood
Salvation, Showers of Blood
Hell of the Harvey
Emsky Chronicles
Methuselah's Hidden Antediluvian Abridgment
American States of China
Unconscious Escapades
11-27
Amazing Truths or Foolish Lies
The Legend of Mu (Lumaria)
American Second Civil War
Psychotic Phantasmagoria Divulgence

Printed in the United States
by Baker & Taylor Publisher Services